7/12

Angela Dracup was born and educated in Bradford and read psychology at Sheffield and Manchester Universities. She is a chartered psychologist and works with education authorities to assess the needs of children with learning and behavioural problems. She is married with one daughter and lives in Harrogate, North Yorkshire.

WHERE DARKNESS BEGINS

When the body of a teenage girl is found in a Yorkshire quarry, evidence points to the senile old farmer who discovered her. But DCI Ed Swift is not convinced . . . His superintendent is desperate to get the case sewn up and Swift is in a race against time to find the real killer. His investigation points to the possible guilt of three people and Swift faces a tangle of lies and deceit to uncover an act of evil which has destroyed the life of more than one young person. And then he must find the proof . . .

ANGELA DRACUP

WHERE DARKNESS BEGINS

Complete and Unabridged

ULVERSCROFT
Leicester

First published in Great Britain in 2004 by
Robert Hale Limited
London

First Large Print Edition
published 2006
by arrangement with
Robert Hale Limited
London

British Library CIP Data

Dracup, Angela
Where darkness begins.—Large print ed.—
Ulverscroft large print series: crime
1. Police—England—Yorkshire—Fiction
2. Detective and mystery stories
3. Large type books
I. Title
823.9'14 [F]

ISBN 1–84617–364–7

Published by
F. A. Thorpe (Publishing)
Anstey, Leicestershire

Set by Words & Graphics Ltd.
Anstey, Leicestershire
Printed and bound in Great Britain by
T. J. International Ltd., Padstow, Cornwall

This book is printed on acid-free paper

For Margaret, with love.

1

It was raining hard and dark as night by the time Ned got home for his dinner. He could see Sadie through the kitchen window, standing beside the cooker. All the lights were on and there was a glow around her head. Ned stood shifting from one foot to the other, drawn to the bright ring of light. Inside his own head there was a slow, ever-deepening darkness, a watery gloom which swirled away his thoughts and memories as he reached out to grasp them.

He pressed his ruddy, weathered face against the window and watched the glow around Sadie's head shiver and undulate as she moved. He tried to think of her name but there was nothing in his mind to get hold of. He tried to think who he was. He scratched on the window to make her know he was there.

'Get inside this minute!' Sadie yelled as she flung open the door and advanced on him. 'You're soaked. You'll catch your death.'

'Who am I?' he asked piteously, cringing away.

'You're Ned Bracewell, my dad, God help

me,' she told him, seizing his arm and pulling him to the door. 'Where have you been? Your dinner's been ready and waiting for an hour.'

He looked at her fearfully. 'Walking.'

'Oh, Dad!' She sat him down in the old Windsor-chair that had belonged to his grandmother and rubbed his wet, grizzled hair with a towel.

He stared at her, subdued and puzzled. 'Where's me mam?' he asked.

Sadie drew in a long breath. Sometimes she could hardly bear to make her lips frame the answer one more time. 'She's dead, Dad. She's been dead for more than fifty years.'

'Well, I never,' he said, looking thoughtful.

'Dad. Your nails!' she exclaimed in dismay. 'What on earth have you been doing?' She turned his hand over in hers. 'You've been digging in the earth!' She put her hand up to her forehead.

He was overwhelmed with desolation. He laid his hand on her sleeve. 'Angel,' he said suddenly, smiling. 'An angel.'

Sadie snatched her arm away. 'I'm no bloody angel,' she snapped, wincing at the sight of his decayed yellow teeth, flinching away from the rank odour of his breath.

She ran hot water into the washing-up bowl, squirted in detergent and soaked a fresh cloth. 'Here,' she said, grasping his hands and making a start on mopping him up. 'Keep still, will you!'

Suddenly overcome with pity for what he had become — that strong, quick, decisive man who had managed to pull a living out of his herds of black-faced sheep when other daleside farmers were turning to safe jobs in the towns — Sadie schooled her movements to be gentle.

She watched the water grow dark and cloudy as the earth beneath his nails dissolved. She noticed streaks of blood on the insides of his fingers. He must have been digging away like a dog with the scent of a meaty bone.

'What did you think you were *doing*, Dad?' she muttered. 'Searching for buried treasure?'

His fingers became still for a moment. It was almost as though he had understood her question. 'An angel,' he said dreamily.

She glanced into his face. He had on a slack, soppy smile. Beatific as though he were contemplating some earthly paradise. Poor old sod, the heavenly visions in his head were the only pleasure he got from life now. She wrapped a tea towel around his neck and fed him stewed shin beef with onions and mashed potatoes. He opened his mouth obediently and chewed like a churning cement mixer. When he had had enough he pressed his lips tight together and refused any more like a stubborn child. He got up from the table and drifted away, muttering to himself. She heard him in the hallway, shuffling, meddling, chuntering.

Sadie turned up the volume control on the television. The sound of the voices from one of the afternoon's soap operas eventually lured him back from his wanderings. He sat in his chair, leaning forward, staring intently at the characters on the screen, all else forgotten. Eventually he fell asleep.

Sadie breathed a sigh of relief. She spread newspaper on the table, upended his jacket and shook out the contents. Bits of dirt, twists of silver foil, a fragment of barbed wire. And some strands of hair clinging to a cluster of little stones and bound together with a thick, sticky substance. Her mind jerked into full alertness. She bent and peered at the pale strands. They were definitely human hair. Long threads of light brown. She bent closer and reached out a tentative fingertip. The dark red stickiness was unmistakably blood.

A flash of foreboding skittered over Sadie's scalp. Her heart made tiny explosions in her chest. She pictured her father on his stumbling, desultory walk. He was so unfocused, so purposeless. What the devil had he been up to?

4

He ground his teeth as he slept, the stumps crunching together. Sadie never took her eyes off him. When he woke she spoke sternly. 'Now don't you go walking out again today,' she told him, knowing that he would understand perfectly and thus do exactly the opposite.

She went to the kennel block and let out the six dogs she had currently boarding into the large secure pen behind the farmhouse. Normally she would take them for a walk across the moor at this time. Today she kept a watch for her father's departure from the house. The dogs would just have to wait.

It was no more than a few minutes before he appeared at the front door. She watched him, hands on hips. Oh, in some ways he was so predictable, so manipulable.

Closing the gate of the pen softly, she followed him out of the yard and down the mud track to the narrow road which snaked along the side of the moor. The rain had stopped now and there was a freshening wind.

Her father went on ahead, his progress slow and shambling, yet curiously purposeful. For a few moments he disappeared from view at the point where the road curved around an outcrop of stone. When he came back into sight Sadie felt the full strength of a westerly wind tearing into her and whipping the brittle tufty grass beneath her feet into waving ripples. Above her, the wind had hollowed a tiny lake of blue in the boisterous grey clouds.

It was February, the depths of the winter here on the Yorkshire moors north-west of Bradford. Clear shining rivulets from the recent rain sparkled and sizzled in the gulleys scoring the flanks of the hills — tiny waterfalls frilled at the edges like lace. And yet it was not cold. Not biting, bone-chilling, back-hunching cold. Sadie felt warmth glowing in her body beneath her thick quilted anorak. She pulled down the zip and looked up again at the sky. It looked like February. The lake of blue had been swallowed up again and the sky was a great grey lid arching over the moors. But the blustery airstream was eerily, unnaturally mild.

All is not right with the world, she thought gloomily.

Her father made a left turn, leaving the road and taking one of the crumbling tracks which led to a disused limestone quarry. Following on, Sadie could just about recall the time when the quarry had been working; the clatter of the stones shifting through the steel feeder into the crushing plant, the film of dust which spread for miles, coating the farms in white.

She hadn't been near the quarry for years. There was something creepy about a working site which had been abandoned and left to disintegrate. Almost as creepy as the drowned church in the reservoir just a few miles to the north.

She came alert, noting that her father had increased his speed, was moving with focused purpose. He eased himself into the wide, shallow basin which formed the top upper rim of the northern side of the quarry. She saw him crouch down. Reach out his arm.

A chill of foreboding chased through her limbs. She had to force herself to walk forward.

As she came near she saw with a thud of shock that what she had most feared was staring her in the face. Death. The pathetic body of a girl clothed in sodden, mud-smeared garments. She was lying face down, strands of filthy pale hair lying over the collar of her anorak. Sadie could not see her face, but she knew without a doubt that the girl was dead.

Sadie felt herself freeze, trapped in the unbelievability of what she was seeing.

Her father had been stroking the girl's back, making little crooning noises in his throat. Now suddenly his arms reached around her and, with a strength which Sadie had thought long gone from him, he turned the girl over, lifted her up and hugged her to his chest.

'Oh my God!' Sadie looked on in horror as the head swung heavily down from the lifeless stalk of the girl's waxy neck. 'Dad! Don't. Don't touch her. Leave her be!'

Her father was oblivious, rocking the corpse in his arms, crooning to it through slack, damp lips.

Sadie sprang forward and lashed out at her father. She grasped his shoulders and shook him, screaming out at him to let the dead girl go. He hung on grimly, thrashing within her grasp, trying to wrench himself free from the iron clutch of her fingers. Suddenly he jerked violently backwards. The girl's head lolled on its stem, the mask-like face staring full at Sadie with its blank, empty eyes.

And, dear God, she looked no more than a child. A small face, the surface of the skin mottled and dirt-streaked against a backdrop as white and modelled as though it had been made of plaster of Paris. The eye sockets were sunken, the chin elf-like and pointed, the nose a putty-like blob.

Her nerves screaming and trembling, Sadie finally wrenched the dead girl from her father's grasp. The body fell back on to the limestone shelf with a dull thud.

Sadie stared at it in fascinated horror. Oh God, they shouldn't have touched her. To do so was disrespectful. It was obscene. And, *of course*, you never disturb anything at the scene of a crime.

Crime. She felt herself tighten. Why should she think that? The girl might have died of natural causes. She looked again at those disturbing blank eyes. Oh, there had been a crime all right.

Her mind was buzzing and hectic. What to do, what to do? Inform the police. Oh, Christ. They'd think her father had done it. They'd find his fingerprints all over the girl. Could they do that? she wondered. Get fingerprints off fabric? Oh, heavens, they could do bloody anything, couldn't they?

She looked at her father, suddenly realizing how secret he was from her now. The father she had known up to a year or so ago had almost totally vanished. Inside his dementing brain he could be anyone.

A murderer?

She squeezed her eyes shut. No. NO.

When she opened her eyes and looked up, the sky seemed to be lowering itself over her. She contemplated the final moments of the dead girl's short life as she looked around her, sensing the vast anonymity of this space surrounding her father, herself and this poor dead creature. Who would ever know this dead girl was here? And if they did, who would ever know that she and her father had found her first?

Just walk away. Easy as that.

Sadie found herself surprised at the waywardness of her thoughts. This girl had parents, maybe brothers and sisters. They would be frantic, hollow with fear and desperation for the young girl they loved.

For God's sake, Sadie, pull your finger out. She rooted around her waistband for her mobile. She'd left it at home. She was always doing that. She wasn't an 'in touch' kind of person. She liked to be quiet, left alone with her reflections. 'Come on, Dad, we've got to get home,' she told him.

Her father was looking longingly at the girl. 'An angel,' he murmured.

Sadie swallowed. Oh Jesus, Jesus! She grasped hold of her father's arm. She schooled herself to be gentle. 'Come on, Dad. Please. Hold on to me.'

There was the usual desperate struggle. In time he gave in. He shuffled behind her, reluctant, defiant, pulling back.

'Come on!' She jerked him so hard he missed his footing and stumbled.

He tried to unhook himself from her. His bottom lip trembled. 'I want me mam.'

2

Ed Swift was considering going home when Superintendent Tom Lister called him into his office and told him there was a dead girl in the Arkwright quarry. That the circumstances indicated the girl had been abducted and murdered. That it was absolutely imperative they get a firm grip on the case before the media swung into action.

Lister was a stocky, ruddy-faced man with small shrewd blue eyes. The tension and exhilaration of the prospect of a big, sensitive investigation fizzed in the atmosphere around him.

'I'd like you to get up to the quarry right away, Ed,' he informed Swift, drumming plump fingers on the desk top. 'SOCOs and the police surgeon already there, so as soon as you've got a sniff of the flavour of the case I need you to go on to interview the woman who has discovered the body.' Lister leaned forward and pushed a paper with the relevant details across the desk.

Swift made a quick appraisal, his intinctive curiosity instantly roused — mingled with a sinking regret that he'd have to telephone

Naomi and tell her that he was going to be late home. Yet again.

As he started on a run-through of the best available officer to accompany him, the superintendent made a show of clearing his throat and came in with a forestalling suggestion of his own. 'I'd like you to take Geoff Fowler with you,' he said.

Swift took in a breath. 'Very well.'

Lister spread his hands. 'Listen, Ed, I know he wouldn't be your choice. But he's here and he's available.'

'Fine, sir.' Swift turned at the door. 'I'll report back straight away. As soon as we've talked to the informant.'

Lister gave a brisk nod of assent, anxious for his colleague to be on his way. 'We need to get this business sorted as soon as possible, Ed,' he said heavily. 'And for a start I'm thinking of pulling in all the males with form in a radius of forty miles so we can question them.'

'Expensive, Tom,' Swift offered, of the view that large-scale samplings rarely came up with significant results. Best to wait for the forensic evidence and channel investigative energy in a more focused way — a suggestion he kept to himself.

'As if I needed reminding,' Lister agreed, looking grim. 'But it's proactive, makes us look as though we know what's what. The last thing we want is the boys from Scotland Yard being called in to teach us how to suck eggs.' His chest heaved and a low grunt rumbled from it. 'I believe the current term is making a *review*.' Lister's tight-lipped emphasis made it quite clear what he thought of that euphemism.

★ ★ ★

Swift asked Geoff Fowler to drive. He'd learned early on in his career with the police that it put defensive officers at ease to be asked to drive. Somehow evened up the uneasy balance of young, graduate boss who had fast-tracked up the promotion ladder and his older inferior.

Fowler sat hunched over the wheel, driving with grim and silent determination. Swift could sense his colleague's dislike, clenched inside him like a tightening fist. Fowler parked the car at the end of the rutted lane which led to the quarry. Heavy rain had been falling for the past hour and the rutted surface of the lane oozed with glistening mud.

Swift glanced down at Fowler's shoes. Polished black loafers. Smart. Verging on the dapper. The sergeant was a man of contrasts, he'd give him that. 'Are you going to be all right?' he asked. 'In those?'

'You've no need to worry on my account, sir,' Fowler said, swinging himself from the car and walking off.

The quarry came into sight. Swift could see the ridged sides of the huge hollowed-out bowl, a startling chalky white. A small beige tent was precariously perched on one of the higher ledges surrounded by a crooked ring of blue and white tape. Two scene of crime officers clothed in baggy white boiler suits were examining the surrounding ground, picking over any items of potential interest. A further two uniformed officers were standing around waiting for specific orders, their bodies tensed and slightly hunched against the wind.

Swift looked up at the sky: vast, majestic and a grim granite-grey. A mean wind moaned across the moor. He contemplated the final moments of the dead girl's short life. What a place to end up in. All alone. Dying. Ending up on the wet, dark earth where worms and animals lived their daily lives.

Lifting the flap of the tent, he drew in a breath then looked in. The police surgeon was already at work, bending over the body and temporarily obscuring the girl's face from his view. He steeled himself, his lips tightening.

The police surgeon turned around. He was relatively new to the job and still not quite sure of himself. Swift gave him a brief smile of acknowledgement.

'She's been dead at least twenty-four hours,' the doctor said, straightening up so that Swift and Fowler had their first glance of the dead girl's face.

Oh God, she looked so *young*. Swift thought of his own daughter, Naomi, just gone sixteen. A chill shot through his nerves.

'There are some injuries to the back of the head',' the doctor told them. 'But as you'll appreciate we won't know the cause of death until the pathologist files a report.'

'Is she carrying any form of identification?' Fowler made the question sound like an accusation.

The doctor shook his head.

Swift felt his hands clench into tight fists in the pockets of his jacket as he surveyed the girl's slight body. With her arms spread and one leg folded beneath her she looked as loose and disjointed as a puppet whose strings had been cut. He bent his head closer to the body, asking himself what sort of mind could have wanted to rob a young defenceless girl of her life. Confronting the body of a murder victim was always a sombre moment, reminding one of the fragility of life and dark side of the human psyche. Behind him, he heard Fowler shift from one foot to the other. He glanced up. 'Did you want to say something, Geoff?'

'Nothing beyond the obvious. Being let's nail the scum who did this. And fast.' Shaking his head in revulsion at the way evil continued to flourish, the sergeant turned away from his superior's questioning gaze.

'I agree,' Swift murmured, projecting ahead to the grim business of getting an identification from someone who knew the girl.

'There are no obvious signs of sexual assault,' the doctor commented. 'But there are stains on the front of her jeans which could well be semen. Perhaps from the perpetrator.'

'Bastard!' Swift heard Fowler mutter. 'Should be bloody strung up.'

There was a short silence.

'If there is a 'perpetrator',' Swift observed quietly. 'We haven't established that yet.'

The doctor blinked. 'No, quite. I've already called the morgue to ask them to collect the body. I hope that's in order,' he said.

'I don't see any point in keeping her here any longer.' Ducking out of the tent, Swift paused for a moment to watch the men in their white boiler suits combing the sodden, caked earth for what it might yield. Mentally he sympathized with the forensics team over their future task of making plaster casts of the scattered footprints etched into the mud.

'So what do you think?' he asked Fowler as they walked back to the car.

'I think we're not going to get much sleep for the next few days,' he observed, heaving himself behind the wheel. 'When I first started in CID,' he said, firing the engine and easing the clutch, 'we used to call these kind of cases 'murder in open ground'. My super used to say they were the most difficult of all to get a lead on. No point doing house to house to find any neighbours who'd been twitching their curtains and seeing suspicious goings on. No passers by. Nothing much to go on at all.'

'Mmm.' Swift unfolded his mobile. 'So where is it we are going to find our informant?'

'Black Sheep Farm, Black Moor Road.' Fowler pushed the engine to full revs as he made a three-point turn in the mud track. 'It's just a five-minute drive.'

Swift called Naomi's mobile. She answered after the first ring. 'Oh, hi, Dad! So what time are they going to let you out tonight?' The tone was mocking, faintly caustic.

'I don't know yet. I'll get back as soon as I can.'

'Trouble in the criminal underworld?' she asked.

'Look, I'm really sorry — '

'It's your job,' she interjected. 'And I'm a big grown-up girl. I can get my own supper.'

'Yes. Fine.' He paused, frowning as the face of the dead girl on the moor swam silently into his head. And then the thought of Naomi. All alone.

'Listen Dad, just get off the line, will you,' Naomi said. 'I'm expecting a rather hot call. From Marcus Carver. The god of the sixth form.'

'Oh! Right.' He clicked off the connection, feeling a twitch on the thread of parental guilt and anxiety. Naomi was savagely self-reliant. She had always been like that. And after Kate died she had kept her grief very firmly to herself, never let him see beyond the carapace of her bravery. Or was it bravado?

He recalled their discussing the move to Yorkshire for his promotion to DCI. Kate had been killed in the interim between the offer and the move and Swift had wondered whether to stay put. It had seemed like an act of cruelty to wrench Naomi from her school and her network of friends.

Naomi had watched him wrestle with his uncertainty. 'Let's go,' she had told him. 'You can be unhappy anywhere.'

18

Fowler, having pointedly ignored his senior's conversation with his daughter, signalled left then turned the car onto a narrow road which wound itself along the flank of the moor.

Swift glanced at the sergeant's grim, grudging features as he drove. 'Black Moor Road,' he mused, reading out the name on a black and white sign.

'Black Sheep Farm,' said Fowler, turning in through wide unvarnished wooden gates. 'End of the bloody world.'

3

Sadie was standing at the window waiting. She watched the car draw to a halt on the cobbled yard in front of the house, vaguely registering that it was sleek and shiny. Under the outside security lights she could see that the officer driving was bulky and dark with bristling eyebrows and a face of granite, the other man a beanpole with auburn hair and eyes which looked both shrewd and sad. They came to the door and introduced themselves as Sergeant Fowler and Detective Chief Inspector Swift.

Sadie absorbed the mouthful of titles. They'd sent in the big guns. Her mouth dried as she sat down and faced them. They asked her to confirm her name. They glanced across at her father, who had ignored their entrance and was still staring intently at the TV. They asked her to confirm his name and the relationship between them.

When they asked about her occupation, she wished she could give them something more exciting than unmarried daughter looking after her father and the rented out farm cottages and the kennels. But at least that was the truth and straightforward.

The chief inspector was calm and courteous. He asked her to describe the circumstances of the discovery. His request was low and measured. But she knew from the word go that he wasn't one to be messed with. She gave him a short and simple sketch of what had happened. The truth as she recalled it, apart from leaving her father out of the picture.

'Did you touch the body?' he asked, his eyes moving around the big room which served as kitchen and living room, always returning to rest on Sadie's father as he sat entranced with the shimmering TV pictures.

Sadie stared at the chief inspector, feeling herself a small, frightened animal caught in the beam of his assessing blue eyes. Her mind flashed up a picture of her father — a gobbet of spittle on his lips as he clasped the girl's dead body in a crazed old man's embrace. 'No.'

The inspector nodded, his calm gaze holding hers.

'Do you know who she is yet?' she asked, unable to bear this awful silence, filled with the suspicions of the police officers.

'Not yet.'

'And you were on your own when you

found the body?' the sergeant put in, terse and challenging.

'Yes.' She'd rehearsed that response. It came out pat, but she knew that they knew she was lying. They'd been right to turn up so promptly, not giving her time to think things through.

'Would your father be prepared to speak to us?' Swift asked.

'You could try,' Sadie said.

'Is he deaf?' the sergeant asked.

Swift shot Fowler a glance and got to his feet. 'Mr Bracewell,' Swift said, leaning down to speak in the old man's ear.

Ned turned his face up, an expression of bewilderment creasing his features and looked into Swift's face. Swift introduced himself, his voice low and steady. 'We've come to ask some questions, sir. To see if you can help us with our enquiries.'

'Questions!' Ned echoed, clutching at the one word which interested him. 'Oh, aye.'

'Would you mind if we turned the TV off?' Swift asked.

Sadie got up. 'Dad, we need to have a bit of peace so we can talk. I'm going to turn the TV off.' She aimed the remote and the picture died. She waited for a possible outburst, but her father seemed not to notice the loss of his TV friends. Dear God, she thought, recognizing a rare spark of curiosity in his eyes as he looked from Swift to the sergeant, is he going to have one of his flashes of lucidity? There hadn't been one for quite a few weeks, but . . .

Swift had dragged the Windsor-chair from a corner of the room and was sitting almost knee to knee with Ned. He told him the sad story of the discovery of the dead girl. He told it like an uncle telling a child a bedtime story. He told it as though he had no expectation that Ned would have already heard a version from his daughter. He told it with a simplicity and sensitivity which was heartbreaking — if you weren't aware of the motives behind it.

Why didn't I put Dad to bed and throw a sleeping pill down his throat? Sadie asked herself. Why didn't I lock him up with the dogs? She thanked God that at least she'd had the foresight to scrub his hands and nails in hot, soapy water until the skin was red raw.

Ned listened, staring at Swift and shaking his head in sorrow.

'It's a terrible thing, isn't it,' Swift said quietly, 'for a young person to die. No more than a child, really. Tragic.'

Ned stared at him, his eyes vague. Sadie held herself very still. It just needed Dad to start making mournful noises about angels.

'Do you know the Arkwright quarry, sir?' Swift asked.

'Me dad used to take me there to watch the machines,' Ned said with perfect lucidity, as though picking out a clean, whole fragment from his shattered brain. He stopped, his brows pulled together in an effort to harvest further morsels.

Fowler took in a rasping breath, preparing to move in with a snappy follow-up but Swift flung his arm out behind him in a warning gesture. 'And do you ever go there now, sir?' he asked. 'For old times' sake?'

Neds eyes filled with anxiety. The distant past was one thing, the present far more problematic.

'Did you go to the quarry today? This afternoon, perhaps?' Swift suggested conversationally.

Ned frowned. Sadie stiffened.

Fowler leaned forward towards Sadie. 'Does your father ever visit the quarry?' he asked. Curt and to the point.

'I don't know.'

'He goes for walks, does he?'

'Sometimes.'

'So he could visit the quarry? It's possible?'

'Yes.' Sadie stood up. 'It's about time for Dad's evening mug of tea,' she said, moving to the sink and filling the kettle. 'Would you like something?' She glanced from Swift to Fowler.

Fowler's habitually bullish expression softened a fraction. 'Thanks, love. Coffee. Milk and two sugars.'

'Nothing for me.' Swift left the old man and moved slowly around the room, pausing to examine the Yorkshire Farmer's calendar on the wall, carefully scanning the framed pencil sketches of a border collie. His mind was working furiously, attempting to put flesh on the bones of the sparse information Sadie Bracewell had been prepared to offer. 'Did your father do these?' he asked.

'I did,' Sadie said. 'I do a lot of sketching. I do animal heads in clay too.'

'Really.' Swift peered more closely at the sketches. 'Do you do it commercially?'

'Yes.'

'Do you make a profit?' Fowler wondered.

'Yes.' Sadie dropped a tea bag into a pint pot and poured boiling water on to it.

'How long have you had the tenancy of the farm?' Swift asked, turning to face Sadie.

'We're not tenants. The farmhouse and the buildings belonged to my great grandfather.' She straightened up, suddenly quite the châtelaine.

'So, you've quite a lot on your plate, haven't you?' Swift observed. 'The house to

25

run and the rented cottages, and your clay heads to make.' He paused. 'And then there's your father.'

'It's better than going out to work,' Sadie said. 'I worked in an office for a month or two after the farm folded up when Dad got . . . ill. I hated the feeling of being shut in, away from the sky and the smell of the moors.' She spooned coffee into a mug, poured on water, then added milk and two teaspoons of sugar. Having stirred the results, she handed the mug to Fowler.

She felt Swift's eyes on her, watching with intense concentration. His expression disturbed her, sent her off balance. Her mind was churning round and round like wheels in mud. The power and intensity of the two police officers seemed to fill the room. For a moment she had the impression they had the power to control and manipulate her so that she might eventually break down and say anything.

She fished the tea bag from her father's pot and put in three spoons of sugar. 'Here, Dad,' she said tenderly, placing the pot on the multi-stained side table beside his chair. 'Leave it to cool a bit.'

Ned looked up. 'Aye,' he said, his eyes wide and helpless.

Sadie leaned down and pressed a kiss on

his forehead. Tears sprang into her eyes. Turning, she met Swift's calm gaze and looked swiftly away.

'Does your father have Alzheimer's?' Fowler asked.

'He hasn't seen a specialist,' Sadie responded, her tone terse. 'Just our GP.'

'And?'

'He says it's some form of senility. Dementia, he calls it.'

'Miss Bracewell?' Swift asked quietly. 'Where were you yesterday between two and six o'clock in the afternoon?'

A pause. 'I was here,' she said. 'I did some cleaning in one of the cottages. And after that I started on the supper.'

'Was anyone here who could vouch for you?'

'My tenant may have been in. I'm not sure.'

'And where was your father?'

Another pause. Just a fraction too long.

'Was he here with you?' Swift prompted.

'Yes. Well, he went out for a short walk. He likes to walk. I try to keep an eye on him, but no way will I keep him shut up like a dog,' she said defensively.

'Of course not,' Swift agreed kindly.

'What time did he go out?'

'He had his dinner. Then he had a doze. It

would have been about 1.30 when he set off, I suppose.'

'Did you see him leave the house?' Fowler put in.

'Yes. I was working on a sculpture in the room next door. I often do that when he's asleep. There's a good view from there into the yard. I can see what's going on.'

'Yes.' Swift nodded understandingly. 'And when did he return?'

'About half an hour later.'

Swift let a pause develop. 'How long does it take to walk to the quarry?' he asked.

She swallowed. 'Around twenty minutes. For me, that is. Dad goes more slowly.' Her mouth and throat were beginning to feel as dry as sandpaper. She got up and went to stand beside her father. 'You can drink your tea now, Dad,' she said, picking up the mug and placing it in his outstretched hand. 'It's cooled.'

Swift walked to stand beside her. 'Miss Bracewell, could you and I go outside for a few minutes to talk in private? Sergeant Fowler will stay with your father.'

Sadie stiffened. Swift heard her swallow. She bent down to her father. 'Dad, I'm just going out into the yard. I won't be long.'

Ned blinked. His forehead wrinkled. 'Don't leave me!' He banged his pot down on the

28

table and clutched at her arm.

'I'm not leaving you. I'll just be by the door,' Sadie reassured. 'I'll put the light on. You'll be able to see me.'

His clutch tightened. She prised his fingers away. 'Dad, just *stay there* and drink your tea.'

He shrank back at the fierceness of her tone.

Sadie turned to Swift and Fowler, who were watching her with the stillness of an audience at the climax in a drama. She jerked her head towards the door. 'I won't have long,' she said, glancing towards her father.

Swift followed her out into the yard. Beyond the circle of yellow from the door light it was black dark. A cold, penetrating drizzle settled around them, glazing their clothes with a soft, wet sheen.

'I want you to be straight with me,' Swift told her. He spoke with great reasonableness, his tone low and soft, but laced with an irresistible authority.

A pause. 'OK,' she said.

'You weren't straight with us before?' Swift asked.

'Yes. But I was afraid. I still am afraid.'

'What are you afraid of?'

'That you're thinking my father could have killed this girl.'

'We haven't said so,' he pointed out. 'We haven't even said she was killed,' he pointed out.

Sadie clenched her hands. 'You're telling me it was an accident! It didn't look like one to me.'

'We'll have to wait for the autopsy finding,' Swift said. 'In the meantime we're treating it as a suspicious death.' He let a pause develop. 'You seem to have the impression we suspect your father of murdering the girl.'

'Yes. Oh, I don't know. You've seen how my dad is. People think if you've got dementia you're a total nutter.' She sighed. 'How would *you* feel in this situation?'

Swift heard the panic in her voice. 'Maybe you have reasons of your own for thinking your father might have some connection with the girl's death?' he suggested.

Sadie shook her head. 'No,' she said dully.

There was a long pause. Swift watched her. He wondered if she might be on the point of breaking down, saying what was really on her mind. The moment came and passed. 'Well,' he said eventually, 'I think that will be all for now.' He walked back inside. Ned was still in his chair, his hands hanging slackly over the arms as he stared unseeingly at the television. Swift gestured to Fowler, who sat stone-like and impassive at the other side of the room. 'Let's go.'

As they emerged from the farmhouse he saw that Sadie was still standing under the lamp, her face a ghastly white. 'Good night,' he said, 'and thank you for your help, Miss Bracewell. We'll be in touch.'

Lines of concern, desperation even, were drawn over her face, distorting its contours. 'Yes,' she said. 'Good night.'

Sadie watched until the car had turned through the gates and then went back into the house. Her father was sitting staring at the flames in the iron grate. He looked up as she closed the door. 'Someone's bin here,' he said.

'Yes, they've gone now.'

'Did you see them?'

'Yes, Dad.'

'I want me tea,' he said in a piteous voice.

'You've had it, Dad.'

'Have I?'

'Yes.'

'No, I haven't.' He put on a sulky and mutinous look.

Sadie dumped the mugs in the sink and began rinsing them.

'Someone's bin here,' her father grumbled.

Sadie drew in a breath. Sometimes the repetitions made her want to batter him. To shout and scream. To stick a knife in him and finally shut him up. 'Yes, Dad. Two police officers,' she said patiently.

'Police? I didn't see any police.'

'They weren't wearing uniform.'

'Have they gone?'

'Yes.' She soaped the mugs, rubbing fiercely at the stains.

They'd gone. But they would be back.

4

The two men were silent for a time as they drove away from the farm.

'I wouldn't like to be in her shoes,' Fowler volunteered eventually.

'No.'

'You could have pressed her harder. Sir.' The sergeant's lips twisted with contempt.

'Yes.'

'All in good time, eh?' Fowler looked as though he would like to spit.

'Time enough when we've got the autopsy report and forensics,' Swift said with careful neutrality. 'Miss Bracewell clearly knows that we suspect her father was the one who found the body.'

'My money's definitely on the father. He's well away with the fairies, doesn't know what he's about. Acting on his animal instincts.'

'That's a possibility,' Swift agreed.

'Murder in these back-of-beyond farms is usually kith and kin stuff,' Fowler reflected, drawing on decades of experience running way back beyond his long career in the police. 'Young blokes settling old feuds, old farmers made crazy with years of trying to grub a living out of this godforsaken moorland.'

'And what would I know of that?' Swift asked with a twisted grin. 'Me, a born and bred townie migrated from the south?'

Fowler gave a grunt of grudging acknowledgement.

'So you think this girl's murder is about kith and kin?'

Fowler frowned. 'Maybe not the murder itself. I'm just asking myself what the daughter's got to gain by putting her father well in the frame?'

'From what we saw and heard she was trying to protect him. What should she have done? Kept quiet about the body?'

'Come on, sir, how about anonymous information? Call from a phone box. No strings, no follow-up.' Fowler gave a shrug. 'She'd still have done her duty. Reported a crime.'

'True.' Swift paused. 'So what's she got to gain from 'putting him in the frame'?'

'The farm and the land, most likely.'

'There could be another heir. A brother or sister.'

'Aye, well, that's summat you can ask her later,' Fowler said with satisfaction. 'I'll tell you this, if I was stuck in that hellhole of a place with a gibbering idiot of a father, dribbling and pissing about the place, making demands on me day and night, I wouldn't be sorry to get him out of the way.'

Swift winced at the viciousness of the sergeant's tone, at the same time agreeing that there was some substance to his observations.

'If the old man gets done for the murder, what'll happen? He'll be put in some 'secure' psychiatric nursing home for half-wits. All found. Five-star board, lodging and medical care on the state. Very cosy, and she won't have to spend a penny of her inheritance forking out for it from selling the farm.'

'True. There's just one thing you've left out of the equation, Geoff.'

'What?'

'Daughterly love.'

Fowler shot his senior officer a look, shaking his head in disbelieving sorrow.

★   ★   ★

It was gone eleven when Swift arrived home. On his return to the station his request for a trawl through the national database for missing fifteen-year-old girls had yielded no satisfactory matches. The personnel from the path lab were working on the body now, trying to come up with an identity photo which would be acceptable to the public on its release to the media. The autopsy was to take place the next morning.

Swift switched off the engine and sat for a few seconds trying to shake off the grimness of his work before going inside and greeting his daughter. Uncertain how he and Naomi would settle in Yorkshire, he had decided against buying a house and taken a twelve-month lease on an apartment in a Victorian mansion on the northern outskirts of the town. The rooms were grand and elegant with elaborate plaster roses adorning the ceilings and wood-block floors gleaming beneath. Naomi had said the apartment suited her aspirations to the high life. Swift, having talked to one or two other tenants, had judged the place suited his wish to be reassured that Naomi was not alone in an empty house on those occasions when he had to work late or through the night.

He let himself in, laying his keys softly on the table in the hallway. Warmth pulsed from the renovated 1920s radiators and he could smell the tang of a freshly peeled orange. He smiled, the pleasure of coming home to his daughter suddenly blotting out the constant gnaw of longing for Kate. He sometimes wondered what would have happened if Naomi too had been taken from him in the rail crash which killed Kate. She had, in fact, toyed with the idea of accompanying Kate to London to visit the art gallery of a friend, but had decided against it at the last minute. If he had lost them both he doubted if he could have retained his sanity.

'No need for hush-hush tactics, I'm still up!' Naomi's voice came from the depths of the sofa in the drawing room.

Swift crossed the room and leaned over to ruffle her dark hair. She was lying on her stomach, holding a book open in one hand and sliding orange segments into her mouth with the other. She was wearing one of Kate's dressing gowns and huge furry slippers with golden retriever heads.

'What time do you call this?' She glanced up at him.

He smiled ruefully and shook his head.

She held out a section of orange for him. 'There's cottage pie in the oven. Still warm and not dried up — I put foil over it.'

'You don't have to cook for me.' He ran a hand through his hair.

'No. I know. That's why I don't mind.' She rolled over, sat up and tucked her legs beneath her. Two sets of golden retriever eyes observed him. 'Just occasionally.'

He went into the kitchen and loaded his plate.

'So what's cooking on the crime front?' she

asked as he returned.

He sat down. A brew of highly unappetizing evil, he thought, anticipating the numb despair and shock of the dead girl's parents when they eventually heard the news. He smiled at Naomi and took up his fork. 'Just the usual.'

★ ★ ★

'When's the autopsy, sir?' Fowler demanded as he arrived at his desk just before eight the next morning.

'Now,' Swift said, glancing at his sergeant and wishing he had stayed at the desk in his own private office. But he liked to be around when his team arrived; sense the mood, pick up some of the throwaway comments.

Fowler sat down and pressed the start button on his computer. 'I thought you'd want to be there.'

Swift noted the implied accusation. He reflected on the gruesome theatre of an autopsy. Pictured the pale, lifeless girl being cut to pieces, her head raised on a wooden block, her skin cut to the bone from ear to ear, the scalp pushed forward off the glistening bone beneath, the skin pulled down over her face like a gruesome blindfold. Then cut from chin to pubis and her organs extracted and weighed on a butcher's scale. 'Squeamish,' he told Fowler.

Fowler looked at him for a long moment, then turned back to his illuminated screen. 'Be interesting to hear what forensics have to say. When they get around to it.'

Swift got to his feet. Fowler's sour cynicism was getting to him and he knew he had to get away.

★ ★ ★

Ned watched Sadie stuff sheets and towels into the washing machine. Her arms moved with quick, fierce jerks and her face was dark and grim. Earlier on he'd seen her lock the kitchen door and put the brass key in the pocket of her jeans. She'd turned to him, her mouth working away, clack, clack, her finger wagging a warning. She was angry with him. He didn't know why.

He sat slumped in his chair beside the fire, a blanket of misery settling around him. He saw the man from the cottage across the yard come along and knock on the door. He was tall and well made. A manly sort of man. Shiny black face and big brown eyes with the whites flashing like snow in the sun. Sadie unlocked the door and opened it. There was talking and laughing.

Sadie swung around. 'I won't be a minute, Dad,' she said. 'Just stay there.'

He watched her cross the yard, the tall man walking by her side. They went into the cottage.

He sat for a few moments, his gaze drawn to the gleam of the key in the lock. A wing of hope lifted inside him. He got to his feet, pulled at the door, and went out into the morning air, shuffling around the back of the farmhouse so she wouldn't see him.

And then he was in the lane, and going down the road which would take him to his angel. And he was free.

★　★　★

Swift made his way down the rutted lane to the quarry. It was raining steadily and his shoes squelched through the thick slimy mud, each step an effort. Looking up at the sky, he reflected that it had been raining on and off for the past thirty-six hours, most likely destroying any evidence the SOCOs were likely to find.

As he came closer to the spot where the girl's body had lain, he saw one of the police dog handlers squatting down on his haunches, examining the sodden earth, whilst his dog sat quietly beside him, looking on.

Swift stopped alongside the ruddy-faced constable. 'Anything of interest?'

The handler sprang to his feet, laying a hand on the dog's head and quieting its low warning growl. 'Very little, sir, I'm afraid. The forensic team have got some footprint casts, but the rain's made a real mess of things. And anyway, this isn't a fenced-off place. Anyone can come here. It looks deserted now, but over the year who knows how many folks come along — with whatever motive in mind. There's no shortage of the usual rubbish hanging around a public place.'

Swift gave a wry smile. 'Empty lager cans, paper litter, underwear, used condoms . . . ' He spread his hands.

'Aye. You name it, sir. It's all been bagged up for analysis. But most likely none of it's anything to do with that poor little lass lying in the mortuary.'

Swift nodded acknowledgement. 'Has the dog picked up any scents?'

'Plenty, sir. But nothing that looks connected with the case. We gave him a scrap of the girl's clothing so he could have a go at picking up a trail. He was interested, but he just ran in circles round the spot.' The handler gave his dog an affectionate pat, clearly disappointed that the animal had been deprived of the opportunity to show what he could do.

'So what does that suggest?'

'Probably that the rain and the scent of other people coming along obscured any scent of the girl. He just didn't have enough to go on.' The dog received another regretful pat.

Swift looked around him, imagining the girl, maybe alone, making her way to this deserted, unforgiving place. Or maybe being forced to come here by someone else. A chill ran through him. 'Why would a young girl want to come to this unappealing place?' he mused.

'With a boyfriend, maybe?' The handler gave a twisted grin. 'After all, if you want a bit of time to yourself, you're not likely to get disturbed here, are you?'

'True. And I suppose there is a wild kind of romance about the place,' Swift agreed, looking around him at the vastness of the terrain and the granite sky above.

Swift looked down the track leading to the road. There were no signs of recent tyre prints beyond the point where he — and the other members of the team — had parked their vehicles. But then maybe the rain had washed away any useful evidence. 'I suppose she could have been dragged or carried here,' he commented thoughtfully.

'Aye, that's a possibility. She was just a little scrap of a thing, wasn't she, sir? Anyone could have heaved her over his shoulder.'

'That, of course, would have made his — or her — prints deeper,' Swift said, already resigning himself to the unlikelihood of getting any evidence from footprints. Unless any deeper prints had been found which could be matched with those of Ned or Sadie Bracewell, and even then it was hardly grounds for making a charge. And once they got an ID on the girl, the field would be wide open . . .

He made his way back to his car, the mud sucking greedily at his shoes seeming intent on dragging him down with every step he took.

★   ★   ★

Shuffling along in pursuit of his goal, Ned rounded the corner of the track which led to the quarry. His eyesight, unlike his mind, was undimmed by age. His body reverberated with alarm to see two men and a dog standing at the spot his angel had lain. Where had she gone? And what were they doing? Where had they taken her?

Fear and suspicion gripped him in a tight,

punishing vice. He had to get to a place of safety. The men mustn't see him. Sadie mustn't find him.

He veered off the track and stumbled into the screen of bushes and scraggy, wind-battered trees which bordered the east side of the quarry. Concealing himself behind a dead but stout trunk, he watched the two men with the intentness of a wild animal observing its predators. In time one of the men walked back up the track and climbed into his car.

An enemy, thought Ned. Everyone was an enemy these days. 'Get away, get away. Be off with yer,' he growled, not daring to move a muscle. Crouching low, he watched the man remove first one shoe and then the other, carefully wiping each one with a bright yellow cloth which swiftly turned a dark sullen grey.

At last Ned heard the sound of the engine firing, and the car moved slowly away, mud spraying from its tyres. Looking down the track he saw that the other man had walked in the opposite direction, his dog bounding ahead.

Ned released the breath from his lungs. He sat for a long while, conscious of an inner emptiness with something dark and unfathomable at its base. Some desperate, unthinkable evil. He tried to grasp hold of it, shape it into something he could understand. But he was grasping at a void. He got to his feet, overwhelmed with a sense of abandonment and loss. They had taken his angel away. Or maybe it was Sadie who had taken her away. Sadie didn't like him any more, he could tell. Oh, the way she had looked at him, her eyes like the sting of a wasp.

He got to his feet and began to lope across the ground. Rudderless and yet fuelled by an undefined intent, he weaved his way through the trees. They arched over him, hugging dark shadows in their thick bare branches, stealing away the light and air. The tangle of undergrowth pulled at his ankles, almost bringing him down, and there was mud beneath the carpet of dead leaves, skiddy and treacherous. But still he pressed on. His memory took him back through the years, to the days he had bunked school and run wild on the moors, climbing higher and higher. His heart was pounding as he took flight across the thick grassy moorland, his feet sometimes sinking deep into patches of bog fizzing with underground springs. In the picture gallery of his head he could see the stone shepherd's hut his dad used to take him to years ago. They'd eat their pork pies and he'd have a drink of pop.

It began to grow dark and the cold

wrapped itself around him and stole into his flesh and his bones, but he didn't notice it. His attention was fixed on escaping from those people who would still be watching him, waiting to pounce.

Frowning, and looking around him for any sign of the enemy, he pushed forward through the dark. In time his eyes seemed to see a light: a shivering line of gold. He followed it, his eyes fixed. A black shape grew up around the light, and as he moved nearer he could see lines of stones. This was the place! He crept up stealthily to the slatted wooden door; the light was streaming out now. He could see the planks were rotten and crumbling, daubed all over with patches of moss. He scratched on the wood with his nails and then furtively pushed at the planks.

There was the sound of scuffling inside, as though he had disturbed a sleeping animal. He took a step back, his nerves shrieking a warning. A dog began to bark.

The door swung open and a figure moved forward, eyes glinting, mouth working. Ned shrank back. He felt a hand reach out.

5

Some hours earlier, around the time Ned had set out on his journey, Swift had arrived back at the station and shut himself in his cubby-hole of a personal office. Within moments he had a visitor.

Dr Aileen Kabinsky, senior pathologist, was not a woman to waste time on social niceties and feminine charms. Somewhere in her thirties, tall and thin with long black hair tied severely back from her face, she reminded Swift of some high priestess used to holding court with respectful and obedient minions.

'I have just a few moments to spare,' she told Swift. 'Would you care to hear a summary of my findings on the dead girl?'

He suppressed a smile. Who would dare say no? 'Indeed I would.' He motioned her to a seat.

She sat, crossing long slender legs. Very shapely ones, Swift noted, as ever surprised that his appreciation of female qualities had not been all snuffed out by the loss of Kate.

'You must appreciate,' she said, 'that we are talking of probabilities and hypotheses — for the moment at least.'

Swift inclined his head.

'The girl died from asphyxiation. Perhaps from having her face tightly covered with a plastic bag, or being wrapped in clingfilm. I suggest that because there are no signs of fibres on her skin or in her hair caused by items of clothing or such things as cushions or pillows which are common methods of inflicting suffocation. Moreover, the colour of her lips would suggest that death was not protracted which would be consistent with the swift and skilful use of clingfilm. There are no signs of a struggle, nor any significant bruising or abrasions on the body. However, there is a contusion and also a network of cuts on the left side of her skull, suggesting that she could have been hit with a sharp stone shortly before she died. The blow could certainly have stunned her, but is highly unlikely to have been the cause of death.'

'Can we entirely rule out the possibility that the blow could have killed her?' Swift cut in, daring to interrupt the smooth flow of Kabinsky's rhetoric. 'In which case she could have simply taken a fall. The death could have been an accident.'

Kabinsky's dark eyes flashed. Swift's glance levelled with them.

'She died from asphyxiation,' she repeated in glacial tones. 'I have no definite proof of the method used because of the lack of actual forensic evidence. As I said before, we are dealing with probabilities, weighing evidence and theory in the balance.'

'Quite,' Swift agreed. 'So — in a court of law, would you be prepared to rule out any chance of this girl's death being caused by the injury to her head?'

Kabinsky pulled back her shoulders and took in a long breath. 'Yes, I would.'

Swift nodded his appreciation. 'The implications of being killed by a blow from a stone as opposed to having clingfilm wrapped around one's face are rather different, aren't they?' he suggested evenly. 'In terms of a possible perpetrator's motives?'

Kabinsky refused to be drawn. 'I don't go beyond the brief of my expertise, Chief Inspector. Motivation is your area of conjecture.'

There was a pause.

'I can, however, tell you,' she offered, 'that according to some recent research findings in my professional journals, the use of plastic wrapping substances is on the increase as a method of killing.'

And a very cold, calculated and cowardly method it is, thought Swift privately.

'The time of death?' he asked. 'Approximately.'

The pathologist flicked through her notes. 'Bearing in mind the time she was reported missing, the climatic conditions she was found in and the process of decomposition, I would suggest that she had been dead for around forty-eight hours at the time I examined her, perhaps a little longer.'

Swift drew in a long breath, twisting the tip of his pencil against his notepad.

Kabinsky was scanning through her immaculately handwritten pages. 'Her body showed no evidence of disease. There were no traces of drugs, but there was alcohol in the blood. Cider most probably.'

'Enough to have made her unsteady or to pass out?'

Kabinsky frowned and shook her head. 'Very hard to say. It's certainly possible she'd drunk enough to make her sleepy.'

'Any signs of sexual assualt?'

She shook her head. 'No. And there was no semen present in the body, neither was she pregnant. However, it would appear that she could have been sexually active. The hymen was broken and the vagina stretched. But, on the other hand,' she cautioned, 'it could be argued that that is normal for a young female and consistent with the use of tampons, exercising in the gym and so on.'

'So there could be a boyfriend,' Swift

remarked thoughtfully.

She held up her hand. 'Yes, but wait, there's something else. Although there were no traces of semen internally or on the body, there were traces on the girl's clothing,' Kabinsky said. 'I got the report from forensics just before I came to see you.'

Swift sat forward. 'On her *outer* clothing?'

'On both her jeans and her anorak.'

'But not on her underclothes?'

'Solely on her outerwear,' Kabinsky confirmed. 'And none on the skin.'

Swift felt the sudden tingle that comes with the whiff of a scent that might lead somewhere. He reached around the back of the chair for his jacket and began to shrug himself into it.

There was a knock on the door and Fowler walked in. 'We've got a possible ID on the girl,' he told Swift, his voice tight with suppressed excitement. 'A couple have telephoned to say they think it's their daughter.'

Swift's thoughts instantly leapt to the parents' shock and confusion. What could be worse than having your child die? Nothing, except the knowledge that the death had been a murder. How did you ever learn to live with that? He took the print-out Fowler was offering for his inspection.

51

Thursday 15th February: 10.54 — Telephone call from Mrs Anita Hoxton who claims that the unidentified murder victim discovered in Arkwright quarry is her daughter Jennifer Hoxton, aged 15 years and 6 months. Mrs Hoxton and her husband on holiday in Lake District. Now on their way back to Yorkshire to make formal identification. No further information. Call came from mobile number, break in transmission — ? battery dead. No further contact so far.

Swift dropped the paper on the desk. 'So what arrangements are being made for the Hoxtons when they arrive to view the body?'

'They're well in the picture. They've been given directions to get to the mortuary.' Fowler's deep jowls had settled in appropriately grim lines.

Swift sighed. 'I've been talking with Dr Kabinsky.'

'Oh yes?' Fowler came into full alert mode, his concentration intense as he listened to his superior's brief outline of the salient points from Kabinsky's findings. As the final details emerged, his body tensed with silent elation. He pondered for a while after Swift stopped speaking. 'I suppose you'll be wanting to meet the parents,' he said.

'Yes.' Swift looked up at the sergeant. 'Although I had been planning to go out,' he told him.

Fowler's expression sharpened. 'Yes?'

'I thought we should get a sample for DNA testing from Ned Bracewell.' Swift knew that he was simply tracking the anticipatory leaps in Fowler's conjectures.

'I'll do it, sir,' Fowler cut in, his eyes alight with new purpose.

'Yes,' Swift agreed. 'I thought you'd be the man, Geoff.'

Fowler shot him a look.

'Get a woman officer to go along with you to do the swabs,' Swift told him. 'And Geoff — take it easy on the old man.'

★　★　★

Fowler's eagerness to get to Black Sheep Farm as soon as possible was bedevilled with frustrations. To begin with his car had been blocked in by a delivery van in the pocket handkerchief of a car park which was supposed to serve a busy station. It took Detective Constable Sue Sallis fifteen minutes to locate the driver. She got into Fowler's blue VW Passat, her face pink with anxiety and effort.

'Sorry, sir,' she said. 'No one seemed to

know who the van belonged to. And I seemed to try all the wrong places.'

Hearing the genuine respect and regret in her apology, Fowler was mollified. The constable was a good-looking young woman. He'd always admired handsome women. And in his heyday he'd had no problem pulling them. He'd been quite a good-looker himself and the uniform had always helped. But the looks had gone now, just like everything else — career progression, the hope of kids, his wife.

Turning out into the main road and pulling up at the traffic lights, he reminded himself that self-pity was a pathetic and useless emotion. At which point the car coming up behind ran into the back of the Passat with a sickening crunch.

'Shit!' Fowler growled, leaping from the car to assess the damage. Fortunately, owing to the Volkswagen's tank-like construction, the damage to his car was minimal. Nothing the paint lad at his garage couldn't put right in a jiff. But the woman driver who'd bumped him needed quite a bit of calming down, and there was all the necessary performance of exchange of details to be gone through. The last thing he needed was to be caught out on procedures following a traffic incident.

'Everything all right, sir?' the constable

asked as he got back into the driving seat.

'Fine. She admitted full liability. Which, of course, is probably the best choice when you've rear-ended someone. Open and shut case.'

'Yes, sir.'

He glanced at her. Had the phrase 'rear-ended' upset her? He supposed it could be taken more than one way.

They finally arrived at Black Sheep Farm at the end of a journey which should have taken twenty minutes and had taken almost an hour. Fowler told himself to stay calm. It wasn't as if the old man would be legging it to the nearest airport, bound for some far-flung refuge from British law like Ronnie Biggs.

He turned the car into the gates with a flourish of acceleration and pulled up with a hiss of tyres. He could feel the adrenalin fizzing in his veins. This was the real stuff. Nailing the prime suspect in a big murder case.

There was no reply in response to his banging on the door. After the second attempt it was clear to both him and the constable that the farmhouse was empty. Or maybe the daughter had seen the car coming and she'd bundled her dad off somewhere to lie low.

'Have a look around the back,' he told the constable. 'Every window you can find. And see if there are any outhouses, sheds or whatever.'

As he looked into the windows running along the front wall of the farmhouse, he heard a man's voice.

'Hello there!'

Fowler turned. The man approaching was a big hunk of a young chap dressed in old jeans and a T-shirt. 'Can I help?' he asked, pleasant and matey.

Fowler produced his identification badge. 'We've come to see Mr Ned Bracewell.'

'Oh. Right.' He grinned, relaxed and at ease. Irritatingly so, in Fowler's view.

'And you are?'

'Godfrey Quarmie. I rent one of Sadie's cottages.'

'Do you know if Mr Bracewell is at home?'

'I think not.'

'Did you see him go out earlier?'

'No, I didn't. And neither did Sadie.' He left a rather theatrical pause, staring straight into the sergeant's face with a pleasantly open expression.

Fowler felt his hackles rising. He wondered what Sadie's tenant knew about the Hoxton murder. 'Just get to the point, Mr Quarmie.'

'Well, neither of us saw old Ned go out.

But he's gone, for sure. Been AWOL now for around — ' He paused to check his watch ' — oh about six hours, I'd say.'

Fowler's exhilaration was wiped out at a stroke. Shit, shit, shit!

The constable appeared from around the far side of the farmhouse. 'No one in, sir. As far as I can tell.'

'No,' said Fowler through gritted teeth. 'They've both gone missing apparently.'

'Not exactly,' Godfrey Quarmie pointed out, eyeing DC Sue Sallis with interest. 'Sadie's not missing. She just went out to find her dad. She'll be back soon, no worries. You're most welcome to come and wait in my place if you'd like.' His lazy, sexy smile made Fowler's fist tingle with the desire to ram itself into the tenant's handsome face.

What to do now? Fowler wondered. To return to the station seemed like a humiliating anti-climax. But there was no point both he and the constable hanging around here in the middle of nowhere. He was just contemplating phoning for a car to come and pick either him or her up, when Sadie's mud-caked Land Rover turned into the drive.

She climbed out of the car, a strong, solid figure, her body slow with fatigue, her face crumpled with anxiety. 'Oh!' she said when she recognized Fowler. She walked past him,

57

selecting the house key from the jangling bunch in her hand. 'You'd better come in.' She stood aside as Fowler and the police constable stepped through the door.

Fowler saw her glance towards Quarmie. It was hard to tell how much he knew.

'Will you be OK?' the tenant enquired of her, his laidback demeanour suddenly giving way to an air of genuine concern.

Something between those two? Fowler wondered, storing the conjecture for later consideration.

'Yeah, fine,' Sadie told her tenant.

'OK.' He turned towards his cottage. 'Take it easy now.'

Sadie made a cursory gesture in Fowler and the constable's direction, indicating that they should sit down. She then went to the sink, filled the kettle and switched it on. She slapped a thick wooden chopping board on the counter, took peeled potatoes from a pan of water on the drainer, and began to slice them with a long cook's knife. From the oven came the rich scent of meat which had been cooking slowly for some time.

Fowler exchanged a glance with the constable. 'Leave this to me,' he mouthed.

Before he could speak, Sadie spun around, leaning back against the counter. 'Well?' she said, eyeballing Fowler with a directness somewhere between challenge and fear. 'What do you want?'

'We've got some important forensic evidence,' Fowler told her. 'From the dead girl's clothing. We've come to get some swabs from your dad. For DNA testing.'

He watched Sadie carefully. Her eyes stared back with the flash of the devil in them.

'It's routine procedure, Miss Bracewell,' Fowler said.

'He's not here.' She delved into a basket of vegetables beside the sink and seized a large winter cabbage wrapped in swathes of clingfilm.

'No, we know that already,' Fowler said, his eyes feasting on the shiny plastic as she peeled it from the cabbage, delightedly noting that the old guy had access to the stuff used in the kid's murder. 'So where is he?'

She threw the knife down on the board. 'I don't know. I've looked in all his usual haunts.' She pushed a hand through her thick brown hair. The strands lifted and settled back in exactly the same position. 'I just don't know. I'm really worried . . . ' Her voice sounded on the edge of despair.

'Come on, now, love,' Fowler objected. 'You must have some idea.'

'No. He does sometimes go missing

59

. . . well, go out for an hour or so. But not for all this time. And he's always back for his supper.' She bit on her lips. 'He'll be hungry.'

'Where are his usual haunts?' the constable asked.

Sadie took a few moments to think. 'He likes to walk across the fields at the back. He goes as far as the old cattle drinking trough that marks the boundary between our land and the Smithsons' farm, and then he comes back. Sometimes he'll walk down the road until he gets to the main junction.'

'And, of course, the quarry,' Fowler reminded her.

'I suppose so.' She picked up the knife and began sectioning the cabbage with strong, clean strokes.

'Does he take food with him when he goes out?' the constable asked.

Sadie shook her head.

'Or money?' the constable pressed.

Fowler grimaced, thinking he could do without the girl farting about asking useless questions and not letting him get a word in edgeways. He sent her a quelling look.

'Hard to say,' Sadie said. 'He doesn't think ahead like that. He just . . . does things.'

'He just . . . does things,' Fowler echoed slowly. 'Like wanking over a young girl's body. Like killing her first.' He was beginning to relish the freedom to conduct the interview in exactly the way he liked. The way he thought best to get a result. Not with one hand tied behind his back by Swift's liking for pussyfooting political correctness.

He heard the constable draw in a breath. Well, she could think what she liked. God! Everyone thought what they liked. The knack was learning not to care.

'No!' Sadie yelled, bringing her fist down on the counter and making the cups stacked beside the kettle rattle.

'His mind's gone, hasn't it, love? His mind's permanently on AWOL. He's capable of anything.'

'No!' She put her hands over her face. 'No,' she groaned.

The kettle had come up to the boil as she spoke. Clouds of steam were billowing from the spout, gradually enveloping Sadie in a white mist. The constable got up and stepped forward to flip the switch off. Sadie remained motionless. Fowler jerked his head, instructing the constable to move away from the stricken woman.

'We'll be able to prove it,' Fowler said, deadly quiet. 'You can't mess with DNA. One hundred per cent reliable.'

'Oh, God!' Sadie moaned.

'Come on, love,' Fowler coaxed. 'You know

he did it, don't you? I can understand your loyalty, but we're talking about a young girl's murder here. This is no time to mess about. And once your dad turns up and we get a DNA match, what happened will be as clear as day. There'll be no point protecting him.'

Sadie stood with her head bowed like a dumb tethered animal awaiting its fate.

'You believe he did it, don't you?' Fowler persisted. 'So just tell us where he is, love. You've put him somewhere safe, haven't you? With relatives maybe, or friends who aren't going to talk.'

'You must be joking,' she said wearily. 'Dad hasn't got anyone left except me. My brother lives in Australia and doesn't want to know about him since things started getting difficult. And it's funny how friends back off when there's any sign of the brain not being quite what it was.'

'Let's try to get this mess sorted out,' Fowler coaxed. 'No one's going to hurt your dad. He'll be well treated. Diminished responsibility. He'll be in clover — '

Sadie's head came up. Her eyes blazed as she stepped up to Fowler, thrusting her face into his. 'Are you totally stupid? Hasn't it occurred to you that I *don't* believe my father is guilty. No, wrong — that I *know* he isn't guilty. Maybe you think I'm frightened about living with the horror of my dad being a murderer. Wrong. What I am frightened of is you lot using your 'evidence' to pin this crime on him and for all the world to believe he's a killer. It's a matter of honour, you see. Of his honour, regardless of the state of his mind. I can't bear for him to carry the stamp of evil with him until he dies. For his memory to be blighted. I won't let it happen.' She moved back, letting out a sigh. 'And what's more,' she added with quiet intensity, 'I have no idea where he is. I am frantic with worry. And if you weren't here the first thing I'd be doing is calling the police.'

6

Swift stood back to allow Jeremy and Anita Hoxton some privacy as they came face to face with the terrible reality of their daughter's death. It was a small bare room they entered, its only feature a large interior window from which red cotton curtains were drawn back. Beyond the glass the small body could be seen lying on a white-draped trolley. She was now wrapped in a winding sheet, her lifeless face waxen and empty.

After a short silence, Anita Hoxton spoke in calm, unemotional tones. 'Yes, that is Jenny.' Her husband nodded acknowledgement. He and his wife exchanged a long look, then Anita Hoxton turned away from the pathetic bundle of the body and walked to the door. She moved with noticeable dignity and grace. Swift was reminded of shots of Margot Fonteyn in her later years: the severe classically swept-up hair-style, the beautiful but skeletal figure, the sad, remote smile.

'You can spend as long as you like with her,' Swift told her quietly.

She shook her head. 'She's gone. There's nothing that can be done to alter that.' She made a slight alteration to the fall of the coral silk scarf around her neck. 'If you would like to speak to us now, Inspector, we'll be glad to answer any questions which might help you with your enquiries.'

Swift wondered if she was on some miracle tranquilizer, her composure was so chillingly intact. Jeremy Hoxton, well made and two or three inches shorter than his wife, put a hand beneath her elbow as they made their way to Swift's office, although she didn't seem to need his support.

'I'd like to offer my sincerest condolences before we start,' Swift told the two of them as they faced him, backs straight, faces impassive and yet at the same time expectant of his interrogation. 'I have a daughter of my own. But I wouldn't presume to pretend that I can imagine how you must be feeling. Only someone who has lost a child themselves could begin to understand that.'

Jeremy Hoxton nodded, resignation and misery dragging down his heavy but pleasantly modelled features.

'How did she die?' Anita Hoxton asked, fixing Swift with her large silvery blue eyes. 'I mean — do you think it could have been some terrible accident?'

'We're treating it as a suspicious death,' Swift told her with deliberate caution. He left a pause, hopeful that the precise ice queen Anita Hoxton was going to hand out quite a bit of information without very much help from him.

'Could it have been suicide?' she asked, eyeing Swift in a manner that would have left a less assured officer with the uncomfortable sense that he should in some way feel guilt about her daughter's death.

'Do you know of any reason why she might have attempted suicide?' Swift followed up.

'She was a teenager,' Anita Hoxton said. 'Moody, uncertain, unpredictable.'

'Are you talking of teenagers generally, or Jenny in particular?'

She gave a faint smile. 'Both.'

'Do you have any other children?' Swift let his gaze swivel to Jeremy Hoxton, wondering when he was going to show any sign of participating in the proceedings.

'A son. He's twenty-one and studying at the Sorbonne.' He bent his head and let out a low groan. 'Oh, God! Poor little Jenny.'

'And our daughter Antonia is sixteen,' Anita said. 'She's still at school.'

'Did they get on well?' Swift asked. 'They're very close in age.'

Jeremy glanced up at Swift, pressed his lips together then lowered his head once more.

'No,' Anita said calmly. 'They didn't get on

well at all. I don't mean that in the sense of their having rows and so on. Antonia and Jenny simply didn't take all that much notice of each other.' Her disturbing eyes fixed on Swift. 'That happens in families, you know. It's not at all abnormal.'

Swift wondered about the atmosphere in the Hoxton household, speculating on Jenny's life with this cold mother, a seemingly ineffectual father and an elder sister who apparently wasn't interested in her. 'You were away in the Lake District when Jenny went missing,' he said to the parents.

'We were never aware that she was missing,' Anita Hoxton responded coldly. 'She was supposedly staying at a school-friend's house whilst we were away.'

'Supposedly?' Swift interposed.

'I telephoned the girl's parents as soon as I saw the report on the television. They said that Jenny had not been to stay with them.' She paused. 'They also said that they had not been aware of any such arrangement having been made. Nor had their daughter.'

Swift noticed the tightness of her lips. It had clearly been difficult for her to make that admission. But was the difficulty connected with how badly the revelation reflected on Jenny, or was the problem more connected with it showing Mrs Hoxton up in a poor light as a parent? 'So, Jenny told you she had made arrangements to stay with a friend whilst you and your husband were away in the Lake District. She gave you details of this friend and her family — but she never turned up there,' Swift observed. 'Is that correct?'

Mrs Hoxton gave a terse 'Yes'. 'You're welcome to check this out with the family concerned,' she told Swift graciously. 'They are a Mr and Mrs York and their daughter is called Rosemary.' She turned her head slightly. 'Rosemary, incidentally, spent her half-term visiting a friend in Geneva.'

'So you didn't check personally on the arrangements with Mr and Mrs York before you left home?'

Anita Hoxton let out a sigh of irritation. 'Jenny was fifteen. The friend in question and her family were people I knew to be very reliable and Jenny had visited their house before. I always tried to give Jenny the impression that I trusted in her as a young adult.' She sounded as though she were reading from a textbook.

'Have you any idea where Jenny might have been staying instead?' Swift asked, reviewing his own likely procedures of checking on Naomi's plans in similar circumstances and discovering they were not as clear cut as he might have imagined. 'Or with whom?'

'No,' Mrs Hoxton said with firm finality. 'It's possible she could have been living rough. She did that once or twice when she was nine or ten.'

'Living rough?' Swift invited elaboration.

'She once made herself very snug on the verandah of the mini golf course in the park just at the end of the road. She'd crept out of the house after she'd gone to bed for the night. We didn't even know she was missing until the police brought her home in the morning.' Mrs Hoxton flexed her long fingers. Her perfectly manicured nails gleamed.

'But to live rough in this weather? In wintertime? For three whole days?'

'Yes, it does seem odd,' Mrs Hoxton agreed. 'But still. Teenage girls can do some very odd things — and show enormous resilience.'

Swift paused, momentarily staggered by this mother's clinical detachment in the face of the violent death of a child.

'I assume you must have got medical reports and so on,' Anita Hoxton observed. 'So presumably you're able to give me an answer to my question about suicide.'

Her ability to maintain her astounding poise led Swift to assume she was exhibiting a severe form of denial, that by some purely subconscious means she had developed a successful mental block about her daughter's death and all the horrors attaching to it.

'We have evidence which strongly suggests she was murdered,' Swift told her.

Jeremy Hoxton flinched but his wife, whilst her face registered a wintry bleakness, maintained her calm. 'She looked so peaceful,' she commented. 'Her face, the way she was lying — there was nothing about her that spoke of violence.'

'So, how was she . . . erm . . . How did . . . ?' Jeremy's voice trailed away. 'Would it have been quick?'

'We believe so,' Swift reassured him.

Jeremy Hoxton's face hardened. He made a visible effort to shake off his torpor, straightening his spine and pulling his shoulders back in a gesture of self-assertion. 'So have you got any ideas?' he levelled at Swift. 'A suspect? One of these paedophiles who seem to be springing up all over the place?' Suddenly there was a light of emotion in his eyes — rage and a desire for the swift tracking down of evildoers.

'We're pursuing a certain line of enquiry,' Swift said carefully.

'You mean you've got someone in the frame?'

'It's too early to say yet. Of course we're also carrying out routine investigative work, trawling through unsolved murder cases in the area from the last twelve months, looking for any similarities with Jenny's case. So far we haven't come up with any matches, but it is very early days as yet.'

'You need to work fast,' Jeremy Hoxton said. 'According to statistics the chance of finding the murderer drops significantly some time around three days after the deed has been done. Isn't that right?'

Swift parried the question with a terse inclination of his head. He looked from one parent to the other. 'Do you feel able to answer some questions about Jenny? What you can tell us about her as a person could be very helpful in channelling our efforts in the right direction.'

Jeremy Hoxton glowered. 'This isn't anything to do with Jenny. This has to do with some nutter out there in 'society'. There seem to be psychos all over the place these days.'

'What more do you want to know about Jenny?' Anita Hoxton asked, ignoring her husband's bitterness. Her face was beginning to register the strain of the situation, but her dignity still remained intact.

'Well,' Swift began gently, 'had you noticed anything unusual in her behaviour in recent weeks?'

Jeremy Hoxton gave an impatient sigh, but

his wife turned her head slightly, a frown of concentration making faint grooves in her forehead. One of her solitaire diamond earrings caught the light, shooting out a tongue of fire.

'She absented herself from home without anyone knowing where she was,' Swift reminded them. 'Was she worried about anything? Did she show any signs of distress?'

'Oh, for God's sake,' Jeremy protested. 'As my wife said before, Jenny was a teenage girl. They're up and down like see-saws, aren't they? All over the bloody place.'

'If anything, I would describe Jenny as unusually animated,' Mrs Hoxton said thoughtfully. 'Excited, on a bit of a high.'

'I never noticed that,' her husband countered.

'No.' His wife turned to him. 'But you never noticed much about her, did you? After all, you're always working or out at your various sports club dinners.' The accusation was delivered with polite and chilling dispassion.

'Did she give you any indication as to what might have been the reason for the behaviour you describe?' Swift lobbed the question into the ensuing tight silence, his eyes not swerving from Anita Hoxton.

She shook her head. 'No, but then she

wasn't in the habit of confiding in me. Hardly at all, in fact.'

'Maybe she confided in Antonia?' Swift suggested.

'I doubt it. Jenny preferred to keep her thoughts and feelings very private. But you're perfectly at liberty to ask Antonia herself if you wish.'

'Do you know if Jenny had received any unusual phone calls in recent weeks? Or arranged any meetings?'

Anita frowned. 'Not as far as I'm aware. I suppose you're referring to possible boyfriend liaisons and so forth?'

Swift made a confirming nod.

'I suppose,' Anita said slowly, 'Jenny could have received 'unusual calls', as you put it. Jeremy and I are not in the habit of supervising our children every minute of the day.' She considered further. 'But she certainly didn't make any. I always check our phone account very carefully. There have been no calls to numbers I don't recognize.'

Swift could not deny that Anita had been unfailingly co-operative, but her glacial composure was having an increasingly deadening effect on the progress of the interview. Making a swift mental review of what had already been covered, he considered his next line of questioning.

'For God's sake,' Jeremy Hoxton burst out, 'if the poor kid was hounded down and murdered, what's the point in going on with this? What does it matter if she was on a 'high' or in a mood or whatever? She went out and got killed by a nutter. That's what everyone we know thinks.' He got to his feet, fixing Swift with a blazing glare. 'So why don't you stop wasting our time and get out there and find him?'

★   ★   ★

Fowler let himself in through the kitchen door and switched off the alarm. He ran through a mental checklist of the past two hours, anxious to ensure that he had set up all the correct procedural arrangements for the early discovery of Ned Bracewell's whereabouts. When it had gone past eight-thirty and neither Swift nor Lister had been available for consultation, he had decided to pack in and call it a day. Going back three years or so he would have had a sure confidence in having covered all eventualities until the morning, and there would have been no worrying and 'what-ifs' churning away in his head. You only had to make one unlucky mistake and all the years of reliable work seemed to be rubbed out. You were no longer fully trusted, and your chances of promotion vanished like the setting sun. And at his age you came to realize that you had crowned the hill and started down the dreary slope to an inglorious retirement on the approach to fifty.

'Hello!' he called into the hallway. 'I'm home.' He took a bottle of lager from the fridge and eased off the cap.

'Hello there, lover boy!' The husky voice resonated in his ear. 'You're late. Had a good day?'

He took a swig of lager. 'Could have been better.'

'Oh, come on. Don't be such a pessimist.' The tone was lovingly chiding.

'Am I getting to be a bitter, warped old sod?' he asked.

'Old! You've got plenty of life left in you yet, my lad.' The voice turned seductive. 'Come here, let me show you.'

Fowler crashed the bottle down on the kitchen table. Tears of frustration and loneliness were building beneath his eyelids. 'Christ Almighty! I'll be heading for the funny farm if I keep on talking to myself like this.'

He picked up his keys, reset the alarm and headed off to his local pub.

After a couple of pints of good Yorkshire bitter the sullen sourness that scoured his innards like an ever-present cancer began to ease and mellow. He lit a cigarette and inhaled deeply. A hand fell on his shoulder. Turning, he saw the smiling face of Phil Kirkham, another regular who liked to put a few pints away after work before going home.

'Geoff! How are you, pal? I'm buying.' Kirkham settled himself on a stool and made instant eye contact with the barmaid. 'Two pints of best bitter here, love.' He loosened his tie. 'So, how's tricks in the world of crime solving?'

Fowler raised his eyes to the tannin-stained ceiling.

'Have you got anything on this Arkwright quarry murder yet?' Kirkham's doggedly amiable expression suddenly sharpened.

'Nothing I'm prepared to divulge to you,' Fowler responded with a wry grin. Kirkham was a reporter on the local newspaper, well known for his tenacity in pursuing a good story and his complete lack of morals in spilling any beans which landed on his plate.

'Oh, come on, Geoff. You must have a suspect.'

Fowler assumed an expression of saintly restraint.

'You have got someone!' Kirkham exclaimed, eyes glittering like gems.

'Just been up to Black Sheep Farm,' Fowler said, pushing his empty glass away and grasping the full one the girl placed in front of him.

'The Bracewells' place?'

'Mmm.'

'Of course! She was the one who found the body.'

'That's right.'

'What! Sadie Bracewell? Are you telling me she's been bumping off schoolgirls? Now that could have the beginnings of a good story.'

'Keep your voice down, Phil.' Fowler stared fixedly into his pint. 'Slander's actionable.'

Kirkham thought for a couple of seconds. 'Not Sadie, then.' He took a long drink of beer. 'Is the old man still going strong?' he said thoughtfully.

'You could say that,' Fowler agreed. 'Lost his marbles, poor bugger. Soft in the head, still sound in wind and limb.'

Kirkham got the drift. He leaned forward. 'Are you going to charge him?'

Fowler stubbed out his cigarette and drew himself up. 'I've said enough. That's your lot.'

'You've said nothing, mate,' Kirkham said with a conspiratorial wink. 'And I never divulge sources.'

On the way home Fowler examined his motives in leaking information to Kirkham, who could be relied on to have it reaching the necessary outlets within the hour.

It was a mish-mash. It was all about enjoying the power of setting a match to a box of fireworks, cocking a snook at prissy, do-gooding Swift, pushing against the restraints which were increasingly strangling police work. Getting the right man nailed. And something more than that, some deep need he couldn't put his finger on. He remembered, way back in detective school, they'd had a psychologist come to talk to them. The bloke had done a session when he'd talked about the 'whole' being more than the sum of the 'parts'. It was one of the few theories the bloke had floated that had made any impression on him. Made sense. He tried to remember the name of the theory but it annoyingly eluded him. Hell, was he going soft in the head like dozy Bracewell?

He drew in deep breaths of the night air. Whatever his real motives in talking to Kirkham, the basic result was he felt good. Maybe criminals who pulled off a job and knew they'd never get caught had much the same feeling.

As he put his key in the lock, his brain spoke to him. 'Gestalt', it said. 'Gestalt!' he responded in triumph. 'Ay, Geoff lad, you're not finished yet.'

* * *

Swift found the apartment in semi-darkness when he arrived home around ten o'clock. The kitchen and the living room had a tidy, abandoned look about them. There was a disturbing lack of any signs of life: no cereal bowls, cigarette packets, magazines or clothes scattered around. And no sign of Naomi. When he had rung earlier the house phone had kicked into the answering service and her mobile phone had been firmly switched off.

His throat was dry as he tapped on the door of her bedroom. No response. He opened the door and moved softly through. He could see the curve of her body under the duvet. Thank God!

He sat on the bed and looked down at her. Her eyes were closed, her breathing steady. He sat watching her.

'I'm awake,' she said.

'You're early to bed,' he ventured.

'Mmm.'

'Are you all right?'

'Yes.' Everything in her tone said 'no'.

He dared to let his fingers trail lightly over her cheek. 'You're not ill, are you?'

'No, I am not ill.'

Aware that she had probably been wishing for him to come home, possibly even wanting to confide in him, he could tell that she now couldn't wait for him to go away and leave her in peace. That's normal, he told himself. That's teenagers. And most likely nothing to do with being alone far too much and struggling with grief. And not having a mother. He got up.

'Sleep well,' he said as he closed the door.

He got cheese, bread and wine from the fridge, then flicked on the television news to see if there was anything about Jenny Hoxton. Her murder came on as the second item, after the main story about a rebellion on the government backbenches. Detective Superintendent Lister was being interviewed by a young woman reporter with a chiselled haircut and fiercely intelligent features. He told her that detectives and forensic teams were searching the quarry area for clues. The reporter kept pressing him for information about possible suspects, making reference to the public concern about paedophiles. But Lister declined to be drawn. Swift was surprised at his patience and fluency in responding to the woman's interrogation. His usual bluff, call-a-spade-a-bloody-shovel approach was well under wraps, his Yorkshire accent barely discernible. The pictures then moved on to the mound of flowers and soft toys being left outside the gates of Jenny's house. Through his concentration on the unfolding account, he was aware of Naomi's bedroom door opening, of the slap of her slippers on the hall floor, of her silent presence standing beside him. A photograph of Jenny came up on the screen. A pinched, solemn face with small features, the hair scraped back from her face.

'This is your current case, isn't it?' Naomi said.

'Yes.'

Naomi looked at the screen for a moment then turned away. She never pressed him about his work, his cases, the victims and perpetrators. He supposed she was simply used to his being a detective — it was what he had done ever since she could remember.

She curled herself on the sofa. The news moved on to a new item.

Swift sat down and assembled a chunky sandwich from the cheese and bread on his plate. Signals of need were coming off Naomi like sparks, but he was unsure how to coax her into confiding. She reacted to stress by retreating into secretive, brittle privacy. She'd been like that from being a small child.

'I *am* all right,' she told him. 'You don't need to worry about me.'

He smiled. 'How's the god of the sixth form?' He held his breath.

'Better than most.' She shot him one of her slanty, wicked glances. 'And that's another thing not to worry about. I'm not going to get my heart broken by some bloke, no matter how god-like. I'm not even going to *think* of going down that road.'

'Fair enough,' Swift agreed non-committally.

'Do you miss Mum really terribly?' she asked abruptly, catching him off-guard.

'Yes.' He put his plate down on the floor and picked up his glass. 'Do you?'

'Sometimes,' she said slowly, 'I dream about her. Not a mixed-up fantasy kind of dream, more like real life. She's there with me, being a mother, knowing things only mothers know.' She looked across at her stricken parent. 'You're in the dreams sometimes too, Dad,' she said as an offering of comfort.

He smiled.

'I wake up,' she said in an absent voice, 'and just for a few minutes I'm all dizzy with hope and longing.'

He closed his eyes briefly. 'Yes,' he agreed.

'So!' she said, putting on a brave grin and shaking her shoulders. 'That's enough of bleeding hearts and confessions for one evening.'

Swift looked into Naomi's knowing face with her mother's vivid blue eyes and was aware of a strange lift in his spirits. Maybe it wouldn't last long, but the brief sharing of feelings with his daughter had kindled a spark of new hope which could, perhaps, be kept smouldering when this moment of unexpected happiness had passed. He leaned back and stretched.

'That girl,' Naomi said, her eyes narrowed in thought. 'Jenny. In the photograph she looked . . . how can I put it, dissatisfied.'

Swift was interested. For him the girl had looked sad. But then he was aware of seeing sadness everywhere. He recalled the words Anita Hoxton had first used about her daughter. *Moody, uncertain.*

'I suppose it's the parents who make the choice of which photograph to give to the media,' Naomi continued.

'Yes, that would normally be the case.'

'I wonder why they'd choose a picture that made their daughter look cheesed off with life. I mean, usually the pictures of murdered kids show them all happy and smiling, tragically cut down in the golden days of their youth and so on.' Her voice had regained all its usual acerbity. Acid sixteen, thought Swift with an internal grin.

'Maybe there wasn't a picture like that available,' he suggested.

'Not one single picture with a hint of a happy smile about it!' Naomi rolled her eyes. 'Well, that's something for you to get your teeth into, isn't it?'

★ ★ ★

Ned scraped at the closed door with his fingernails. He didn't know where he was. It was dark. The door wouldn't open. The wind was moaning through the cracks, piercing him with darts of freezing air. It was cold, so very cold. His fingers and toes hurt.

Thoughts drifted through his mind like clouds blown on the breeze. He started to cry and then he couldn't remember what he was crying about. His memories were blocked by thick grey clumps which kept moving silently into his head. There was someone he needed, someone who could help him. He didn't know who. He began to sob.

7

Twenty-fours had passed. Twenty-four hours of futile searching for Ned Bracewell. For Lister it had seemed like a lifetime.

He called Swift into his office. 'How can an old man disappear into thin air when the whole of the nation's police force are aware, and a significant proportion of the local crew are combing the landscape?'

Swift appreciated the diminishing likelihood of an early discovery now that the initial search had been completed. Having lost their prime suspect, they would now have to start interviewing known paedophiles in the area from the Sex Offenders' Register. More delay, more expense. More griping from the press about a lack of progress on the case. More pressure from the powers that be. And the response to an appeal for any sighting or information about Jenny's doings or whereabouts in the days before her death had also drawn a disappointing blank.

'We had a case of a young woman going missing a couple of winters ago,' Lister said gloomily. 'She'd been out for a drink. Phoned her family around midnight, pissed, to say she was lost in some sort of woodland. We went through all the surrounding woods with a toothcomb. She was found nine weeks later in a rhododendron bush at the back of a long garden just down the road from where she lived. She'd passed out, then died of hypothermia.' He paused, frustration crackling from him. 'Nine weeks, Ed. Nine bloody weeks!'

Swift was becoming accustomed to his new superior's irascibility in the face of setbacks. He had come to realize that the most effective response was one of unruffled calm.

'I think it would be worth my talking to the dead girl's family again,' he said, framing the plan more as a polite request than a foregone conclusion. 'There seems to have been some friction between Jenny and her sister.'

Lister's impatience mounted; Swift could see him struggling to restrain it like a rider wrestling with a wayward horse. 'It's a bugger when we have to waste time and manpower going down blind alleys when we know pretty damn well who our man is.'

'We need to be seen to be proactive whilst we're waiting for Bracewell to turn up,' Swift pointed out. 'Maybe we could call in one of the Home Office criminal analysts to compile a profile.'

Lister threw his gaze up to the ceiling.

'They are police officers,' Swift pointed out.

'A bloody strange new breed of officers, if you ask me. Christ Almighty. The last thing I want is some trick cyclist hanging around. Mind you, I'd give a grand to someone who read the tea leaves if I thought they could lead us to the old bloke's hideout.' Lister's jowls sagged with despondency. 'Well, there certainly seems no point going through all the pantomime of press conferences and a mock-up of the girl's last movements.' He rested his chin on his clenched hand, his face creased with anxiety. Irritated beyond endurance when the phone on his desk rang, he snatched it up and shouted into the mouthpiece. 'I said not to put through any calls until I've finished this meeting.'

Swift waited for him to slam the phone down, but instead he saw Lister give a grimace, then sit a little higher and run a hand over the dome of his head as if he expected the caller to look through the receiver and see him. There was the low rumble of a man's voice at the other end. Lister pulled the receiver closer to his ear and with his other hand touched the knot of his tie. 'Good morning, sir,' he said. 'Yes, yes, I'm well, thank you. And you?'

As the voice rumbled on, Lister reached for

the pen which lay beside his pad. 'No, sir. I'm afraid not. We're making an intensive search.' He paused and more words floated to him over the phone, reaching Swift as no more than a dim murmur.

'Yes, sir. I agree, it's very unfortunate for a key witness to go missing.' He looked across at Swift and raised his eyes to the ceiling in despair. There was an accelerated eruption of words from the other end. Lister winced, tapping the pen rhythmically on his pad. 'Of course, sir. I appreciate that.' He shot a look at Swift, then glanced down at the tapping pen and forced himself to lay it down on the desk. The voice continued, an unstoppable stream of authority. Lister opened his mouth once or twice to speak but the distant voice gave him no gap into which to proceed.

Eventually the torture ceased. 'I'll keep you informed,' Lister managed in a tight voice, replacing the receiver gently on its rest. His body sagged as he looked across at Swift. 'The assistant chief constable,' he said. 'handing out what I think might be termed a 'right bollocking'. On top of which he wants me to talk to the press again later today.'

Swift assumed a neutral expression and kept silent.

'OK, then,' Lister said eventually. 'You go and do a bit of digging with the family, Ed.'

He looked up, the hint of a smile softening his features. 'Proactive seems to be the current buzzword. And just keep things low key, will you? I don't want any more ear bashings. Not for the next twenty-four hours at least.'

★   ★   ★

The Hoxtons' house was in a broad road, bordered by a generously wide pavement with long-established trees growing out of it. It was an imposing detached Victorian villa built of sturdy Yorkshire stone which spoke of comfortable affluence and restrained taste. Swift could see the hand of Anita Hoxton all over it.

He had taken with him the young Detective Constable Sue Sallis, who had previously been paired with Fowler. They spoke to Antonia in the drawing room amongst elegant antiques shaded from the slanting winter sun by stylishly faded brocade curtains. She had answered Swift's ring on the doorbell and had shown neither surprise nor discomfiture when he introduced himself.

'My parents are out,' she told him. 'Talking to the vicar about a memorial service.' She had looked at him, sizing him up with a shrewd, cool gaze, noting the presence of the woman detective behind him. 'Do you want to come in?' She stood aside as they stepped into the hallway. She was tall like her mother, and even in her teenage uniform of baggy sludge-green combat trousers and a grey lycra top she projected an aura of style and grace.

She curled herself on the sofa, tucking her bare feet beneath her. She fitted perfectly into her surroundings: a tall, white-painted room with elaborate plaster mouldings, parquet floor polished to the brilliance of a newly fallen conker, a nine-foot Steinway in the corner, the lid propped open, a book of Chopin nocturnes on the stand. And flowers everywhere: velvety irises, pale pink carnations and great bowls of white lilies whose thick, sweet fragrance filled the room.

Swift noticed the rows of condolence cards crowded together on the marble mantelpiece. 'I'm sorry about your sister,' he said.

She made a small movement of her head. 'Yeah. Thanks.'

Swift watched her, wondering how long she would tolerate the silence. She curled a strand of highlighted blonde hair around her finger. 'Have you any idea who killed her?' she asked.

'We've nothing definite as yet.'

'Do you think you've any real hope of

catching whoever it was?' She unleashed the strand of hair and took up another.

As cool as a cucumber, Swift thought. Like mother, like daughter. Or was this simply a defensive adolescent front? 'What makes you say that?'

'Well, isn't it true that lots of murders remain unsolved?' Her eyes challenged him with an unswerving gaze.

'Some do,' Swift agreed. 'But modern techniques of forensic pathology have given our detection success rates a good boost.'

'Sure.' She gave a little sigh, as though bored with this line of discussion. Pushing her hair behind her ears, she waited for the next question.

'Where were you, Antonia,' Swift asked in neutral tones, 'when you heard about Jenny's death?'

'I was staying with friends while my parents were away. They rang me there to tell me.' She uncurled her legs slightly, her eyes still holding his. A beautifully boned filly, her hair slightly dirty, her face bare of make-up, everything about her oozed high-class sexiness.

'Did you know Jenny was missing before that?' Swift asked.

'No. She'd gone to stay with a friend. I thought she was there. Didn't Mummy tell you all this?'

Swift ignored the demand. 'Did you know who she was staying with?'

'I knew who she was supposed to be staying with. But apparently, she never went there at all.' The silly bitch, her face seemed to say.

Swift waited. 'Where do you think she went instead?'

'I've no idea.'

He made his face austere and unforgiving. 'Come on, Antonia. You and Jenny were sisters — don't they always know each other's business?'

Her eyes flickered with glints of angry displeasure. 'Maybe. But we two didn't happen to fit that cosy mould.'

'Which of Jenny's friends was she most likely to be with? In your opinion?' he persisted.

'I don't know. She didn't really seem to have many friends. And she certainly didn't talk about them to me.' She glanced at him in defiance, then relented. 'I'm sure Mummy could give you some names. She's very organized about that sort of thing.' Her eyes were once again fixed on his. Silvery-blue gimlets like Anita's.

'Did Jenny have a boyfriend?' Constable Sallis asked.

Antonia's lips parted in a gesture of

92

incredulity. 'No. She wasn't interested in boys and they weren't interested in her.'

Swift and his constable kept quiet, their eyes on Antonia.

'She was, sort of, immature,' Antonia said eventually. 'You know, she still had posters of pop idols and TV stars on her bedroom walls.'

'Did Jenny carry a mobile phone?' the constable asked.

'No. My mother doesn't approve of them.' Antonia's eyes swivelled briefly in the woman's direction and then moved back to Swift.

She's learned always to deal with the top man, he thought with grim irony. 'Do you have one?' he asked.

'Yes.' She looked at him with faint challenge. 'But I'm sixteen. And I bought one for myself with money my grandmother gave me.'

Swift made a mental note of this indication of parental discrimination. 'Did you catch the first news reports of a girl being found at the Arkwright quarry?'

'Yeah.'

'What was your reaction?'

She shrugged. 'I suppose . . . kind of sorry that yet another kid had ended up dead at the hands of some nutcase. But it happens all the time, doesn't it? There are kids reported going missing most weeks.' She wound another strand of hair through her fingers. 'Mainly girls.'

'Did you link the quarry murder with Jenny?'

'Of course not,' she flashed back. 'I told you, I'd no idea she'd gone missing.' You won't catch me out like that, her scornful glance indicated.

'Did you talk to anyone about it?'

'Just to Pippa. She was the friend I was staying with. We heard about it on one of the local radio news flashes.'

Swift tried to imagine the conversation. *Hey, listen to this! A girl's been found dead in some old quarry. Do you think she's been murdered, poor bitch?*

'Mummy rang quite soon afterwards to tell us . . . what had happened. It was a shock,' Antonia offered, as though reading Swift's reflections on her unsisterly-like behaviour and reactions.

'Was anything troubling Jenny?' Swift asked. 'In recent weeks?'

Antonia dipped her head, then lifted it again. 'No, I don't think so.' Still her face gave nothing away.

'Did she seem in any respect different to how she was normally?'

There was a brief undecipherable glimmer

94

in Antonia's eyes. A flash which vanished almost as soon as it had come. 'No. She was just like her usual self.'

'Which was?'

'A bit of a loner. Keeping things to herself.' She spread her long fingers and touched around a slender silver ring on her right hand. 'I didn't really see so much of her. I'm round at Pippa's a lot. And we go out together. Shopping and clubs.'

'What about your school work? Where do you do that?'

Antonia smiled. There was a hint of contempt for his adult misconception of the modern student's work habits. 'I get most of it done in school in the lunch hour. You can get through quite a lot if you make yourself really focused.'

'And so then you're free in the evenings and at weekends?'

'Yeah. Mostly.'

'What was Jenny interested in?' DC Sallis asked. 'Did she have any hobbies?'

'Hobbies!' Again there was a glimmer, a chord struck which seemed to symbolize disdainful amusement that such a suggestion could be made. 'Not really. She watched a lot of television.'

'By herself — or with friends?' Swift followed up.

'I've already said, I don't know about friends. She certainly didn't bring them here. She tagged on with a crowd at school, but I don't think there was anyone special. Like I said, she was OK being on her own.' Antonia's relaxed disinterest was almost shocking. And Swift was not easily shocked.

He glanced at the constable, indicating that they'd gone as far as they could for the moment. 'Fine,' he murmured, getting up and turning towards the door. Ignoring the constable, who was gathering up her bag, Antonia followed him, her bare feet slapping on the polished parquet in the hallway. She held the front door open.

'Thank you for your help,' Swift told her.

'That's OK.'

He stood back to let DC Sallis go first. He swivelled round. 'Do you miss her?' he asked Antonia, tossing out the biggest question of all in the guise of an aside on leaving.

For the first time the girl hesitated, at a loss. He wondered about following up by asking if she would like her sister back. But that really did seem unduly brutal. Besides which, he thought, as he followed his colleague to the car, it was not too difficult to predict what the response would be.

'How did it ever get put about that women are the weaker sex?' the constable remarked drily as Swift fired the engine.

'I've never been a fully paid up subscriber to that particular doctrine,' he told her, his face relaxing into a smile. 'Miss Hoxton certainly doesn't fit the stereotype of the devoted sister, does she?'

'Nor the ugly step-sister,' Sue Sallis commented. 'She's a very good-looking girl. And from the pictures I've seen, I'd put Jenny down as the ugly duckling. Well, plain Jane, at least.'

'Yes,' Swift said slowly. 'You've got a point there. So do you see Antonia Hoxton as a suspect?'

'Too openly hostile. She's a bright kid in my book. And a canny killer would make sure to be as sweet as sugar.'

Swift nodded, thinking it was good to see promising material coming up in the CID ranks.

* * *

Sadie had got up at six and made her way across the yard to the kennels and let her canine boarders out to run in the field. It was still dark and the shapes of the dogs were like grey ghosts in the beam of her torch as they bounded over the rain-sodden grass. She checked the state of the individual enclosures, filled a bucket with water and set about swilling out those pens in which the dogs had urinated.

Work is what gets you through the day, she thought, as she squeezed the mop against the drainer then wiped it over the floor. Being active is one of the main pleasures of life. Doing things. Keeping yourself busy, as her mother used to put it. Sadie had never minded work — hard, sweat-making physical labour. She'd learned over the years to cultivate the capacity for turning the most menial tasks into something pleasurable and satisfying. She had found them a pretty effective remedy for life's disappointments. Today they were definitely the best way to ward off a looming sensation of dread.

Around 7.30, as lightness was creeping into the sky, she knocked on the door of Godfrey Quarmie's cottage — or rather her father's cottage which Godfrey was renting. It struck her that in reality it was now her cottage. She had dealt with all the business of letting it, all the rent collection arrangements, all the checking and organization of repairs. Her father was no longer in this world. What was to be hers in his will was already in her possession. Was her responsibility. She pushed back the thought that he was probably dead. He had been gone for a day and a night.

Vanished into thin air. No one had seen him. How could he survive away from home and her care all that time?

Godfrey took some time to answer her knock. When he did he more than filled the doorway. He was six foot two and big with it. He was wearing a towel wrapped around his waist and his feet were bare. 'Hi,' he said.

'Sorry to come so early,' she told him.

'That's quite OK. What can I do for you?'

'You'll get your death of cold standing out here on the step with hardly a stitch on,' she told him, wondering why an icon of such stunning male beauty and sexiness should have chosen to live up here on the side of a moor betwixt a number of geriatric mill towns. She would have thought an out-of-work actor taking casual labour where he could would choose a gentler part of the world.

'You're right.' He looked up at the leaden sky and grimaced. 'Come on in,' he said, standing to one side. Sadie stepped forward, her nose almost touching his muscled chest as they squeezed together into the narrow passage hallway. He led her into the sitting room and gestured to the old fat leather sofa that had once belonged to Sadie's grandparents. 'Make yourself at home.'

'No, no. I'm not staying.' She paused.

'So . . . how's things?' he asked, helping her out.

'Could be better,' Sadie told him. 'Did you go for another audition yesterday?'

'Yep.' A raising of eyebrows. A crooked soap-star grin.

Take a pair of sparkling eyes, thought Sadie. Except I'm past it. And weighed down with trouble. 'Did you get it? The part?'

He put up two fingers almost touching. 'That much between me and the guy who landed it.'

'Aah, I'm sorry. You'll get one soon. Bound to.' She couldn't imagine anyone would be daft enough not to hire him. Even if he couldn't act his way out of a shoe box.

'Sure,' he said easily. 'I will. No worries. In the meantime I'm quite enjoying myself pulling pints at the Shepherd's Dog.'

'All human life is there,' Sadie observed drily.

'Yeah. I'm getting in some good research on the rich tapestry of human behaviour.' Godfrey grinned. 'All grist to an actor's mill.'

'I suppose so.'

'What's wrong?' Godfrey said, observing her with curiosity. 'You don't look too great.'

'Dad's still missing,' she said, sitting down abruptly on the battered sofa and putting her head in her hands. A wave of despair engulfed her.

'Hey! Come on now.' Godfrey sat down beside her, placing a comforting arm around her shoulders.

'He's been gone since yesterday morning. He's never out for more than a couple of hours. Always back for his dinner and his tea regular as clockwork.' She sighed and rubbed her eyes. She recalled how he'd taken his chance to slip away whilst she was laughing and chatting with Godfrey. But, bloody hell, surely she was entitled to the occasional few minutes of fun!

'No way should you lock him in,' Godfrey said. 'Look, don't beat yourself up about this, Sadie. He's an old man, but he's still a free agent.'

'Do you think so? I'm not sure any more. I always used to believe in 'respecting the rights of the elderly' and those poor creatures who went senile. I couldn't bear to think of patronizing my dad. He'd run a farm and been a good husband and a father. He was an adult, for God's sake. A senior citizen with the right to his dignity.' She rubbed at the moisture beneath her eyes. 'I closed my eyes to the fact that our roles had reversed, that he'd become the child and I the mother. But that's the truth of the matter. And I think that's what he wanted. Just to shake off all his worries and be cared for like when he was a

101

kid. Safe from all the evil of the world.'

'You did all that,' said Godfrey. 'You still do. You're a saint.'

'There's more,' said Sadie. 'I wasn't going to tell you . . .'

'Go right ahead!'

Swiftly she told him the bare bones of the story. The scene at the quarry, the dead girl, the visits from the police. The nightmare of it all.

'He didn't do it,' she said in conclusion. 'At first I wondered about it, even though I hated myself for it. But then I thought of him the other day. I went into the bathroom and he was standing against the toilet struggling to open his trousers. He was whimpering with frustration. I don't think he *could* kill anyone. And I don't think he *would*, even though he's not the person he was. As I see it he's fighting every minute of the day to hang on to his status as a human being. He's using every scrap of his energy just to survive. He simply wouldn't have enough strength left over to kill someone.'

'Yeah.' Godfrey looked thoughtful. 'Yeah, that figures. I'll buy that.'

There was the sudden sound of wheels screeching to a halt in the yard.

'Oh, God!' she groaned, watching Fowler and a sturdy uniformed male officer climb out of the car and pause to look at the farmhouse. They looked like something from a newsflash of a dawn raid.

She stood up, wiping her cheeks dry, smoothing her hair. 'Maybe they've found him. Oh, please God no one's hurt him.'

'Do you want me to come along for moral support?' Godfrey asked.

Sadie looked at him and had an absurd impulse to break into hysterical laughter. 'No, I'll be OK. I'll shout out if I need back-up.'

She walked out to face the two officers, hauling her composure around her like a coat. She glanced around her at the ring of farm buildings and the surrounding land. Mistress of all she surveyed.

Fowler was looking uncharacteristically amiable. 'Good morning, Miss Bracewell.'

'What is it?' She squared up to him, not prepared to be disarmed by a friendly smile.

'Can we go inside?' Fowler asked. 'It's a bit parky out here.'

Sadie's breath stopped in her chest. Oh no! Bad news. They were always really nice to you when there was a bitter pill to be swallowed. She pushed open the door and went ahead of them. 'Have you found him?' she demanded. 'Just tell me. No need to pussyfoot around.'

'No, we haven't found him yet,' Fowler said. 'We were hoping perhaps he'd come

103

home on his own.' He made the statement on a rising inflection, his questioning gaze levelling with Sadie's.

'No,' Sadie told him sharply, pretty sure that both officers still suspected her of having hidden her father somewhere where they couldn't find him and start taking samples of his DNA.

'Have you thought of any other places where he might have gone? Ones you didn't mention before?' the uniformed officer asked.

'No. I've wracked my brains, believe me.' Sadie found the young man's attitude subtly intimidating. Maybe it was the uniform.

'Relatives? Friends?' he persisted.

'We went through all that before,' Sadie protested.

Things went on like that for a time, Fowler and the uniformed officer using a pincer movement strategy to try to grind her down with their repeated questions.

Eventually they looked as though they had had enough. They progressed to the door. Fowler turned. 'Could I possibly use the bathroom?' he said with a hint of apology.

'It's just opposite the top of the stairs,' Sadie told him, simply wanting them both to leave her alone as soon as possible so that she could try to make some sense of the clutter in her brain.

'I'm sure we'll find your dad soon,' the uniformed officer said formally. 'We've got a lot of manpower out there looking for him.'

'I don't doubt it,' Sadie said. 'I'm sure you won't leave a stone unturned when it comes to finding your prime suspect.'

The young man assumed the impassive expression of a person in authority when faced with churlish behaviour from a member of the public.

Sadie considered apologizing for her ungraciousness and instantly dismissed the idea.

'Thanks for your time, love — that's been very helpful,' Fowler told her as he ran down the steps. She watched the two officers walk to the car, the briskness in the sergeant's step suggesting that he was probably as glad to be quitting Black Sheep Farm as Sadie was to see him go.

Godfrey was standing in the doorway of his cottage observing the proceedings. 'Hey,' he called out to Sadie, 'how did it go?'

She walked across the yard to join him. 'Nothing new,' she said. 'They haven't found him yet.'

'So why the big flourish?' He raised a quizzical eyebrow. 'Two of them turning up before it's properly light?'

'They're just desperate for something to

happen, I suppose,' she said. 'They can't move things along with this investigation whilst Dad's missing. They'd pinned all their hopes on it being him. They just needed to get some of his DNA to match with stuff the forensic people have found, and bingo! They'd got their man. But he's vanished. They're as stuck as if they were wading through treacle. They can't get on with arresting the man they want, and I guess they can't do much else very useful either until the issue of Dad gets sorted.' She took a tissue from the pocket of her jeans and blew her nose. 'Rather like me.'

As they stood together on Godfrey's doorstep another car turned into the gates. Sleek and silver, with a black soft top, braking to a screeching halt and setting all the dogs barking.

Sadie turned, her heart accelerating. Two figures uncurled from the car, a man and a woman. There was a flash, dazzling her eyes, reverberating in her head.

The woman came forward, bright cropped red hair, an emerald coat, glossy high heels. 'Miss Bracewell, what do you say to your father being the prime suspect in the Jenny Hoxton murder case? Has your dad been found yet? Do you know where he is?'

Dazed, as though stunned with a blow,

Sadie stared at the woman with incomprehension. She felt Godfrey's fingers around her arm, his voice low and urgent, saying, 'Leave it, Sadie. Come inside.'

'No!' She shook him off and stepped forward, squaring up to the redhead, eyes like guns. 'My father didn't murder Jenny Hoxton,' she said in fury. 'He's an old man, and he wouldn't hurt a fly. And no, I don't know where he is. Now bloody get off my land or I'll set the dogs on you.'

The woman hesitated. Her photographer was already backing off. Spurred by instinct rather than thought, Sadie sprang forward, tore the camera from the young man's shoulder and threw it on the cobbles before storming back to the house and slamming the door shut behind her. Safely inside, she collapsed against the door, every nerve in her body screaming.

The dogs were still barking outside. And then there was the roar of an engine, another squealing of tyres. They were gone.

'I'm going to brew you coffee,' Godfrey said. 'I'm going to cook you breakfast. The full works. Don't even bother saying no.'

* * *

'We didn't get far there, did we, sir?' the uniformed officer commented eventually to

Fowler as they drove in silence back to the station. 'Bit of a waste of time, don't you think?'

'Oh, I wouldn't say that,' Fowler responded.

The cheery affability of his tone prompted the younger man to shoot him a sharp glance, wondering what could have put him in such a good mood.

* * *

Lister drummed his fingers on the desk top as he listened to Swift's account of his interview with Antonia Hoxton.

'It's interesting stuff, Ed,' he agreed. 'Especially if you favour the psychological approach. But, be honest with me, what have we got of any substance here? OK, both the mother and the sister seem to be cold fishes. The mother says the dead girl was secretive. The sister says she was a bit of a loner. The photograph the parents released makes the poor kid look like some miserable waif from the back streets.' He spread his hands. 'So? Can we make a case from that? I doubt it.'

'Anita Hoxton said Jenny was excited about something,' Swift mused. 'In the weeks before she died.'

'Adolescent girls, for Christ's sake! Their hormones could uproot trees,' Lister said with the feeling of one who had had experience of these things.

'I have an instinct there's something to pursue here,' Swift said. 'Something odd in the family. Or maybe something wrong in Jenny's peer group. Something we shouldn't ignore.'

'Are you sure you shouldn't have gone in for psychiatry?' Lister suggested drily. 'Look, Ed, we've got some DNA from the girl's clothing. A good, reliable sample. And it doesn't match up with any of the two million samples on the national database of villains. *We just need to find Bracewell.* God help us.'

'According to the sister, the parents are planning a memorial service for Jenny,' Swift said.

'Probably a good idea. It doesn't look as though the body will be released for a while. Do you know when it's likely to be?'

'Quite soon, I would guess. I'll follow it up and get the date.'

Lister pursed his lips. 'I take it you're thinking of joining the throng?'

'I think it could be profitable, sir,' Swift said steadily.

'In other circumstances I'd have a three-line whip out for you to go,' said Lister, his face a portrait of weary resignation. 'But as things are I hate to think of you wasting your time. Of all of us wasting our time. I don't suppose there's any way I could persuade you to get your wellies on and join the troops searching for the old man?' He glanced up at Swift. 'Just joking,' he said hurriedly.

'I think Geoff's got that operation well covered,' Swift remarked with a wry grin. 'From what I can tell he's taken to directing the troops with a will.'

★   ★   ★

Sadie put her knife and fork together on the plate and looked up to meet Godfrey's unashamedly interested gaze. 'That was exactly what I needed.'

He had fried her eggs and bacon and tomatoes. There had been crispy fried bread too and warm pancakes with maple syrup. 'I aim to give satisfaction,' he said, resting his head on his hand. His brown eyes were like headlights.

I'll bet you do, she thought, surprised not to find herself more irritated by his blatant flirting. More often than not these days she treated men who came on to her with a look of pitying sorrow which said very clearly, 'Drop dead.' Few risked a second rebuff. 'I've got to *do* something,' she burst out impulsively.

'Yeah?' he said encouragingly. 'You mean do some more searching for your dad? Looks like the police have got that well in hand.'

'I agree. No, I don't mean that . . . God, I feel so helpless. And now this business with the press.'

'Do you ever feel it would be a relief if he didn't come back?' Godfrey asked quietly. The question was one which should have had her hackles springing up like knives. But the way he asked it had nothing offensive about it. And suddenly she wanted to talk.

'When I was a kid,' she told him, 'my dad got a border collie puppy that promised to be a brilliant dog and then turned out to be a rogue. It started attacking the sheep. It was always running off and chasing cars and cyclists in the road. It was a hazard and a menace, and totally useless as a working dog. But my dad loved that dog. He got another dog to replace it as a worker with the sheep, but he hung on to the rogue. There was something about it that made him want to protect it. I think he thought if he gave it enough care, then in time it would become the dog he had always believed it was going to be. Eventually the vet diagnosed it with a brain tumour: parts of its brain had been wiped out by an enormous growth. I can remember the night my dad came home and told us. He cried that night. I could hear him in the bedroom. My strong stiff-upper-lip, never-show-your-feelings father crying like a little child. The next day he took it to be put down. He was heart-broken. 'I did the right thing,' he kept saying. 'He didn't suffer.'' Sadie paused to stir her coffee. She gave Godfrey a rueful smile. 'Some shaggy dog story! The point being that there have been moments when I've hoped they'd find Dad's body somewhere up on the moors, that he'd just slipped away without suffering.' She looked steadily into Godfrey's face, relief rolling away from her as she made this confession. 'But then sometimes I want him back so much I can hardly bear it. I just want to care for him and let nature take him away when she's ready.'

'You're a saint,' Godfrey said. 'I mean it.'

'No, I'm just doing what seems right, what I truly feel I want to do. Not that you'd believe a word of it if you heard me yelling at him when he drives me mad.'

'You said you've got a need to *do* something,' Godfrey reminded her. 'What?'

She linked her fingers together and her knuckles grew white as she squeezed them. 'Try to find out who really killed that girl, I suppose. It's not just about Dad, you see. I'll never forget the feeling I got when I saw her lying there dead. I keep seeing her face . . . '

'How would you go about finding out?' Godfrey asked.

She shook her head. 'No idea. I wouldn't even know where to start.' She paused. 'Any ideas?'

'Two heads are always better than one,' said Godfrey, pouring freshly brewed coffee into her cup.

⋆ ⋆ ⋆

Fowler paused by the door to Dr Kabinsky's office. The adrenalin rush he had felt as he left Black Sheep Farm was still with him. But there was also a needling voice of caution at the corner of his mind demanding to be heard. A voice that pointed out the fine line between taking initiative and acting as a loose cannon.

He thought then of Ed Swift, more interested in wanking around digging into family issues and chasing red herrings than finding old Ned Bracewell.

He thought finally of Lister, his long-time senior colleague for whom he had both respect and affection. He pictured Lister's face when he gave him the result he wanted. Anticipation glowed within. He gave two sharp knocks on the door.

★   ★   ★

Swift's phone rang early the next morning.

'It's Saturday,' Naomi complained, placing a mug of hot coffee on his bedside table.

'It's Tom,' said Lister's voice on the other end of the line. 'Have you seen a morning paper yet?'

'No.'

'Well, go and get one. Not a serious one, one of the tabloids. Any one you fancy for God's sake! Bloody hell!' That was it.

Swift dressed and ran down the road to the nearest mini-market. Back in the apartment, he spread a selection of the day's tabloids on the kitchen table. A fuzzy picture of Ned Bracewell, looking a year or two younger and somewhat fiercer than the man Swift had seen, stared up at him and Naomi from huge, shouting headlines.

'MISSING FARMER PRIME SUSPECT IN JENNY MURDER.' And more worrying: 'POLICE POISED TO ARREST JENNY'S KILLER.' And nastiest of all: 'IS THIS THE FACE OF A MONSTER?'

He scanned through the reports. They were all very hazy. There was mention of a Yorkshire farmer, Ned Bracewell, being the father of the woman who had found Jenny's body. Mention of Bracewell being questioned

114

immediately by the police following the grim discovery — an old man with Alzheimer's, a man with a mental condition that meant he was an obvious prey to the forces of evil. Mention of the likelihood of ominous forensic evidence soon to emerge to prove Ned's guilt. There were some sketchy accounts of Ned's life as a farmer: an apparently blameless life, though in his young days he'd been noted as having a fiery temper. Reports all ended with an exhortation to the general public to help find the old man. One paper offered a £20,000 reward for genuine information, arguing it was in the interests of the safety of children everywhere for Ned and his like to be off the streets and safely confined.

'Ugh!' said Naomi. 'But it does make irresistible reading,' she added thoughtfully.

'It's a typical piece of journalistic hype,' Swift said with resignation.

She looked up from the newsprint, questions hovering on her lips. Her father shook his head. She spread her hands in a gesture of surrender. 'It's OK. I'm not going to go there. Forget I even thought about it.'

Fortified with a cup of strong black coffee, he returned Tom Lister's call.

'If there's one thing gets me going it's wondering if we've got a snitcher in the police ranks,' Lister brayed. 'Still, it might not be all bad news. At least the public know we're doing more than just sitting on our arses. And maybe it'll do the trick in flushing the old guy out from wherever he's landed up.'

8

The church had been built in the mid-nineteenth century to serve the needs of the fine houses being put up for the wealthy middle classes on the fashionable outskirts of the town. It was a building of substance. And it was packed. Every pew was full and rows of metal chairs had been ranged along the side and back walls to accommodate the huge congregation.

The morning was grey and dark and Swift found himself temporarily blinded by a dazzle of candles as he passed through the big oak doors into the body of the church. There were flowers everywhere; great banks of white lilies and carnations spiked with the gold of spring daffodils.

He made his way to the back and sat amongst a group of girls in their early teens clutching handkerchieves, their expressions a mingle of anguish and intense excitement.

The service started with a brief address from the minister, followed by prayers for the dead girl. There was a deep, doleful silence at the end of each prayer, with just the occasional sound of a smothered sob from the ranks of school students packed into the pews.

The minister based his words of comfort around Saint Paul's much quoted words from Chapter 13 of the sermon from First Corinthians. *If I speak with the tongues of men and of angels, but have not love, I am become sounding brass or a clanging cymbal* . . . He went on to give his own address, his voice heavy with sorrow and sympathy for all the mourners. But it was clear to Swift that Jenny had not been known personally to the minister, whose words seemed to focus more on the grief of the parents than the individual qualities of their child. There were then some words from the headteacher, who made reference to 'the unique spirit of Jenny Hoxton', to the school's 'terrible loss' and a need for all concerned 'to find the strength to maintain their belief in the fundamental decency of human nature in order to move forward into the future.'

No one from the immediate family spoke, but her year tutor said a few words about how Jenny would be missed by her friends, and how she had been a valued member of the school community. They were thoughtful words, carefully strung together and spoken with warmth, but they could have applied to anyone elevated to a higher sphere by the mystery of death.

Recalling Kate's funeral and the haunted, lost face of Naomi as she spoke of her mother, her voice thick with love, Swift felt a chill at what was now unfolding at this remembrance service of a girl who had been brutally removed from the great game of life before she had even become a full player.

The next to speak was Nick Ashton, the head boy at Jenny's school. He spoke in the low, clear tones of someone who might be considering a career as a Shakespearean actor. Offering quiet regrets for not having known Jenny personally, he went on to talk of her family and how the hearts of everyone in the school went out to them. He spoke of the pain and horror of losing a fellow pupil and how the shock of Jenny's death had reverberated throughout the school. He said that he had talked to some of Jenny's friends and that he had been moved by their despair and bewilderment in getting to grips with how they were going to get along without her. 'But we must all be brave and go forward,' he said. 'That is what she would have wanted.'

He paused and turned to look at the coffin with its one simple wreath of white roses. Seconds beat by, the atmosphere now electric. He looked up, sweeping the congregation with his clear, frank gaze. And then he concluded by reciting Christina Rossetti's poem 'Remember'. He spoke without a text, facing his audience and speaking as though to each one individually.

> Remember me when I am gone away,
> Gone far away into the silent land;
> When you can no more hold me by the
> hand . . .

It was a bravura performance, magnetizing. When he walked back to his pew, half the church was in tears. The girls beside Swift clutched each other for comfort, openly sobbing. Swift swallowed down the thickness in his throat.

The minister recited the final prayers and the congregation began to file out, wet eyes and handkerchieves much in evidence.

Swift moved into a side aisle and took a place in a vacated pew. He could see Anita and Jeremy Hoxton leading the departing procession. Jeremy's shoulders were hunched, his face pale and set in lines of pain. Anita, regal and elegant in black, held herself straight, staring directly ahead, her face a blank canvas so that you could project on to it any emotion you might care to choose. And behind her Antonia Hoxton looked like a beautiful facsimile of her parent, aside from the thirty or so years which separated them.

Slowly the line of relatives and friends and peers filed out of the church. Swift watched and wondered. Was it possible the murderer was here amongst the mourners? Someone harbouring a rage that had taken root in some inner void and grown like cancer? Of course it was.

Outside in the churchyard the day was oppressive: drizzling, damp and bleak. On the horizon the hills of the Dales were shrouded in a white fog, insubstantial and mysterious like memories from another life, isolated and disconnected in the mist. The church bell was tolling, pealing out its message of death and desolation.

Swift watched as people straggled to their cars. He noticed a woman standing on her own by the lychgate. She was engaged in the same occupation — observing the crowd. Her dress and her demeanour were quiet and unobtrusive so that she seemed to blend into the grey background of the day. But Swift recognized the intensity behind her low-key surveillance, could almost hear the hum of speculation as she gathered up the crumbs of information this grim feast was yielding. He also recognized her instantly as Sadie

Bracewell, even though in a sleek grey coat and plain black court shoes she was a transformed woman from the bulky farmer's daughter in her jeans and sweatshirt and trainers.

He waited until the main throng had left the churchyard before making his way to stand beside her.

'Hello, Inspector Swift,' she said, clearly having noticed his presence some time before. 'I wondered when you'd spot me.'

Swift nodded an acknowledgement, wondering if she was aware that a significant percentage of murderers put in an appearance at their victim's funeral or memorial service, and reminded himself that she was, of course, still in the frame.

She did not flinch under his calm, steady gaze. 'I needed to come,' she said. 'I keep seeing her face. Her poor dead face.'

'Yes, I can understand that,' he agreed.

'My father didn't kill her,' she said with sudden passion. 'He's not a murderer. I know he didn't kill her.'

Swift waited.

'But he's still the main suspect.' Her face hardened. 'Isn't he?'

'We can't rule him out of the investigation as yet,' Swift said formally.

'There's still no news about him,' she said

resignedly. 'They'd tell me, wouldn't they? Straight away. If he'd been found?'

He could hear the panic in her voice. 'Of course.'

'I want to be with him. If he's to be questioned. He couldn't manage on his own, you see. He can't deal with any anxieties. He'd just collapse under pressure.' She swept a hand through her thick hair. 'Oh, God! Poor old Dad. What's happened to him? It's such hell not knowing.'

'There will be no question of his being harassed or put under pressure,' Swift reassured her. 'I give you my word on that.'

She slid him a glance of steel. 'But you're not the only one on the case, are you? You might be a dove, but there are some hawks around too. I've seen them.'

★   ★   ★

Swift drove from the church to Middlewood High, Jenny Hoxton's school. It was late in the afternoon and whatever activity there had been in the school that afternoon was now finished and the building looked empty apart from the team of cleaners assembled in the reception area, preparing to work their way through corridors and classrooms.

Guessing that the head would by now have

returned to the school to catch up on administration work, he followed the signs to his office.

'Ivan Hewlett', said the small gilt plaque on his door. 'B.A. Hons, M.Ed.'

Hewlett opened the door himself. Once apprised of Swift's name and rank, he shook his hand in a brief, firm grasp and ushered him in. 'Do sit down, Chief Inspector.' He had the easy yet vigilant expression of a man with clout. Reinforcing his words with an eloquent gesture of hospitality, he slipped behind his vast desk and lowered himself into a tall chrome and black leather chair.

A touch throne-like, Swift thought, automatically sniffing out the vibes and emotional ambience of his surroundings and its inhabitant. Ivan Hewlett was a tall, fair-haired man projecting a quiet but powerful aura of authority. In his dark suit, white shirt and sombre burgundy tie, he looked very much the part of the-buck-stops-here man heading up a big organization. He struck Swift as typical of the new breed of high school headteachers who ran their empires with the cunning, panache and grandeur of the wiliest captains of industry.

'How can I be of assistance?' Hewlett asked, going straight on to say, 'This is a terrible business. What those poor parents must be going through. And, of course, I don't need to tell you this is a headteacher's worst nightmare. A pupil being cruelly mown down in the prime of their life. But thank God she — ' He stopped abruptly, suddenly wrong-footed.

'I think I'd appreciate it if you finished what you were going to say, Mr Hewlett,' Swift told him with a faint smile.

'I was going to say how glad I was that Jenny wasn't killed on the recent school trip. And that sounds self-seeking and heartless, I appreciate, but that really is a headteacher's worst nightmare.'

Swift nodded his agreement. 'When was the school trip?'

'Half-term week, the same week this dreadful tragedy occurred. A party set off on the Sunday up into the Dales on a three-day field expedition.' Hewlett frowned and tapped his fingers on the desk. 'So have you found any leads? Do you think it's possible Jenny could have been abducted?'

'We haven't yet sufficient evidence to make a comment on that,' Swift told him, noticing how Hewlett had automatically assumed the role of question asker rather than responder. 'Do you have reasons for thinking abduction is likely?'

'Not at all. It just seems to be a growing

hazard in our culture. Don't you agree, Chief Inspector?'

Swift put on a thoughtful expression and made no comment. 'I'd like a list of all the pupils in Jenny's class group,' he said.

'Naturally. I'll get one sent in right away.' Hewlett pressed a button on his desk phone and murmured some soft instructions into it.

Almost instantly the door opened and a woman walked in with a slim folder which she laid on Hewlett's desk. He nodded thanks to her, checked through the contents of the folder and passed them across to Swift.

The secretary was hovering, wanting to speak. She was looking at Swift. 'There's a call for you come through to the office,' she said. 'From Superintendent Lister. It sounds urgent.'

Pulling his thoughts away from his next line of questioning with the headteacher, Swift excused himself.

'Ed,' came Lister's voice down the phone, agitated and excited. 'Don't bother going any further with investigations at the school. I want you back here. We've got some vital new evidence.'

★ ★ ★

Sadie had watched Swift walk away from church and make for his car. She hung on for a while beside the lychgate, watching the final stragglers leave. There was a girl who had particularly caught her attention during the service. Having arrived very early, Sadie had positioned herself alone at the end of a row in a side aisle close to the front. From there she had been able to observe the family and a small group of girls who she guessed must be classmates of Jenny's. The girls had been solemn-faced and dry-eyed at first. After the final address from the head boy three of them had huddled together sobbing whilst the fourth girl sat on her own, her face still and blank.

And, now, fifteen minutes or so after the service had ended, the girl was still hanging around. Sadie had watched her wander around the neatly tended lawns on the west side of the church. She had disappeared for a few minutes around the back and then re-emerged, walking slowly, kicking at imaginary stones with her scuffed clumpy black shoes. She was pale and skinny, her face framed with long brown hair that looked as though it needed a wash. Her grey padded anorak looked similarly in need of care and attention — the seams were torn and stretched and white stuffing was squeezing out all over. In one hand she held a single pink rosebud. Noticing Sadie's scrutiny, her expression immediately became guarded and hostile.

'Hello,' Sadie said, smiling.

The girl walked a couple of paces forward. 'Lo,' she muttered.

Sadie kept very still as though she were talking to a suspicious animal who might dart away if she alarmed it. 'My name's Sadie Bracewell. I used to know Jenny when she was a kid.'

'Oh.'

'Were you a friend of Jenny's?'

'Yeah.' The girl looked haggard and haunted and desperately sad.

Sadie pulled her coat collar up. 'I'm really cold. Do you know anywhere near here to have a coffee?'

'There's the Coach and Horses pub just down at the junction. They're open all day. They do food and coffees and stuff.' The girl's eyes showed a fleeting flicker of expectation.

'Would you show me?'

'Yeah. OK.'

They walked along together. 'I hope I'm not making you late for getting home,' Sadie said.

'I don't like to go home before five. Me

mam doesn't get home till then, and my brother's a pain.'

They walked along in silence. 'How did you know Jenny then?' the girl asked.

'Oh, not well at all. I was a kind of distant cousin.'

Sadie winced at the lie. She recalled Godfrey's advice: 'When you're playing a part, whatever you say, believe it at the time. Whatever you pretend to feel, then really feel it. Your face will reflect it. That's the secret of good acting. And it's not really that difficult.'

'Oh, right,' said the girl. 'I've got some cousins. On my dad's side. But I never see 'em. Nor him neither.'

They reached the pub. The lights inside looked gold and welcoming. 'Maybe you'd like a hot drink too,' Sadie suggested as they stood at the open door. 'My treat.' She hoped she didn't sound patronizing. Or like a would-be abductor. 'But only if you want to.'

'Why not?' the girl said. 'I'll have a filter coffee with cream, please.'

Whilst Sadie ordered at the bar, the girl wandered over to the fruit machine and dug around in the pockets of her padded jacket. She slid a coin into the slot and pushed the buttons. The coloured fruits rolled. And then stopped. No winnings.

'You always lose on those machines,' Sadie

said, bringing the coffees to the table.

'No, you don't,' the girl said. 'Once you get to know a fruitie it kind of tells you how to play it. They're all different, you see. Like dogs. And you can count the reels on your fingers. Like with that one, there's three more symbols before the cherry. And you have to knock the buttons quite hard. You need strong hands. I just didn't do it quite right that time.'

Sadie was intrigued. She dropped the change from the bar into the girl's palm. 'Go on then.'

The girl smiled. A real smile. She moved to the machine, slipped a coin in the slot, then paused for a few moments before activating the cycle. Sadie watched the symbols begin their dazzling dance, then turned her attention to opening the little tubs of cream to pour into the coffee. She turned, hearing the sudden clatter of coins as they spilled out into the tray.

'Jackpot!' said the girl, returning with her hoard. She sat down, her palms full of glinting coins. 'Here, half of this is yours.'

'No. I gave you the stake. Your bet, your win.'

'Oh, all right, then.' She looked at Sadie with faint doubt. 'Well, thanks.' She poured the coins into the pocket of her jacket, then grasped her cup in both hands, using the frayed edges of her grey jumper as a heat glove. 'Cheers!' She took a gulp and gave a sigh of satisfaction. 'I'm Crystal, by the way. Me mam named me after some 1980s Hollywood soap star. How sad can you get?'

'It's a pretty name,' Sadie said.

'Exactly! And look at this ugly mug!' She put a finger against the tip of her nose.

'Did Jenny play the fruities?' Sadie asked.

'Oh, aye. Once I showed her how to do it. She never used to go to pubs and stuff before we got to be mates. They're posh, her parents. Not like me and me mam.'

Sadie had already been wondering about the differences between the two girls and their families, having seen Mrs Hoxton on a TV news report. A very classy lady. Whereas Crystal looked like a kid who'd been taken off the streets as an act of charity. So what had drawn Jenny and Crystal to each other?

'She didn't get on with them, you know, her parents,' Crystal said. 'They made her have cello lessons and join the youth theatre.'

'Is that bad?' Sadie asked.

'Well, not really, no. But if you hate classical music and reciting Shakespeare it's not good, is it?'

'What did Jenny like doing?'

'Oh, you know. Just messing around.

Hanging out. Just . . . living.'

'Yes,' Sadie agreed.

'We used to go out together when she could get away. I don't like being at home if I can help it. The police are forever coming to hassle my brother.' Her eyes narrowed with venom. 'They're bastards, the police. Once they came at six in the morning. They turned the place upside down. I had to get out of bed and stand there while they stripped my bed. And they don't put things back, you know. My mam and me, we hate 'em. Mind you, my brother's a stupid sod, messing about with drugs and stuff. Deserves what's coming to him.'

'That must be bad for you.'

'Yeah.'

'You'll miss Jenny,' Sadie said gently.

'Yeah, she was me best mate.' She pulled down her sleeves and grasped her cup again. 'But we hadn't been out together so much the past few weeks,' she said, sliding a glance at Sadie, almost as if she wanted to be asked to say more.

'Did you fall out?'

'No.' Another pause.

Sadie could see the tension in the girl's face. She was convinced that Crystal had something on her mind and wanted to unburden herself. A spark of excitement lit inside her. She found herself holding her breath.

'Who did you say you were?' Crystal asked, a little frown creasing her forehead. 'Jenny's cousin?'

'Yes.'

'Was that from . . . ?' She stopped.

Sadie stared at her, at a loss as to what to say next.

'No, forget it, it doesn't matter,' Crystal said. 'I'm glad you came along. Jenny would've been pleased. You know, that you'd remembered her.' She picked up the rose which she had been carrying earlier. 'I wanted to leave this somewhere. For Jenny. But I didn't know where to put it. You see people throw them onto the coffin, don't you? In films. But they said that was going to be later on. And private, laying her to rest and stuff.'

'Perhaps you could just keep it yourself. Something to help remember her.'

'Yeah.' Crystal laid the rose back on the table. 'Are you married?' she asked. 'Do you have kids?'

'No, not married, no kids.'

'Why not? You must have been a good-looking lass when you were . . . '

'Young,' Sadie laughed.

'Yeah. Sorry.' She finished her coffee. 'Where did you say you came from?'

'I live up on the moors. Black Sheep Farm.

It's quite near Brontë country.'

'Oh,' said Crystal, her eyes flickering. 'I'd like to live in the country. Some day.' She sat for a while, her face sad and lost. 'Would you like another coffee?' she asked, standing up and jangling her pocket. 'I'm rich.'

9

Whilst Swift was driving away from the church, making for the school, Fowler sat in the incident room, staring at the shimmering screen of his computer, restlessly turning the pen in his fingers around from end to point.

His mobile pealed. He grabbed it. 'Fowler.' Breathlessly he waited for Dr Kabinsky's carefully enunciated tones.

'Get here into my office,' Lister's voice barked. 'Now!'

Fowler shrugged on his jacket, his mind racing. The summons from Lister suggested that either something unbelievably big had turned up, or that Kabinsky had sneaked straight to Lister with her findings. The devious, tight-arsed bitch.

He found Lister standing at the window of his office, staring down into the car park and smoking a short, chubby cigar. The DS swung around. 'Geoff. Sit down!' His eyes blazed with feeling. 'What the bloody hell do you think you've been doing? What put it into your head to go behind my back, giving vital evidence to Dr Kabinsky without a word to me? And what's more, how the heck did you get it?'

Fowler wondered if there was a hint of triumph beneath Lister's anger and indignation. He couldn't read his boss's expression. But he certainly looked awful. Suit rumpled, a haze of stubble around his chin, his cheeks grey with fatigue. This investigation was taking its toll.

'I took some hairs from Ned Bracewell's hairbrush when I last visited to speak to the daughter,' Fowler said, deciding directness was the best line of approach, and making sure to keep his voice low and steady. 'I needed a leak. The brush was there on the shelf over the washbasin. I simply lifted off the hairs sticking out from it.'

'I take it you didn't bother asking the daughter for her cooperation. Or her permission.'

Fowler sighed. A clear enough answer.

Lister pulled heavily on his cigar. Fowler could hear the other man's breathing, heavy and rasping, no doubt mirroring the exertions going on in his head. 'It was hard to resist it, sir. Evidence to provide DNA just offering itself up on a plate, so to speak.'

'Yes, well, you might like to call it initiative, and in many ways I'm with you on that. But you were skating on the edge, Geoff. Suppose

Miss Bracewell decides to make a fuss. Gets her solicitor to make a case against us. Even a lawyer not normally known as a Rottweiler could have a field day.'

Geoff pressed his lips together; he had the impression he could ride this. He raised his head. 'What was the result of the test, sir?' His body and limbs clenched. Oh, please God!

'There was a match,' Lister said. 'The DNA from the semen found on the girl's clothing and that of the hairs on the brush matched.' He looked at Fowler and his eyes lit with a gleam of intense exultation.

'Got him!' Fowler slammed his hand down on the desk.

'Except we haven't,' Lister said. 'The old bloke's still missing. And,' he added with heavy warning, 'nor do we have proof that the hairs on that brush belonged to Ned Bracewell.'

'Oh, come on, sir.'

'We'd need corroboration from the daughter. Which she could well refuse to give. At least before she'd talked to her solicitor. We still need the old guy to turn up to make a watertight case.' Lister paced the floor, drawing on his cigar, looking like a man at the end of his tether. 'To be honest, Geoff,' he said, 'I'm damned if I know the best way forward.'

Fowler relaxed. The DS rarely admitted to a dilemma regarding decision making. Fowler allowed himself to take the confession as a sign of Lister's tacit approval of his overstepping the bounds of initiative in illicitly helping himself to scraps from old Bracewell's tufty nut.

★　★　★

Swift was tired when he got back to the station. He had a sense of swimming against the flow of the team he was working with. He doubted there was one of them who had any real reservations about Ned Bracewell's culpability. Although whether it was belief, or a need for the triumph of a conviction which fired them, he was not certain.

Lister's news about the DNA match and the way it had been achieved did not surprise him. Nor did Lister's total conviction that the case was now more or less sewn up — it was just a question of selecting the most appropriate way to proceed.

Swift stood looking out of the window after Lister had spoken to him, his eyes moving over the wasteland at the back of the station; an overflowing skip, a row of large metal bins with black lids, some splintered planks heaped in a haphazard pile. He knew that he should have kicked up a storm about Fowler's activities, taken the high moral ground. Instead the revelation of the sergeant's devious and cowardly procedures had merely induced a sensation of weary resignation.

Turning away from the dreary view, he sat at his desk and disciplined himself to tap an account of his unrewarding interview with Hewlett into his computer. Then he closed the machine down and headed back to his car.

★ ★ ★

Fowler opened the door with a look of closed defensiveness on his granite-like features. He had obviously seen Swift's car pull into the drive.

'I'd like to come in, Geoff,' Swift said.

Fowler stood back, then ushered his superior officer through a small, thickly carpeted hallway into the front room. He gestured to a dainty chair upholstered in silver brocade, then sat down on the sleek, dusky-rose sofa.

Instantly absorbing the style and ambience of the house and this immaculate room, filled with delicate ornaments and two perfect arrangements of fresh flowers, Swift felt a jolt of surprise. He was not quite sure what he had expected, but certainly not this. He knew that Fowler lived on his own, and had always imagined him in some stark man-alone kind of setting. Maybe he had a very good cleaner. Or an obsessively house-proud girlfriend.

'Do you want a drink, sir?' Fowler asked with exaggerated formality.

'No.' Swift levelled him an unsmiling glance. 'You know why I'm here, Geoff?'

'Yeah.' He paused and took in a long breath. 'About the DNA results.'

They sat in silence for a time, uneasy and at odds. 'I'm not sure I want you on my team any more,' Swift said eventually.

'No. I can understand that. But I don't regret what I did.' Fowler's glare acknowledged the blunt challenge of this remark and at the same time endorsed his right to say what he thought. 'The DNA evidence against Bracewell proves he's the murderer. In my opinion, anyway — and in Lister's. It's a pity the old man's missing, because if we'd got him in custody, all we'd have to do now is prove his guilt before a jury. And I think we will. If I stretched the rules a bit to get that evidence, well, I'd have thought most people would understand that. And approve what's more. The vast majority of people in this country want to see child killers put away somewhere very safe.'

Swift drew in a long breath.

'I've said my piece,' Fowler said. 'I've told you just where I stand. And I'm getting too old now to change my views.'

'Yes.' Swift shifted position in his chair. 'It's not so much the way you got the evidence that bothers me — it's your sure conviction that Ned Bracewell is guilty.'

'Oh, aye.' Fowler's eyes glittered with contempt.

'There's no motive — '

'No *rational* motive,' Fowler cut in. 'The old man's away with the fairies. He does whatever comes into his head.'

'No clear motive,' Swift said steadily. 'No previous convictions. And the callous method of the killing has all the hallmarks of an act that has been thought out and planned.'

'You're entitled to your own view, sir.'

'Yes.'

'What do you think the governor'll do next?' Fowler wondered tentatively.

'Confer with his superior officers, most probably. Get legal advice.'

'If Bracewell would just turn up,' Fowler mused. 'Poor old sod.'

'Let's hope he turns up alive and well,' Swift commented. 'After those press reports suggesting it's a national disgrace to have mad old men like Bracewell on the loose posing a threat to families and children — well, it just takes a paedophile vigilante to recognize him from the picture . . . ' He turned and faced Fowler, an unspoken accusation on his face.

Fowler's responding look was one of deep and dangerous affront. 'I have never spoken Bracewell's name to anyone outside the team,' he hissed. 'You've no right to come here with your half-baked accusations.'

Swift got to his feet. He'd said enough — as much as he wanted, at any rate. Fowler had registered the warning. 'This is a pleasant room,' he commented, looking around him.

Fowler looked at him suspiciously. 'Yes.'

'Nice flowers.' His eyes locked with Fowler's bleak, hollow gaze.

'My wife always liked flowers. She'd spend ages fiddling with them, getting them just right.'

'Where is your wife, Geoff?'

'She's living in Cheshire with her new bloke.' Fowler's face twisted as though he were in pain. 'I like to keep this place nice, just like she used to.'

'Bloody hell,' Swift muttered to himself as he walked to his car. Cursed or blessed with a psychological double vision that urged him to see two sides in any one situation, he was unable simply to write the sergeant off as an embittered, burned-out has-been.

* ★ *

'You've had a bad day,' Naomi said when she saw him. She was curled on the sofa amongst a pile of cushions, eating Coco Pops and watching a cookery contest programme on the TV.

'I'm not going to argue with that,' he said, staring at the amazing feast that was being cooked up on the screen.

'I could rustle up a sort of Spanishy-style omelette,' Naomi told him. 'You could open a bottle of wine.'

'Best suggestion I've heard all day.' He ruffled her hair as he started to make his way to the kitchen. 'Are you sure you haven't something more exciting to do?'

'Nope.' Crisp, definite.

His hand stilled, the familiar anxiety about his daughter's happiness surging up.

'It's OK, Dad. I'm fine.'

Swift's hackles rose. If that lad she'd been seeing had given her grief, by God, he thought he'd strangle him.

'I dumped him. Marcus the mouth-watering god of the sixth form.' She put another spoon-ful of Coco Pops into her mouth.

'Are you going to tell me why?'

'He was showing signs of being a pompous plonker.'

'Better to find out sooner rather than later,' Swift suggested, wondering if the bright, caustic quality of Naomi's tone was nothing more than a defence.

'Certainly is.'

Swift found himself rooted to the spot. Wanting to say something to comfort her. The idea of her having been hurt and made to suffer was unbearably painful.

'Dad! Stop worrying. It's OK. I really did dump him, not the other way round. It makes things a whole lot less traumatic. And as I've told you before, no way am I going to be ground down by a spot of man trouble.'

Swift supposed not, not after her recent experience of being thrown into the dark torture-pit of grief by losing her mother. 'No.' He gave an inner sigh.

'I've got girlfriends and a mobile phone. Which adds up to quite enough sticking plaster to patch over any little cracks in the heart department,' she said, swinging her legs off the sofa and stretching herself upright in a series of graceful movements identical to those of Kate's.

Later, as they sat together eating, she asked him how the murder investigation was going.

'Nowhere very productive,' he said grimly. 'Apart from the fact that it's more or less wrapped up.'

'Wrapped up. That was quick work.' She laid down her fork and looked hard at him. 'But you're not looking one bit pleased.'

'I certainly am not.'

She stirred her food thoughtfully with the tines of her fork. 'Has Farmer Ned turned up yet?'

'No.'

'But there's 'trooble at mill', as they say in these parts?'

'Correct.'

'Am I allowed to know more?' She took up her fork and speared a cube of red pepper. 'You know I can be relied on to be silent as the grave as regards your police business secrets.'

He gave her the bare bones. They'd be public knowledge soon enough. 'Farmer Ned, as you call him, is our prime suspect — at least in the eyes of my colleagues. He's in his seventies, he has some form of senile dementia, he has no previous convictions whatsoever, nor any motive. And he's still missing.'

'I can see why you're not running around cheering. What's the evidence for bringing a charge?' she asked.

'A DNA match between traces found on the girl's clothing and samples taken from the suspect.'

'D-N-A,' Naomi chanted. 'Deoxyribonucleic acid. The basic material of existence. The stuff that differentiates each living creature from all its fellows. The stuff of uniqueness.'

'You can't argue with DNA matches,' Swift agreed. 'They're supposedly one hundred per cent reliable. We've moved light years away from matching fingerprints.'

'Do you think I've overcooked this?' Naomi wondered, dangling a strip of omelette from her fork and squinting at it through narrowed eyes.

'No,' he said, 'it's perfect.'

'Yes,' she agreed with a witchy grin. 'It is. Just testing you!' She searched around her plate for another cube of pepper. 'So, you've got one of your 'feelings' about this case?'

'I think we should be looking nearer home. I can't accept that this is a random murder committed by a stranger. And certainly not by the demented old man we're about to pin it on.'

'Family or friends, then?'

'Maybe.'

Naomi reached for his empty plate and stacked it on her own, lining the forks neatly together. 'But if the old man gets charged, you'll be off this case and on to the next?'

'Exactly,' he said.

'And not a happy man?'

He took up his glass and gave a faint, wry smile.

* * *

Sadie pulled her Land Rover to a halt in the yard and went straight to Godfrey's cottage.

'Hi, there,' he said, appearing at the door in old ripped jeans and a bright fuchsia-pink sweatshirt. 'My, you're looking very city smart. I didn't know you did heels!'

'They're killing me,' she said. 'Is this an inconvenient time to talk?'

'Not at all. Come right in.' He led the way to the living room and settled her on the old leather sofa. 'I fed the dogs and let them out in the field like you said,' he told her. 'Two of them got collected by their owners around an hour ago.'

'Thanks,' she said. 'I really appreciate that.'

He grinned down at her. Kept grinning.

'You look pleased,' she said.

'Yep. My agent phoned earlier. Some guy's dropped out of a Yorkshire TV series. And I'm in. Filming starts tomorrow. Six-part series. Could be big.'

'Well done! That's great, Godfrey.'

'Thanks. Drink?' he asked.

'Yes, please! What have you got?'

'Whisky, gin, brandy, vodka, schnapps, red wine. You name it.'

'Brandy. A large one.'

He padded off to the kitchen. She could hear his bare feet slapping on the tiles. She leaned into the soft back of the sofa. He had lit the fire and a beautiful smoky warmth filled the room. Light from the flames rippled on the walls. She slipped off her punishing court shoes and wriggled her toes.

Godfrey returned with two large tumblers and a bottle. He dropped several chunks of ice into each tumbler, then glugged in a stream of golden brandy.

'Cheers! Here's to your success. Congratulations.' Sadie raised her glass to him and took a long drink. 'Aaah!'

Godfrey sat on the floor and crossed his long legs beneath him. 'Well?'

'It wasn't difficult at all,' Sadie told him, frowning slightly as she reviewed the events of the afternoon. 'Finding the best friend. She's called Crystal.'

'Did she buy your story? About being a long-lost cousin? Or did you go for the outlawed black sheep of the family angle?'

'I don't think she was really bothered who I was. She just wanted to talk. We went to a pub and she got the fruit machine to cough up the jackpot. Apparently it's easy when you know how. Did you know that?'

'Nope,' said Godfrey. 'But I'd sure like to find out.'

'I liked her,' Sadie said. 'Very direct; calls a spade a spade.'

'Takes one to know one,' Godfrey remarked. 'What else did you find out?'

'She seemed lost and forlorn. A lonely kid. She's not happy at home, didn't seem in a hurry to get back there at all.' Sadie stared into the amber depths of her brandy. The excitement and anxiety which had fuelled her to attend Jenny Hoxton's memorial service and do some amateurish sleuthing had begun to evaporate. Earlier in the afternoon, whilst she was talking to Crystal, gaining her confidence and befriending her, she had been filled with a sense of purpose, had felt she was making some kind of progress. But now doubt was stealing up on her. What had she discovered of any substance?

'I don't suppose I found out very much at all,' she told Godfrey gloomily. 'And I can't say I've many bright ideas about where to go from here.'

'Hey! Chin up. Let's be positive,' Godfrey commanded. 'Take yourself back through your talk with Crystal, focus on what she said about Jenny and tell me anything you come up with.'

149

'OK, let's see. Crystal said Jenny didn't get on with her parents.'

'How old are these guys?'

'Fifteen.'

'At that age, I'd say getting on with your parents is fairly peculiar.'

'I suppose so.' Sadie willed her memory to work. 'She said Jenny's parents were 'posh'. They made her take cello lessons.'

'Child abuse, no less.'

'She said Jenny just liked messing about and hanging out.'

'It's all sounding distressingly normal.'

Sadie closed her eyes in concentration. The brandy was working on her, at the brief, pivotal point of enlivening memories before muzziness took over. 'She said that she hadn't seen so much of Jenny in the past few weeks. She looked pretty sad about that.'

'They'd had a fight?'

'No, not so. Crystal particularly mentioned they hadn't fallen out.'

'Mm. Sounds like Jenny had had something, or someone else, on her mind. Anything more?'

Sadie shook her head. 'Can't think of anything.' She swirled the liquid in her tumbler and took another sip. 'You know, Crystal has a lost, forlorn look about her, rather like Jenny has in that picture they use in the TV reports. And how she looked when we saw her at the quarry. Me and my dad.' She put her glass down on the floor. Her hands were shaking; there was a fullness in her throat. Suddenly tears were running down her cheeks, making glistening tracks into her hairline.

Godfrey seized her in a great bear-like hug and rocked her against him.

Later, when she was calmer, she stood up, smoothed her crumpled blouse and skirt and began to make a little speech about getting back to her own place. Godfrey stood looking down at her, shaking his head in mock despair at her bravery and self-reliance.

'Do you know what I'd really like?' she said, aware that her head was spinning. 'A nice warm bath, and then a lovely, long, slow screw to follow.' She groped about for her bag. 'It's all right,' she reassured him. 'Take no notice of me. I'm just drunk, that's all.'

'I thought you'd never ask,' Godfrey said.

She stared at him in astonishment. 'Oh, come off it. Look at me! I'm carrying around two stones of spare flesh and I'd need a complete makeover to raise any interest in the most desperate man alive.'

'Come with me,' said Godfrey, reaching for her hand. 'I'll run you a bath.'

10

Swift swung into the incident room, rescued Detective Constable Sue Sallis from her drudgery at the computer and took her along with him to Middlewood School. They made their way to the office and spoke to Ivan Hewlett's secretary.

Swift asked her if she could give details of the route taken by the school party who had been on the half-term trip to the Dales.

'I should be able to — my daughter was on it,' she said. 'They went up to Malham Cove and then spent two days tracing the course of the River Aire. After they'd completed that they ended up at Haworth to take a look at the Brontë museum. My daughter said it was fascinating. She's a great fan of the Brontë sisters' novels.'

'Me, too,' Sue Sallis agreed, smiling at the secretary and creating an easy atmosphere of trust.

Swift remained silent and abstracted, his mind taking a rapid mental sprint around the possibilities that were opening up:

Fact: Jenny Hoxton was missing during the three days the trip was taking place.

Fact: She was found dead on the day after the final afternoon of the trip.

Fact: She was found in a location less than three miles from Haworth and the Brontë museum.

A thrill of elation shot through him. He held it in check, his cautious, coolly reasoning self still firmly in control. There was a very long way to go before he could start congratulating himself on having at last found a fruitful lead which would make some sense.

'I thought the case was all solved,' the secretary said, looking from one officer to the other with a gleam of expectancy in her eyes. 'I saw it on the news — it was on both local and national. They say poor little Jenny was killed by some old man with senile dementia. It's terrible.' Her face shone with horror and excitement.

'We need to fill in a few gaps,' Sue Sallis told her.

'Oh, I see.'

'I'd like to look at the names of the students who went on the trip,' Swift told the secretary. 'Do you have those to hand?'

She looked at him, initially doubtful. 'Yes, yes, of course.' She plucked a folder from the filing cabinet behind her desk, rifled through the sheets and handed him the list he'd requested.

153

Swift made a quick scan, noting there were around fourteen names, all with addresses and contact numbers. He asked if she would make him a copy to take away with him.

Concern creased her face. 'Oh! I don't know about that. I think I should ask Mr Hewlett, but he's away at a conference. Shall I get the deputy head?'

Swift shook his head. 'This is a murder investigation,' he told her with quiet emphasis.

She hurried instantly to the copier. 'Of course, of course.'

'Who was Jenny's class teacher?' he asked, smiling thanks as she handed him the sheet warm from the copier.

She looked startled and then smiled. 'Mr Walker. Toby Walker. He's not in school at the moment. He went skiing at half term. He broke his leg!' She smiled in an indulgent 'boys will be boys' kind of way. Swift had the impression Walker must be young and popular. 'He's in the district hospital,' she carried on, into the swing now of helping as much as possible. 'Orthopaedics.'

As Swift and Sue Sallis returned to the car, he gave her a terse summary of his thoughts to date. The constable was instantly interested in the connection between the place the murdered girl was found and the location of the last day of the trip.

'It could be coincidence,' Swift commented, scanning again through the list as they went out into the car park.

'There speaks the voice of caution,' she responded with a grin. 'It looks like something important to me.'

Swift gave Sue the car keys and slid himself into the passenger seat. Freed from driving he could channel all his mental energy into the imaginative leaps necessary to begin making vital connections. He spread the list out on the dash-board for the two of them to look at together. He noted that Nick Ashton, the head boy who had spoken so eloquently at Jenny's funeral, was on the list. But none of the other names meant anything yet.

Sue then pointed out that one of the pupil's addresses was in a road about a minute's drive away. Swift followed the progress of her finger as it tracked the name — Imogen Barclay, 16, Seymour Drive. 'Fine — might as well start there,' he decided. Sue fired the engine.

The house they wanted was one of a pristine group of mock-Tudor residences on an estate built in the early 1990s. Open-plan gardens, immaculate lawns, carefully pruned rose bushes.

The face of the woman who answered the

door crumpled into anxious concern as she looked at the solemn faces of the two visitors and listened to Swift's introductory explanations. 'Oh dear! I don't really know if Imogen can help you, Inspector. She hasn't been very well. But . . . do please come in anyway.' Her face remained lined and fretful as she ushered them through to a comfortable sitting room. Swift was immediately struck by a huge photographic portrait of a dark-haired girl with big hazel eyes in pride of place on the mantelpiece.

'Is that your daughter?' he asked, nodding towards the portrait.

Mrs Barclay nodded. 'It was taken on her eighteenth birthday two months ago.' Pride glowed in her eyes for a moment, to be rapidly replaced with the strain he had seen before.

Swift sat calm and still, his expression thoughtful, as though composing himself before embarking on the questions he had come to ask. Sue Sallis followed his lead and there was a short silence.

'I don't think Imogen will be able to tell you . . . help you very much with your investigations,' Mrs Barclay said. 'Well, how could she?'

Swift looked at her, inviting an elaboration.

'I mean, the poor girl was obviously

abducted by some madman. You hear about it all the time, don't you?' She let out a long sigh of regret. 'Imogen's taken it very hard. Jenny's murder, I mean. The whole idea of a schoolfriend being killed in such a wicked senseless, *horrible* way. It's not easy for a young person to come to terms with, is it?

'No, indeed,' Swift murmured. 'Were Imogen and Jenny friends?'

'Well, not close, no. But Imogen sometimes walked part of the way home with her after school. The Hoxtons' house isn't very far from here, you see. Apparently Jenny used to get quite nervous and jumpy in the winter when the dark evenings came along. It's terrible to think of what she must have gone through . . . ' Mrs Barclay's hands had been laid in her lap like two plump white moles. Now she began to twist them together, literally wringing them.

'Has Imogen been seen by her doctor?' Swift asked, phrasing the question to allow for the girl's possible need for privacy. Although his guess was that Mrs Barclay was the sort of hands-on mother who would want to have as full a control as possible over the details of her daughter's life.

'Oh, of course,' Mrs Barclay responded. 'I called the doctor the day after she . . . became unwell.' She stared at Swift, clearly debating how much she was prepared to reveal. 'To be honest, I thought she was having some sort of breakdown. I hope you'll keep that confidential. I've told the school she has a virus.'

'Have you any idea what might have caused Imogen's distress?'

'Well, no.' Her hands were working again, the fingers twisting round and round. 'Of course, everyone's upset about this horrific business with Jenny. And, in fact that's the first thing I asked Imo. You know, I wondered if she needed to have some counselling or suchlike. But Imo just went inside herself. When I mentioned the counselling again she got quite angry at the suggestion.' She unlaced her fingers and began to rub her knees as though she were kneading dough. 'It's usually work pressures or boyfriend problems, isn't it, at this age?' she mused. 'But as far as I know she's no problems with her coursework. I mean, she works hard, but she's always seemed on top of things. And Nick's been so sweet since she's been off school. He phones every evening, and he's been round to see her.'

'Nick is her boyfriend? Nick Ashton?'

'That's right. He's head boy and she's head girl. They make such a . . . superb couple.' The maternal pride broke through again. 'They've both got offers of a place at Oxford.'

Swift gave an appropriate nod of approval. 'When did Imogen become ill, Mrs Barclay?' Sue Sallis asked gently.

'About a week ago.'

'Was she ill when she came back from the trip?' Sue followed up.

'No, she seemed all right when she came back. She was tired, of course. But then they'd done a lot of walking and I suppose they'd have had a lot of late nights as well. Although, I must say, she'd usually take that in her stride. She's very fit and athletic. Last year she came second in the Yorkshire Junior Ladies' Marathon.' She frowned, a woman who seemed genuine in her wish to give as accurate information as she could. 'It was on the Wednesday, the day after she came home, that I noticed something was wrong. She might have been working up to it, of course, whilst she was away. But I didn't begin to be really worried until that day.' She gazed in appeal at the young woman officer. 'The doctor says there's nothing organically wrong. It's just nervous strain. Imo worked terribly hard before her interview at Oxford last December. It was quite an ordeal, you know. And then there was the waiting for the results. And now she's got her A-levels coming up in May.'

'Of course,' Swift agreed. 'We would like to

speak to her,' he reminded Mrs Barclay.

'Oh yes.' He could sense her anxiety like a silent scream. She stood up. 'Yes, I'll go and get her. I won't be a moment.'

Swift and Sue swapped a glance as they heard Mrs Barclay knocking on an upstairs door. There was the sound of the door opening, then closing again. Swift could just make out an exchange of low voices, intermingled sounds of cajoling and responding protests.

The door opened and closed once more. There were footsteps on the stairs.

'Oh, dear! I can't persuade her to come down,' said Mrs Barclay, standing in the doorway looking desperate with anxiety and frustration. 'She's been in her room for over a week, you know.' She bowed her head. Her hands started their wringing routine again. 'She's in a dreadful state. I'll have to get the doctor to see her again. She hasn't eaten anything for days.'

As she was speaking, there was the sound of footsteps coming down the stairs. A leggy, rumple-haired girl appeared in the doorway. She was bundled in a cream towelling robe and her eyes in her white face were like huge black holes. She was recognizable as the handsome girl in the photograph on the mantelpiece, but only just. She looked at

Swift and Sallis, blinking as though she had only just woken and needed to clear her vision and bring herself back to reality.

'I'll make some coffee,' Mrs Barclay said. 'I'll be just there in the kitchen,' she assured them all. 'If you need me.'

Imogen sat opposite Swift, huddled in a corner of the sofa. She glanced at him, her face filled with uncertainty and apprehension.

Swift was wondering what had prompted the girl to come out of hiding. What had made her brace herself to come downstairs and walk into the lion's den, so to speak. There was surely only one reason powerful enough.

He introduced himself and Sue Sallis, sketching a brief and deliberately bland explanation for their visit. He spoke very softly, as though Imogen were a nervy horse he might frighten with loud words and sudden movements. 'We're planning to interview all the pupils who were on the Dales trip,' he reassured her. 'It's good of you to come and talk to us. We appreciate that you're not well.'

'But Jenny wasn't down for the trip,' Imogen said. 'She wasn't there.'

'She was found only a few miles from the Brontë house in Haworth, where the trip ended up,' Sue Sallis observed.

161

Imogen hunched her shoulders, shrinking down into her robe. 'It's like a nightmare,' she said abruptly. 'It's all so awful. I can't believe this has happened. Murders don't happen to people you know.'

'Were you a friend of Jenny's?' Swift asked.

'Not really.'

'Your mother said that you sometimes walked part of the way home with her after school.'

'Yes. She used to . . . hang around and wait for me sometimes.'

'Isn't that rather strange?' Sue Sallis asked quietly.

Imogen stared at her, a frown pulling her brows together. She shrugged.

'I mean,' Sue persisted, 'isn't it unusual for a sixth former — and a head girl at that — to walk home with a year ten pupil?'

Neat angle, Swift thought. He knew that Naomi would have made the same point given the information.

'Well — I — she — ' The words seemed to stick in Imogen's throat. 'She just kind of tagged along.'

'Maybe she had a crush on you,' Sue said.

A sound between a snort and a laugh escaped Imogen's lips. 'No. Absolutely not.' She wrapped her arms around her waist and looked down at her bare feet.

'What did you talk about?' Sue wondered, leaning forward slightly.

'What?' The word was a shrill bark.

'You and Jenny — what did you talk about, when you were walking home from school?'

Imogen tensed. A nerve fluttered in her cheek. 'I don't really remember. Just . . . general things.'

'Girl talk,' Sallis suggested with a smile.

Imogen's face was suddenly thundery. 'If you must know, I didn't want her tagging along. She was a pain.' Her voice died away as she realized she had made a bad mistake. 'I'm sorry, that sounds cruel and wicked now she's dead. But that's how I felt about her.'

'Are you quite sure Jenny was not on the Dales trip?' Swift asked.

There was a silence like the aftermath of an explosion.

'No! Of course not, she was never down to go. I already told you.' The girl's protest was jagged and angry.

'Maybe she decided to gatecrash. It's not unknown,' Swift suggested.

'No. She didn't. She wasn't there.'

'When did you last see Jenny?' Swift continued.

Imogen considered. 'I'm not sure. Maybe a few days before half term. I used to see her around school. Just like I see hundreds of other people. Listen, she wasn't a friend of mine,' she said with shaky desperation. 'And I can't tell you anything about . . . how she died.' There was a tremor now, on her chin.

'Fair enough,' Swift said. 'Imogen, can you tell us where you were on the afternoon Jenny was killed?' he asked in calm, even tones.

Imogen looked at him with sheer panic in her face. She swallowed hard. 'I was with all the others in Haworth village. We went to the parsonage and then we got on the coach and went to Skipton for a snack and coffee. And then the coach brought us back to the school car park.'

'I see,' Swift said. He gave the tormented-looking girl a kind smile and then rose to his feet. He took a step towards the doorway, then turned back. 'I hear from your mother that you and your friend Nick Ashton have both got a place at Oxford in the autumn.'

'Yes, that's right,' Imogen responded with a notable lack of enthusiasm.

'Congratulations,' he said. 'And thank you for talking to us. I hope you'll soon feel better.'

She took in a long breath. 'Yes. Thanks.' As they left, Swift saw her sink back on the sofa cushions, drained and exhausted.

Mrs Barclay was lurking by the kitchen door. 'I thought I wouldn't disturb you with coffee,' she said. 'Would you like some now?'

Swift made a gesture of thanks and shook his head.

'You seemed to get her talking a little,' Mrs Barclay said, her face hopeful. 'It's more than I've managed.'

'She was very helpful.' Swift was moving purposefully to the door.

Mrs Barclay nipped neatly ahead of him and stood with her hand on the door handle. 'You surely don't think Imogen knows something about this dreadful murder?' She was rattled now. 'I thought you'd got a suspect.'

'We need to get the fullest picture possible,' Swift told her courteously, stepping out on to the path and wondering how many times he had resorted to that trusty euphemism.

*   *   *

In a pub just down the road from the Barclay residence Swift ordered coffee and sandwiches for himself and Sue Sallis. He'd politely requested that she gave him some space to think as they drove away from the house and he could tell she was brimming over with eagerness to share her theories with him. They sat in a draughty corner of the pub, away from the crackling log fire and the handful of other early punters.

'Questions running through your mind,' he commanded the constable. 'No more than three if possible.'

'Who is she protecting? What is it she knows about Jenny's murder that's stopping her sleeping at night? Why would a smart, sexy eighteen-year-old walk home with plain-Jane Jenny who hasn't yet got her full hormonal credentials?' Sue bit hungrily into her coronation chicken baguette and eyed her boss with a degree of concern to ascertain how many points she'd scored with this analysis.

'I'm with you on all of those,' he said. 'And in answer to the first point, I'd like you to go and exercise your perception and female empathy on Nick Ashton.'

Sue Sallis coloured with gratification. 'Sure. Right now?'

Oh, yes, thought Swift. Once Ned Bracewell's found, there'll be a big problem in pursuing this line of enquiry. 'I think you should finish the baguette first,' he told the constable.

'And you, sir?'

Swift took a sip of coffee and savoured the hit of the hot, burned-toast flavour. 'I'm going to talk to Mr Toby Walker, Jenny's form tutor. I'll drop you off at Ashton's place. Get a taxi back to the station and charge it up to expenses.'

Sue looked as though she couldn't wait. 'Any prior briefing, sir?'

Swift drained his cup and pushed his chair back. 'Just use your instinct, Sue. I think I can trust in that.'

★ ★ ★

Toby Walker was lying flat on a spinal bed, surrounded by a lake of unread magazines and newspapers. A traction frame loomed above him.

At the sight of Swift and his police identification, Walker's animation increased by around one hundred per cent. 'Someone to talk to!' he exclaimed. His smile was infectious and Swift smiled back, drawing a chair up to the bed. 'I'd heard you'd broken a leg,' he observed, eyeing Walker's prone body.

'There are hip complications,' Walker responded, grimacing as he made a slight adjustment to his position. 'But I'll be fine to hobble around on crutches in a few days — according to the powers-that-be. At least I'm alive and feebly kicking, which is more than can be said of poor Jenny Hoxton. What do you want to know?'

'I'm trying to find out what Jenny was doing in the last few days before she died — '

'I can't offer much there,' Walker cut in. 'I

was away in the Alps, hell bent on doing damage to my infrastructure.'

'You might be able to help, nevertheless. Mrs Hoxton said Jenny was due to stay with friends known to and approved of by her. The Hoxtons left for the Lake District on the Saturday morning at the start of the half-term week under the impression that Jenny was going to her friend's house early that afternoon. But she never turned up there. That leaves three days during which her whereabouts are unaccounted for.'

Toby Walker sucked in a loud breath of dismay. 'God! That's bad.' He let the breath out, equally noisily. 'Who was she supposed to be going to stay with, as a matter of interest?'

'Rosemary York.'

Toby's amiable features registered amazement. 'Rosemary York!'

Swift smiled. There was something about Toby Walker that generated goodwill. 'Why the surprise?'

'Rosemary York's an intellectual and social high flier, with the body of Venus and a liking for mixing with the A team.'

'And Jenny?'

'Jenny was an also-ran with her school work. And she was spiky and awkward as far as relationships were concerned. Some of the other staff thought of her as a loner, but I'm always wary of those kind of labels. Anyway, in no way were she and Rosemary York friends.'

Swift was preparing his follow-up question, but Toby Walker stopped him with a quick lift of his hand. 'Hang on a minute,' he chimed in, his face screwed up in thought. 'Come to think of it there was a bit of a spark between them back in the autumn term. Jenny tagged along with Rosemary for a few weeks. She had a tendency to do that — latch on to one of the popular, glamorous kids. The kind of friends her mother would have approved of, come to think of it,' he added with a twisted grin. 'But it never lasted.'

'Jenny got dumped?'

'Basically, I suppose that's what happened. But you have to remember that fifteen-year-olds are a remarkably fickle bunch when it comes to friendships. They're like pieces of coloured tissue in a kaleidoscope, forever forming groups then splitting up and re-forming.' He crinkled his eyes, thinking things through. 'Have you got any kids?' he asked Swift.

'One daughter.'

'Not with us?'

'She's in private education.' When they had moved, Kate's grieving parents had insisted on paying for an independent school, concerned about the dangers in Swift's job and its spinoffs for Naomi.

Toby Walker smiled. 'It's a free country.'

Swift waited, wondering if some memory of Jenny's place in the shifting pattern of friendships was filtering through.

'Our school is quite an interesting social mix,' Toby Walker observed. 'We're heavily weighted with a bright, well-heeled lot heading for starred A grades in the sixth form, but we also have a group of kids from the run-down part of the Briarwood estate who are struggling to keep up — both academically and socially.'

'Jenny, I presume, fell into the well-heeled group,' Swift suggested.

'Oh yes. And Antonia Hoxton fits the stereotype perfectly.' Toby Walker looked reflective.

'And Jenny?'

'She didn't really fit with either group. Odd that.' He sighed. 'Poor little Jenny.'

'Would the brief friendship between Jenny and Rosemary explain why Mrs Hoxton was satisfied with Jenny's story that she was going to stay at Rosemary's place?' Swift queried, returning to more concrete ground.

'Probably. Mrs Hoxton is something of a remote figure when it comes to mothering.

She believes in keeping her distance and letting youngsters learn by experience.' Toby Walker gave a wry grin. 'Some of the kids with more protective mothers would probably be delighted to swap.'

'What was Jenny's mood like in recent weeks?' Swift asked.

Toby Walker's eyes became pensive once again. 'It was uncharacteristically good. In fact I'd say that in the past few months Jenny was beginning to come out of herself. Blossoming even, whatever that means.'

'A romance?'

'Not that I knew of. Which isn't saying much, of course. We teachers pride ourselves on having a god-like insight into our pupils' lives and their hopes and fears. But in reality I suspect we know very little.'

'Apparently Jenny had attached herself to Imogen Barclay in recent weeks — '

'What?' Toby Walker interjected. 'Our saintly head girl? Are you sure?'

'The information came from Imogen herself. Jenny and Imogen walked part of the way home together on a number of occasions.'

Toby Walker's face came alive with the delight of one not ashamed to own up to loving a nugget of gossip. 'I'm dumbstruck! Jenny and Imogen, trotting home together like mates! That's even more incredible than the notion of Rosemary York pairing off with Jenny. Year tens and the sixth form just don't connect with each other socially. It's a kind of unwritten law. Almost a taboo.'

Swift had been hopeful that Toby Walker might have a stab at guessing what had brought the two girls together. He waited but was disappointed. It struck him that he still didn't seem to be able to get a handle on the sort of girl Jenny was. Or what she had been doing in her final days.

And so far, apart from Jeremy Hoxton, he hadn't met anyone who seemed to be genuinely upset about Jenny's death.

11

Swift laid down his pen and pushed his sheet of scrawled notes to one side as Sue Sallis appeared by his desk. She was carrying two steaming mugs of coffee. The one she placed in front of him was just as he liked it, strong with a drift of milk and no sugar.

She dug in her bag and took out a packet of Rolos. He shook his head as she offered one. 'I'm four and a half weeks into not smoking,' she said, lining up three of the little chocolate drums on the desk. 'Chocolate's the only substitute.'

He opened his hands in a gesture of acknowledgement. 'So tell me about Nick Ashton.'

Sue slid her notebook onto the desk beside the chocolates, flicked through the pages and then ignored it. 'He has all the necessary male equipment,' she said with an elfish grin. 'He's tall and nicely muscled, he has floppy, shiny, dark hair, he has beautiful golden brown eyes, an intelligent expression and a sympathetic manner. And when he speaks it's like Kenneth Branagh meets Laurence Olivier. He's every girl's dream — to die for, as the saying goes.' She took a sip of her coffee and frowned. 'Sorry, sir, that was in really bad taste.'

Swift smiled. 'He's what my mother would have called a dreamboat,' he observed. 'I saw and heard him at Jenny's memorial service. Your description fits perfectly.'

'He's an only child,' Sue continued. 'His mother is a part-time speech therapist and his father is a partner in Ashton and Fieldhouse estate agents. I didn't meet either of the parents — Nick was in the house alone. He was working on an essay when I arrived — writing by hand at the kitchen table. He was wonderfully polite and welcoming, offering a choice of tea or coffee, getting out the biscuit tin, stating his willingness to help in any way he could regarding the investigation.'

'Too good to be true?' Swift suggested.

'Mmm — you could say that!' She bit off half a Rolo and popped it in her mouth. 'But he hadn't much to say about Jenny. He didn't know her personally, and thus he couldn't say anything about her personality, her friend-ships or her social life — which is probably fair enough.'

'And in line with what just about everyone else says,' Swift put in.

'Did he know about Jenny's tagging along with Imogen on the way home?'

'Yes. And he seemed to think the idea of Jenny having a crush on Imogen was a plausible enough reason. Apparently it happens to both of them quite a bit.' She pulled a wry face.

'What about the last time he saw Jenny?'

'Same kind of answer as Imogen. He couldn't really give a precise day.'

Swift nodded.

Sue Sallis reached across to her notebook and flicked over the pages. 'I was basically trying to follow the same line of questioning we took with Imogen, sir, so the next thing was to gauge his reaction to the coincidence of Jenny having been found in a place relatively close to where the trip finished up.'

'And?'

'He freely admitted it was strange, but he claimed to have no idea at all of why it should have happened like that.' Sue turned her head slightly, clearly searching through the images in her head, reliving the moments she was describing with her interviewee. 'He answered very frankly and steadily. There was no break in his voice, no guilty body language, no eye-contact evasion. And he also volunteered the information that the pupils on the trip have been feeling pretty jittery about it and there's a pretty bad atmosphere all round.'

'Pupils looking at each other with suspicion, and so forth,' Swift commented. 'Not good at all.'

'I asked if he could recall anyone having been missing from the trip at any time,' Sue said, picking up the second half of the broken Rolo, eyeing it contemplatively, then replacing it on the desk.

'Nothing like putting him in the hot seat,' Swift said, sensing a slight charge in the air as Sue prepared to deliver her next piece of information.

'That's more or less what he said and I got the impression that he'd find it difficult to grass up a mate. But it didn't come to that. He maintained that he couldn't give a reliable answer to my question. Because,' and here she paused for a second, 'he himself went AWOL and took a four-hour walk over Haworth moors after lunch on the final afternoon.'

Swift leaned forward. 'Reason?'

'He said he'd done the Brontë thing a couple of times before. He likes walking. And he fancied being on his own.'

'Not unreasonable. Did anyone see him?'

'He said not. He also volunteered that he'd got the OK from one of the staff to go off on his own. I've already verified it.'

'Good.'

Sue took a sip of her cooling coffee and polished off the Rolos. 'I looked on the map, sir, and it would certainly have been possible for him to get up to Arkwright quarry and back within the time scale we've got for Jenny's death.'

'Mmm. And Imogen stayed back at the Brontë place?'

'Yes.'

'I asked him if they'd had any kind of fall out, but he said not.'

Swift nodded. 'Right.'

Swift considered for a few moments before inviting Sue Sallis to offer her theories so far.

She screwed her face into a perplexed grimace. 'I haven't really formed any,' she said, sounding annoyed with herself. 'Ashton's story could be perfectly truthful. After all, if you haven't got a tight alibi, it's always more sensible to say so.'

'Yes, indeed.'

'On the other hand, the circumstances look odd, to say the least. I'd be worried if it were me that had been missing at the time of a murder. If I knew the victim, and the times fitted for me to have had the opportunity to kill them.'

Swift smiled. 'But we're CID! Our

reactions are hardly representative of the general public.'

'No — but you know what I mean, sir.'

'Yes. But he didn't seem worried to you?'

'No, he didn't. Very calm and composed.'

'Maybe he's simply a very good actor. You did mention Branagh and Olivier earlier on.'

Sue did not pick up on the faint provocation in his tone; her face was still crumpled with thought. 'Imogen Barclay,' she said. 'Do you think the state she's in has something to do with her thinking he might have killed Jenny?'

'Possibly. Have you any thoughts on what motive Nick Ashton might have had for killing Jenny?'

'No. But that's for us to find out,' she said, her face flushing with eagerness and purpose.

'Yes,' Swift agreed, feeling suddenly old and a touch cynical. 'So, what do you think?' he demanded. 'Do we include him in the frame? Or does his charm and saintliness put him beyond suspicion?'

Sue Sallis hadn't yet seen this whimsical side to Swift. She was pleased he was dropping his guard. 'I think like you do, sir.'

'Which is?'

'Apart from the missing Ned Bracewell who's got himself placed bang in the centre, with a label screaming 'DNA match' hung around his neck, it's a wide open frame. And at this stage, I wouldn't be prepared to exclude anyone who knew Jenny. Especially those who were in the vicinity of the place she was found at the time of her death.'

'Exactly,' Swift agreed. 'Which probably indicates that we need to interview all the rest of the group on the Dales trip.'

'Yes!' Sue responded with undisguised anticipation.

Swift glanced at his watch. It was coming up for seven o'clock. 'Have you no home to go to?' he teased the keen young constable. 'Husband? Children?'

'Just a hubby,' she said. 'So far.'

He nodded, his thoughts swerving to the preciousness of a whole and steady family group. 'I think it's time to get back to him,' he told her gently.

After she had left he drew his handwritten notes towards him, an entirely private summary on the case to date.

Jenny Hoxton: Murdered by asphyxiation aged 15 years and 7 months old. Found in Arkwright quarry by Sadie Bracewell (? found earlier and/or at the same time as Sadie's discovery by Ned, her father)

Possible murder suspects:

Ned Bracewell: Evidence:
DNA match — semen
found on victim's outer
clothes
no other DNA match found
no other significant forensic
evidence
Opportunity:
Yes
Motive:
No clear convincing motive.
But suspect suffers from
senile dementia, thus raising uncertainties about his
behavioural patterns

Sadie Bracewell: Evidence:
No DNA or other forensic
evidence
Opportunity:
Yes
Motive:
No clear or likely motive
— no known connection
with victim

Antonia Hoxton: No evidence,
Sister   unlikely opportunity, but

might have a motive i.e. dislike (? hatred), jealousy of her sister.

Imogen Barclay: No evidence, but a ? possible
School contact opportunity, no clear motive but was being ? 'harassed' by Jenny.

Nick Ashton: No evidence, but opportun-
School contact ity. No known motive. But a link between him, Imogen and Jenny. ? what lies behind this link.

Parents ??? (very low possibility)
Other school contacts ???
Non-school contacts ???

Shrugging on his jacket, he folded the paper into three, slipped it in an inner pocket and went out to his car. Before starting the engine he telephoned Naomi. There was no answer so he left a brief message to say that he'd be home soon and he'd take her out to the restaurant of her choice.

Driving out of the car park into the road, he pushed back a stab of anxiety about Naomi's whereabouts. And then he began to question the fatherly presumption that she'd want to go out dining with her tired, bereft parent. And, of course, maybe she'd have other plans.

By the time he got home she was very much in evidence. Her coat and the fat canvas bag she used to carry her books around in were tossed on the hall chair. Her favourite music was blaring from the stereo system in the sitting room, and when he walked in he found her locked in the entwining embrace of a young man with spiky blond hair and very long legs. 'Hi,' he said, running a finger down the exposed nape of her neck, then heading for the kitchen, the fridge and a bottle of chilled wine.

She appeared a few moments later, rumpled and sparkly-eyed. 'Caught with my tongue down the throat of a member of the opposite sex,' she said cheerily, making her father ashamed of his own discomfiture. Then as he looked at her, a wing of happiness opened inside to see her safe and well, and looking so animated.

'Name and credentials?' he enquired, uncorking a bottle and pouring himself a large glass. He got out another two glasses. 'Want one?'

'Yes, please. And he probably would too.' She leaned to whisper in his ear. 'The name is Marcus. Credentials: god of the sixth form.'

'I thought he'd had his dismissal notice.'

'I've forgiven him,' she said with glinting sweetness.

'What for?'

'I'd prefer not to say right now. But it's not a capital offence, or the passing on of a dreaded disease.'

Swift swallowed. She's sixteen, he reminded himself.

'He'd love to be taken out to dinner by a wise and brilliant sleuth,' she said with outrageous coquetry. 'And so would I.'

12

Geoff Fowler was keeping his head down. He had organized and participated in the search for Ned Bracewell with a will, but without giving the combing of the local territory or the trawl through the computer files for paedophile vigilantes any flavour of a witch-hunt.

He had maintained a neutral approach when communicating with Swift. No more had been said on the subject of his being taken off the Hoxton case, and Fowler knew that Swift was generously giving him a second chance. Other senior officers of Swift's ultra politically clean persuasion would have probably instigated an enquiry involving the internal investigation boys. He would have been forced to retire at the very least, his reputation and the fatness of his pension being punctured like burst balloons. The thought of it had hollowed out his stomach with dread. True, he often wished he was out of modern-day policing, but the notion of the reality of retirement — its emptiness and the tedium of some low-level security work or parking VIPs' cars in airports — appalled him.

Tonight he had decided to work a late shift and collate all the computer information on paedophile hounds to put on Swift's desk the next morning.

Around ten o'clock the sergeant on the front desk rang through to Fowler's extension with the information that he had Mr Jeremy Hoxton at the desk requesting to speak to one of the officers on the murder enquiry.

Fowler registered an internal buzz of pure adrenalin excitement. 'I'll come around and pick him up right away.'

'He's asking for the top man,' the desk sergeant offered laconically. 'And he's had a few. Whiskies would be my guess.'

'No problem.' Fowler slid on his jacket, shot his cuffs, smoothed his hair and headed down the corridor with energetic purpose.

On arriving at the reception area his gaze worked rapidly around the sad bunch of losers waiting there. Even though he had only seen Jeremy Hoxton briefly on the day he and Anita Hoxton had come to do their grim identification task, he recognized him straight away, sitting on a chair against the wall, hunched and desolate-looking.

Fowler walked up to him. 'Mr Hoxton, I'm Detective Sergeant Fowler. Would you like to follow me? We can talk in my office.' His words reverberated in his head: polite, authoritative yet compassionate. He was pleased with that.

Hoxton looked up.

'Where's your boss?'

'Superintendent Lister went home some time ago, sir.'

Hoxton got to his feet, lumbering and unsteady. 'Not him, the thin one with the long face. Red hair.'

'Chief Inspector Swift has gone home too, sir.' Fowler felt a spark of anger for Hoxton's arrogant assumption that police officers should be working round the clock.

'Holding the fort, then, are you, Sergeant?' Hoxton slouched along behind Fowler, somehow managing to match the other man's brisk pace. 'No, don't bother to answer that. I'm half cut, as you can see. I keep hitting the bottle, hoping my feelings will get as pickled as the rest of me, but somehow that doesn't seem to happen.' He sat down in the chair Fowler gestured him towards, drew a packet of panatellas from his jacket and proffered one in invitation.

Fowler shook his head, at the same time pushing an ashtray across the desk for Hoxton's use. He recalled from the file notes that Hoxton was a partner in the town's most exclusive estate agency. It struck him that Hoxton was dressed as though he had just come back from the office: navy suit, pale pink shirt, deep shimmering burgundy tie held down with a small diamond stud.

Fingers shaking, Hoxton clicked a lighter and inhaled. 'When you lose someone you love, your life seems to turn into some second-rate TV drama,' he observed. 'You keep stumbling round looking for the thing you've lost, wondering why all this pain has been handed out to you. You keep trying to get someone to take the pain away. Your wife, your daughter, your pals at the golf club.' He leaned forwards, peering hard at Fowler as though trying to remind himself who he was. 'But guess what, it doesn't work.'

'No,' Fowler replied softly.

Hoxton sucked on his cigar like a child seeking the comfort of a thumb. 'I don't suppose he's turned up yet, the old guy everyone seems to think did it?'

Fowler shook his head. 'You say 'every-one'.' He connected with Hoxton's glittery drunken gaze. 'Does that include you, sir?'

'Do I think he did it? I've no idea. I'm not the investigating offi . . . ossi . . . God that's a bloody difficult word to say when you're bladdered.' He laid down his cigar. 'Speaking of which, is there somewhere . . . ?'

Fowler pointed the way to the staff toilets just across the corridor. When Hoxton had disappeared behind the door, he took a small tape recorder from the top drawer of his desk, set it to record and slipped it to stand just inside the narrow opening to the drawer.

Hoxton reappeared and seated himself again. His cigar had died, and he clicked on his lighter to reactivate it. 'Do you want to know something for free?' he demanded of Fowler. 'My wife hasn't cried once since Jenny died. Not once!' His eyes were full of challenge; bloodshot and muddy. *'Not once!'*

Fowler held himself very still, understanding that some revelation was imminent.

'Always the perfect lady, my wife. Never shows her feelings, never lets her hair down. Never makes a prat of herself. Not like me. Oh no. I'm the one who lets the side down. Gets plastered, can't keep my dick in my trousers.' He heaved again on his cigar. 'At least I'm good for bringing home the bacon. Good thing too. Anita and Antonia aren't the cheapest of ladies to run.'

Fowler saw that the drink had made him maudlin. Suddenly tears welled in his eyes and then rolled down his cheeks unchecked. 'Poor little Jenny. Poor, poor little Jenny! Those two glamourpuss duchesses couldn't stand her. Couldn't bear the sight of her, in fact. And I was no better. Didn't give her any 'quality time'.' He wiped at the moisture on his livid, veined cheeks. 'Mind you, I don't think she was all that interested in me in the past year or two. Not since she started eyeing up the boys.'

Fowler was wondering where all this was leading. Probably nowhere, he thought with an internal sigh.

Hoxton ground his cigar into the ashtray and lit up another one. 'You coppers must get to hear all kind of things you wouldn't get to know otherwise,' he remarked with grim relish. 'The whole tapestry of life must be constantly spread out before you. Well, here's some grist to your mill, Sergeant. My little Jenny wasn't Anita's child. She was the bastard child of a girl who worked on the shooting gallery of a travelling fair.'

Fowler's heart gave a tiny leap. So the murdered girl had been an adopted child. That surely opened a whole can of new worms. His mind leapt through the possible scenario of Jenny trying to find her natural parents, maybe provoking all kinds of unwanted memories of a dark past, stirring up a forgotten cauldron of turbulent emotions. For a split second Fowler's firm belief in Ned Bracewell's guilt wavered.

'Yeah,' Hoxton continued. 'I knocked down three plastic ducks, won a cuddly pink teddy and got my leg over with the fair girl in the park when the roundabouts and the dodgems had all gone quiet.' He sucked hard on his cigar, a whisper of a smile tilting his lips. 'She was a little tiger. Knew what a chap wanted — know what I mean, Sergeant?'

Fowler nodded. Hoxton was beginning to disgust him. He glanced down at the recorder, hoping he'd set it up properly. Its red eye winked reassuringly.

'We had a hot little fling for a few days, and then she was off. On to the next place. The next bloke, most likely.' Hoxton leaned back in his chair, more relaxed now, in full story-telling mode. 'The fair came round again six months later. I went along to the shooting gallery to find her. I couldn't stop myself. I needed to see her. And there she was. With a bun very clearly in the oven.' His eyes clouded over with remembered feeling. 'She was just a little thing,' he mused. 'Her name was Liza. She was no more than sixteen, and not a looker by any stretch of imagination. But when I saw her that night, I was all filled up with a need to protect her, to look after her.'

Fowler gave an internal sigh. 'What happened next?'

'I pretended I hadn't seen what I'd seen. She was busy with a load of tipsy punters, so she couldn't get to speak to me. I took some pot shots at the ducks and missed them all. And then I went home — to my beautiful, virtuous wife. I told myself to forget all about the affair and little Liza. Let her sort out her own problems; she'd probably been screwing a different bloke in every port of call. That's what I told myself. Nice sort of fellow, wasn't I?' he demanded, his eyes filling up once more with tears. 'Anyway, I didn't have long to curse myself for being a rat and a coward. Little Liza turned up at the front door. She'd followed me home.'

'You'd walked home?' Fowler interjected.

Hoxton nodded. 'Drink driving isn't one of my vices.' He shot Fowler a glance. 'Believe it or not. Anyway, to get back to the point, Liza was standing there on the doorstep and Anita was taking her credentials. And then she was inviting her in.'

Fowler imagined the scene and winced silently.

'Liza got straight to the point. Told me and Anita she was six months gone, and the kid was mine.' He rubbed his chin, the stubble rasping beneath his hand. His fingers moved down to check on the straightness of his tie. 'And I believed her. I'd already been over the whole issue in my mind, right from the moment I realized she was pregnant. I had a gut feeling that kid was mine.'

Fowler nodded sagely, not for the first time

amazed at the gullibility inherent in human nature.

'Yeah. And as it turned out, I was probably right. Jenny was very like her mother, but there was enough of me about her to make me know she was mine.' He paused, his eyes filled with a desperate, empty sorrow.

'So you offered to help her, after all?'

'I said I'd take care of any medical bills connected with the birth and I'd pay maintenance for the kid afterwards.'

'And what was your wife's reaction?' Fowler asked, thinking that his ex would have been none too pleased to have discovered he'd been frequenting funfairs and making teenage girls pregnant. Not to mention mortgaging himself with the expense of an illegitimate child.

Hoxton looked up, his face baleful yet shrewd. 'My wife has a policy of taking the high moral ground,' he said, suddenly sounding much less drunk than he had before. 'She is a 'committed Christian', you see.' He placed malicious emphasis on the descriptive words. 'And a keen supporter of the church. She likes to be noble.

'We sat there, the three of us. And my wife did what she always does. Took charge of the situation and handled it perfectly. She spoke very quietly and kindly to Liza. Managed to extract her family history from her in a matter of minutes — which was bloody awful, by the way. Both parents dead, Liza living with a sister who resented being lumbered with her and so on.' He paused and lit yet another cigar. 'Told you it was like a TV drama, didn't I?'

Fowler said nothing. The red eye of the tape recorder twinkled and then was still as a silence fell.

Hoxton resumed his tale. 'Anita told her that we would both be prepared to help her, but that she would need to speak to certain people before we could make specific commitments. I'm not sure Liza had a clue what she was talking about. But after Anita had plied her with cocoa and sponge cake, Liza agreed to let Anita walk her back to the fairground, with the promise of meeting her again after the fair closed the next evening.'

Fowler leaned forward. 'And then?'

'Oh, I got a grilling and a wigging,' Hoxton said, waving his cigar, 'and the next day Anita consulted the vicar and our solicitor. The wondrous idea of adopting Liza's baby was born.'

'Your wife's idea?'

'With good support from the vicar, and less so from the solicitor, I'd guess,' Hoxton said with irony rather than bitterness.

'And you were in agreement?'

Hoxton laid down his cigar and eyed Fowler with a disturbingly piercing gaze. 'You don't argue with Anita,' he said. 'Especially when she's got you well and truly over a barrel.'

'What was in it for your wife?' Fowler asked, keeping his voice low and impartial, although his curiosity was now twitching.

'A whole bloody jackpot. Doing good Christian works, getting me to face up to my responsibilities, making sure I had my nose rubbed in the mess I'd made for the rest of my life.' He sucked heavily on his cigar. 'There's a saying about making a rod for your own back. Well, I did that, and how, when I married Anita. And then there was Jenny . . .' His voice cracked into a pitiful whine.

Fowler felt nothing but contempt for Hoxton. His own wife had not been the easiest to please. He'd never been able to give her what she wanted: he hadn't been successful enough in his career and had failed to provide the lifestyle she wanted, so she'd ditched him for someone who could. But for all that he'd never badmouthed her, not to anyone, not even himself. Hoxton's disloyalty to his wife made him a very small man in Fowler's eyes. And the feelings for the dead daughter seemed a good deal more like self-pity than genuine remorse.

Hoxton made a gagging sound in his throat. Dropping the cigar onto the floor, he made a sudden dash for the toilets. Fowler retrieved the cigar and carefully extinguished it. Sounds of vomiting rumbled from across the corridor.

Hoxton eventually returned, white-faced and utterly sober. 'Look here, Sergeant,' he said, standing beside the desk, his self-possession fully retrieved, 'it goes without saying that all of that stuff I was telling you was strictly off the record. I just needed to unburden . . . Well, I'm sure you appreciate that.' He spread his hands in a gesture of man-to-man matiness. 'Thanks for listening.'

Fowler connected with Hoxton's gaze, his own expression impassive.

'I've lost my little girl,' Hoxton said. 'I've lost her because I didn't take enough trouble to find out what she was doing with her life and how to protect her. I've got to live with that. Every day.' He stared hard at Fowler. 'So just find the chap who did it and put him away for a long time, will you? And quickly.'

Fowler sat pondering, listening until Hoxton's footsteps had died away. Hot air, he concluded. The whining whingeings of a drunk. He tapped a four-line summary of the interview into his computer. And then he took the tape from the recorder and slipped it into an inner pocket of his jacket.

13

On the morning of 21 February, eight days after Jenny Hoxton's body had been found, an early-morning runner pounding the deserted town streets found an old man collapsed and tethered to a lamppost by a dog collar and leash. Pinned to his coat was a torn piece of newsprint, over which the words 'LET JUSTICE BE DONE' were scrawled in red felt pen.

The runner ascertained that the man was alive, untied him and then alerted the police on his mobile phone.

★　★　★

When Swift woke to the sound of the phone it was still dark outside. His eyelids felt heavy and glued together. He groped around. 'Yes.'

'Ed. I want you round at the station right away. We need to talk. There's been a real turn-up for the books.' This time Lister's voice was laced with an unmistakable tinge of exhilaration. 'Ned Bracewell, in fact.'

★　★　★

Swift listened thoughtfully as Lister gave him the grim details of Ned Bracewell's discovery.

'You see the freakish side of human nature in this job,' Lister observed. 'But to think of someone chaining an old man to a lamppost like an abandoned dog. Well, it takes some beating.'

'What state is he in?' Swift asked.

'The officers who went to pick him up said he was dazed. Not speaking. But there were no obvious signs of assault. We'll know more when the medics have had a look at him.'

'He's in the local hospital?'

'Yes. We've got a couple of DCs keeping an eye on him.'

'Does his daughter know yet?'

'No. I wondered if you'd be the best one to go and see her . . . '

'I'll go right away.'

'Excellent!'

Swift could see that Lister, despite his sombre demeanour, was in his element. Newly shaved and dressed in a well-pressed grey suit, the DS looked like a chief of operations who was confident he had every weapon he needed in his arsenal. Swift guessed that the superintendent was silently simmering with relief at being released from the dilemma surrounding the use of Fowler's vital evidence and the risk of running up against the howl of protest from the do-it-by-the-book-boys and the human rights lot. He sensed too Lister's quiet jubilation at the prospect of bringing a charge against the prime suspect in the Jenny Hoxton case. Suddenly this minefield of a case was taking a turn for the better.

'I've asked for medical and psychological reports on Bracewell's condition,' Lister went on. 'Naturally those will need to be taken into account before we proceed further. Oh, and I've called a press conference for this afternoon.'

Swift nodded. Lister's mood was becoming almost festive.

'Listen, Ed,' Lister said, his tone sympathetic and confidential, 'I know you've never been happy about the way this investigation is going. But I believe we have enough to take to the CPS.' He began to tick off the various points on his fingers. 'We've got Bracewell's DNA over the girl's clothing. We know he was familiar with the territory where she was found. He had the opportunity, he had the means . . . '

Swift did not think it worth offering up further objections at this stage. Things were moving inexorably in one direction only. 'The DNA evidence certainly carries some weight, I can't disagree with that.' He paused. 'So do you want me to tell Sadie Bracewell that we are intending to charge her father with murder?'

Lister cleared his throat with a little grunt. 'It's not an easy one, Ed. I know you'll handle it with your usual professionalism.'

'Do we have any information on where Bracewell has been for the past few days? What's been happening to him?' Swift asked.

Lister shook his head. 'Nothing as yet. Although we do have a report from one of the search team that there's an old broken-down shepherd's croft a few miles up the hill from the Bracewells' place which looks as though someone's been using in the past few days. Empty lager cans, remnants of food, ashes from a fire . . . '

'I'd be surprised if Ned Bracewell could plan ahead to get all that stuff together,' Swift remarked. 'Let alone light a fire.' But the information interested him, nevertheless. 'This cryptic message,' he said to Lister. 'What are we supposed to infer from that?'

'Some paedophile hater?'

'Stirred into a frenzy by Saturday morning's newspapers? Or am I being fanciful?' Swift added with more than a touch of grim irony.

Lister gave a wincing grimace.

'On the other hand, it doesn't seem too

likely that Ned Bracewell was simply stumbling around in a mental fog — an obvious target for paedophile haters to recognize and apprehend,' Swift said thoughtfully. 'The length of time he was away, together with that message, make it look more like a kidnap.'

'What?' Lister responded sharply.

'Well, if not an abduction then holding Ned against his will,' Swift suggested, knowing Tom Lister was not at all pleased to be distracted from his main objective — namely to nail Ned Bracewell as soon as decently possible. 'Just a thought, sir,' he added. 'Who knows? And if so we might need to open a separate investigation . . .'

He left the superintendent standing beside his desk, his brow furrowed with concern. But Swift doubted that he had spoiled Lister's morning — he had merely sent a grey cloud scudding temporarily over the sun.

★ ★ ★

There was no reply to Swift's knocks on the farmhouse door. He went across the yard and looked towards the kennels. One of the dogs was barking hysterically, but he could see no sign of Sadie Bracewell. Looking across the yard he saw the door of one of the tenanted cottages open. Sadie stepped out, her thick hair rumpled, her eyes heavy with sleep. She came swiftly forward.

'Inspector!' Her eyes were suddenly wide awake, the pupils shivering with expectation and dread. 'It's Dad!' she burst out. 'Is he all right?'

'Yes. Can we go inside?'

'Keys!' she said, running her hands helplessly over her skirt but finding neither pockets nor house keys. She gestured towards the cottage. 'We can talk in there. My tenant won't mind.'

Swift's detective's antennae gave an automatic twitch, running through one or two possible scenarios between Sadie Bracewell and her tenant. On meeting Godfrey Quarmie in the hallway of the cottage he instantly knew which theory to drop and which to run with. Although he doubted it mattered in relation to the issue of Ned and the murder of Jenny Hoxton.

'Hi!' Godfrey greeted him, as though he were an old friend. 'Go right along into the sitting room. You won't be disturbed. I'm out of here in a minute or so. There are TV dramas to be made. Take it easy, you guys.' Planting a kiss on Sadie's nose tip, he made himself scarce.

'When can I see him?' Sadie asked Swift urgently.

'Any time you like. He's in the district hospital.'

'Oh, thank God!' She closed her eyes. 'Thank God he's safe.' She started to ask the expected questions about where her father had been and how he had been found.

'We don't have any details as yet,' Swift told her. 'He was found by a man on a morning run.' He paused briefly, then sketched out the scene Lister had described.

'The bastards!' Sadie exclaimed in fury. 'To tie him up like a dog.' She sat down abruptly on the sofa. 'Who would be so bloody cruel, so evil?'

'We'll find him,' Swift told her. 'Is it possible this is someone your father knows? Someone with a grudge against him, perhaps?'

Sadie frowned. 'I can't think of anyone. I mean, for the past couple of years his life has been . . . well, not much of a life at all. You have to be active and purposeful, don't you, to stir up grudges?'

'Someone from the past, then?'

She shook her head. 'He was always pretty well liked around here. He had quite a temper on him sometimes. But he was never nasty, never cunning or slippery. With Dad what you saw was what you got.'

'Sadie,' Swift said quietly, 'we've got

evidence to link your dad with Jenny's murder. DNA matches.'

She lifted her face, her eyes registering weariness rather than surprise. 'Yes,' she agreed. 'It was Dad who took me to the quarry. When he took me to the quarry to show me the body, he was grasping and hugging it. Rocking it like a baby. Literally drooling over her. There'll be plenty of evidence.'

'There were traces of semen on Jenny's clothing,' he said.

Her body drooped. The silence in the room was absolute. 'Had she been assaulted? Sexually assaulted?' Her voice was strained and faint.

'No.'

'Thank heaven for that.' She hesitated a moment before her eyes met Swift's assessing gaze full on. 'Have you got enough evidence to convict him?'

'Conviction is for the courts to decide. But we have enough evidence to make a case against him. To charge him with Jenny's killing.'

'And are you going to do that?' A flash of hate lit her eyes.

'It seems very likely.'

He saw her struggling with her thoughts, realizations of the likely shape of the future rolling up one after another like an army of dark threats.

She wrapped her arms around her chest and then got slowly to her feet. 'I'd like to go and see him now,' she said. 'Will you drive me? I don't think I'm in any fit state to be in charge of a vehicle.'

★   ★   ★

Ned was lying in bed, perfectly still, his body beneath the sheet seeming as insubstantial as a cardboard cut-out. His hands on the outside of the sheet were pierced with intravenous lines attached to little tubes, pumping him with fluids and linking him to a winking monitor. Although his eyes were open, they were dulled and unfocused as if the essence of him was absent from the little room in which he was placed centre-stage.

Sadie sat down beside the bed and took his hand. 'Dad. It's me. Sadie.'

There was a beating pause. A muscle flickered in his jaw and then was still. His face seemed to have shrunk and collapsed since she had last seen him. His skin hung in a series of deep folds as though all the flesh and muscle that had once supported it had been sucked out.

Sadie felt her stomach drop away, felt a

lurching premonition of grief, as though her father had already left the world of the living and gone away for ever.

'I'm here, Dad,' she kept whispering, pressing his hand. 'It's Sadie, I'm here.' The bird-like brittleness of his bones shocked her.

The duty nurse came along. She checked Ned's temperature and pulse and fiddled with the bottles and tubes. Her glance towards Sadie was full of kindly pity. 'He's not doing badly,' she said, in direct contradiction to what her face was conveying. 'He was suffering from dehydration when he came in, so we're putting lots of fluid and vitamins into him. It's surprising what a difference that can make. The doctor'll be round to speak to you before long. We're just so busy this morning.'

They brought Sadie coffee and biscuits. Then they brought Ned's lunch, a surprisingly enticing-looking cottage pie with cauliflower cheese. It was like offering food to a block of wood.

'He's not going to eat that!' Sadie protested.

'We'll just leave his dinner there for the moment,' the nurse said, lining up the knife and fork on the bedside table. 'You never know, he might be tempted . . . '

Sadie loaded the fork and placed it under her father's nostrils. Not a flicker. Eventually she ate the food herself.

A young, hunted-looking doctor came to talk to her. He said little, beyond the fact that her father was traumatized and the next twenty-four hours were critical. There were no clinical indications of any serious problems. Her father was in a frail condition but he was stable. They were doing all they could. Sadie tried to frame questions, but she could see that he was already poised to move on somewhere else. It was like talking to someone leaving on a train when you were still standing on the platform.

Later on, a woman with long floppy hair and a gentle smile came along. 'Has your dad spoken yet?' she asked Sadie, looking intently into Ned's face.

'No. He seems totally out of it.'

'The doctors say there are no signs of a head injury, or any neurological disease,' the woman said helpfully. 'And it doesn't seem that he's suffered a stroke.'

'So he might just wake up?'

'Hopefully.'

'Were you hoping to do some sort of assessment?' Sadie wondered.

The psychologist showed her the test form she was carrying: *Battery for the Assessment of Neuropsychological Status*. 'It's a bit of a mouthful,' she apologized. 'It helps us draw up a profile of the patient's neuropsychological difficulties, so we can advise on treatment and rehabilitation.'

Sadie wondered what that meant in terms of her father's psychological 'fitness' to be charged with the murder of a young innocent girl. She drew in a long breath.

'I don't think we're going to be able to get very far at the moment,' the woman suggested sympathetically.

'No,' Sadie agreed. 'I don't know how far you would have got anyway. He's been getting steadily worse mentally over the past two years. Sometimes I don't think he's even sure who he is.' She stroked the back of his hand with feather-light touches. 'He's like a shell, with bits of him still rattling around inside.'

The woman nodded. 'Neat description.'

'Do you think people with dementia are capable of murder?' Sadie asked.

There was a slight hesitation. 'It's hard to give a generic answer to that.'

'You've read the notes, haven't you?' Sadie challenged. 'His case history. What do *you* think? The police are itching to bring a charge against him.'

'I can't say. I don't know him well enough. I haven't sufficient clinical information to give a balanced opinion. I'm sorry.'

'It's all right,' Sadie said wearily. 'I'm just

thrashing around in the dark here, and I don't seem to be able to find the light switch.'

The woman put her hand briefly on Sadie's shoulder. 'I'll come back later.'

Sadie sat through the empty hours. To start with her focus had all been on her father's helplessness, lying there still and prone, sinking further and further away from life. She was filled with a sense of pity of what he had become, the tragedy of the brutality he had been made to suffer at the closing of his days.

From time to time she covered his hand with hers and talked to him. Talked as she used to do when his mind was whole and healthy. 'It's me, Sadie,' she kept reassuring him. 'I'm here.' Just occasionally she could swear there was a tiny wing-beat of recognition on his features, the faintest pressure from his fingers.

In time, when she had forced herself to face up to the full extent of his tragedy and her own impending loss, her mind became free to move on. And it was not hard to reach a conclusion as to what needed to be done. No, the immediate way forward was simple. Her numbing indecision subsided, falling away like a dead branch.

She went out into the hospital grounds and

telephoned Swift at the station. He was in a meeting.

'I need to speak to him. Urgently.'

'He *is* very busy,' the woman on the end of the line said with headmistressly sternness. 'We have a major investigation in progress.'

'I know. I'm the daughter of the prime suspect,' Sadie said with some energy. 'And if I don't get to speak to him, I think you might find he'll be pretty angry when he hears I've been given the brush-off.'

There was a little sniff, a short silence. 'Please wait a moment.' More silence and then a muffled conversation with a third party. Sadie thought she heard the word 'stroppy'.

'Inspector Swift will call you back within the next few minutes,' she was told. 'Do we have your contact number?'

'Yes. My mobile number. It's in the file.' Sadie swiftly clicked off the connection before the other woman had the satisfaction of doing so.

Pacing the squelchy grass and eyeing the stunted rose bushes in the damp, lumpy earth, Sadie waited, her mood jagged and full of foreboding. She felt as though there were fireworks hissing in her head. Her eyes were dry and hot and gritty. As she looked around her, everything seemed ephemeral and impossibly far away; there was nothing real enough to grasp on to.

And then she was aware of a figure coming across the grass. Making straight for her. She scraped her fingers through her hair, trying to get back to some kind of normality. The figure became a recognizable form. It was Swift, his face fixed in grim lines.

'Oh God, things are bad!' she burst out. 'Really bad.' Now that she was faced with the task she had set herself, bubbles of panic were rising up.

He put his hand under her arm and began to guide her in the direction of the hospital entrance. 'Let's find somewhere to sit down.'

He found an empty outpatient clinic and steered her into one of the consulting rooms.

'You can't charge him with this murder,' she burst out.

'We're not going to do anything for the present,' Swift told her, his voice calm and firm.

'For the present! What does that mean?'

'That we're not going to proceed any further until we've got a full report on your father's medical condition.'

'Have you seen the state of him?' Sadie insisted. 'How he is now? He's in a really bad way.'

'I'm sorry.'

Sadie believed him, but she hadn't finished yet. 'And how come you've got DNA evidence when Dad hasn't yet given a sample for testing?'

Swift turned his head away, but not before she'd seen the look of regret cross his features.

'If any of your lot took a sample this morning, then they damn well shouldn't have done without asking me,' she pressed on. 'But it takes time to process DNA, doesn't it? So you must have got it before. Yes?'

Swift sighed.

'OK, OK,' she said. 'I've no wish to accuse you of some misdeed that someone else should be taking the blame for. And I've a pretty shrewd idea who that someone should be. Your sergeant was not at all pleased when he came along to get a sample and found Dad had gone missing. It doesn't take a great intellect to work out that he took something away with him when he went to the bathroom. He asked so politely,' she reflected with bitter sarcasm. 'To use the lavatory, I mean, not to infringe human rights.'

'Yes,' Swift agreed tersely.

'If you or any of your colleagues come to charge my father with Jenny Hoxton's murder, then I want myself and my solicitor to be there with him.' Reality was kicking in with a vengeance. She was well into her stride now.

'That is your right,' Swift interposed. 'There would be no question of our acting without your knowledge.'

'And if anyone starts saying their piece to him about 'not being obliged to say anything' and so forth, I'd take the opportunity to lodge a strong complaint against the police for taking samples without permission. I'd guess in these days of increased rights for Mr Joe Public that that kind of thing is illegal, pure and simple. So perhaps you'd tell that to your boss.'

Swift nodded.

She stood up. 'I think I've said all I wanted.' She glanced down at him. He looked exhausted. He looked as though he needed to sleep for a week.

'It's not personal,' she told him. 'All that anger and pushiness. I know you're on my side.'

He was still sitting there when she left, leaning against the back of the bench, his face grey and drained.

★   ★   ★

She walked through the hospital, making for her father's little room, when she realized she had lost her bearings, had no idea where she

212

was going. She had to retrace her steps to the main entrance and read the signs once again.

Her legs felt heavy as she walked. Everything seemed so difficult; there were so many complications, so many hurdles. She needed to pull herself together to find the strength to deal with them all.

He was on his own when she re-entered the room, no staff checking his pulse, no one delivering tea and biscuits.

She sat down beside him and laid her hand on his. 'I'm doing my best, Dad,' she told him. And then her glance connected with his eyes. They were dulled and fixed, the faint light in them all snuffed out. He had gone.

14

She stayed with him until it grew dark. The doctor came to speak to her, the same doctor she had talked to earlier. He was grave-faced and informative. He made her feel he had all the time in the world to talk to him. After she had asked the few questions she could think of, she felt empty and dizzy with fatigue. She drove into town to the Tandoori takeaway and ordered an extra hot prawn curry with sweet chutney and sour lime pickle.

Getting out of her Land Rover at the farm, she saw Godfrey at the door of the cottage slotting his key into the lock. There was a woman with him, a young blonde, her hair gleaming in the moonlight.

'Hi there! How's things?' he called out.

She shook her head. There was a sudden impulse to collapse into hysterical laughter. 'See you in the morning,' she said.

She ate the curry to the accompaniment of a large brandy and soda. She was aware of savouring each spiced mouthful, somehow finding a seed of joy amongst her bleak sadness, the intense gratefulness to feel oneself beating and alive after having been brought up close with death.

When the food was finished she poured another brandy and went to inspect her canine clay heads. She had done no work on them for days. Their sightless glass eyes glittered as she flicked the light switch. She stood for a few minutes then flicked the switch off and went out to the kennels to let the two remaining boarding dogs run in the field. She took them back to the house to feed them. They could sleep in the kitchen. Keep her company. Tomorrow she would get the owners to come for them, or make alternative arrangements. She needed to be free. Free to drive all her thoughts and energy into what needed to be done next.

There was a tap on the window. Godfrey's face pressed against the glass, mouthing to her.

She flung open the door. 'Come in. Bring the blonde.'

He stepped inside and laid a hand on Sadie's shoulder. 'Her train was cancelled. She's waiting for her boyfriend to collect her.' There was a ghost of whimsical rebuke in his smile.

'Sorry,' she said.

'What's going on?' he asked

'Dad was found this morning,' she told him. 'Tied to a lamppost with a dog lead. He died this afternoon. And I'm kettled.' She collapsed onto a chair. He knelt beside her and rubbed her hands in his. She smiled at him, reflecting that in the midst of calamity there can be a terrible calm. She wished she could rage, she wished she could cry. Her emotions were all locked up.

★ ★ ★

'Poor old bugger,' Lister said the next morning, glancing at the notes e-mailed from the hospital. 'A pulmonary embolism most likely. He went just like that!' He snapped his fingers and made a little 'thwock' sound. 'There'll need to be a post mortem, but it's an open and shut case.'

'Yes,' Swift agreed. What else was there to say?

'Suspect dies before we can catch up with him,' Lister mused. 'Well, maybe it's for the best.' He was smart again in a dark navy suit, a white shirt and a sombre burgundy tie. All ready for the TV cameras. Alert, confident and all set to handle the flood of questions that would be lobbed at him.

'For him?' Swift wondered. 'Or for us?'

'Oh, come on, Ed. We've got all the forensics we need to be sure he was the killer. We've got a result. We'll need to tread

216

carefully at the press conference, of course. It's all a bit sensitive. But don't be under any illusions, the bulk of the general public will be pretty pleased to think of one less crazed child killer on the loose. We've come up smelling of roses all round,' he said, his tone almost gleeful. 'Got the vital evidence, got our man, set the parents' mind at rest and all the way through showed some respect for the suspect's age and the pathetic state he was in.'

Swift made a non-committal noise and stared over Lister's shoulder into the wasteland of the car park. It struck him that if they had moved just a little faster and charged old Ned before he went missing then he'd now be alive and safe in some secure institution. 'Sadie Bracewell's guessed how we got the DNA sample for matching,' he told Lister. 'And who got it — where and when.'

'Jesus!' Lister's face crumpled. 'Is she going to file a complaint? Sue?'

Swift shrugged. 'Who knows? She's likely to be in a very vulnerable state in the circumstances. And probably pretty volatile as well. Who wouldn't be?'

'Hell,' Lister exclaimed, his fingers tapping urgently on the desk, his mind racing.

'She hasn't said anything about the press

coverage,' Swift went on reflectively. 'Yet.'

Lister sucked in a breath through his teeth.

'I've asked forensics to give us anything they can on the collar and dog leash Ned was wearing when he was found,' Swift said. 'It could give us a lead on whoever tied him up. And I've got the impression Sadie Bracewell would be very supportive of our making a prompt investigation into what happened to her father whilst he was missing.'

Lister pushed out his lips, considering. He brightened. 'Good,' he said crisply. 'Yes. Excellent.'

'I've also got Geoff to visit all the pet shops in the town to see if they can throw any light on who might have purchased the dog gear. And I've asked him to go through each and every report of the officers involved in the search for Bracewell. With a fine toothcomb. There could be something we've overlooked that needs following up.'

Lister glanced at him with a foxy smile. 'There's a bit of the devil in you, Ed, isn't there? Under that mantle of saintliness.'

★   ★   ★

Sadie felt herself on hold. She had been able, at last, to cry, but there was a strange detachment about her grief. It was as though

218

she was somewhere deep inside herself, that all the automatic things her body did were not quite real. She just knew that she would never see her father again. She would grow old and die herself, and no matter how long that took she would never see him. Never feed or scold or comfort him.

There was just one thing to hold on to. Finding Jenny's killer and clearing her father's name. She stood still for a few moments, looking out into the grey mist filling the yard and considering possible strategies.

After that she stoked up the fire, stirring the coals into a bright, hissing blaze. Then she moved purposefully to the fridge, took out bacon, sliced black pudding and pork sausages and dropped them into the frying pan. When things began to sizzle she tossed in tomatoes and mushrooms, then cut thick slices of spongy white bread from the giant white loaves her father used to be able to demolish in a day's eating when he was in his prime. Having spooned hot fat from the pan over them she put them under the grill. The eggs she broke into the remaining fat spat and hissed, their white edges frilling instantly into a crisp gold ribbon.

'Breakfast!' she shouted up the steps. 'Now!'

The kettle began to whistle and she poured the boiling water over the tea leaves she had spooned into her grandmother's brown enamel teapot.

Almost instantly, Godfrey appeared, rumpled and sleepy, dressed in a pair of jeans. He raised his head and sniffed the complex scents of Sadie's cooking. 'Wow!'

'A full English breakfast,' she told him as he kissed the back of her neck. 'Don't go too near the pan,' she warned. 'The fat spits and it's hot.' She turned around, looked him up and down and shook her head.

'I know,' he said, 'don't tell me, I'm going to catch my death of cold — as your mother used to say.'

'If my mother could see you now,' Sadie observed, 'she'd have a lot more to scold you for than simply being about to catch your death of cold. Naked chests have rarely been seen in this house, apart from the odd heatwave that happens around every fifteen or so years.'

'Are you all right, Sadie?' Godfrey queried, concerned to hear the brittle hint of hysteria in her voice.

'I've got to keep busy,' she said, handing him a steaming loaded plate. 'Cooking's a good way. And so is changing the bed linen and making up a fire. And at some point I'll have to arrange Dad's funeral — when they release the body.' Her heart pounded, heavy and bruised. She took in a breath, made herself steady and calm.

'Sure.' He took the wedges of fried bread she offered. 'I dip 'em in — is that right?' He plunged a hunk into a glistening yolk with the conviction of a working man who has lived in the north of England all his life.

Sadie poured tea into the sturdy stone mugs her father had always preferred to fiddly little cups. She sat down. 'I'd like to go on television,' she said.

Godfrey grinned. 'Wouldn't everyone?' He chewed on a slice of black pudding and looked thoughtful. 'Are you wanting to say something about your dad? Put across his side of the story?'

'Yes. And maybe, if I do that, someone will remember something. Something connected with Jenny's death.'

'Yeah.' He nodded in agreement. 'Yeah, that could well be.'

'I thought you might use your influence,' she said. 'Now you're on the ladder to TV star status.'

Godfrey grinned and worked his eyebrows. 'Now I'm getting to know people who know people.'

'Quite.'

'This is a high-profile story,' he pointed out. 'One phone call from you to the local newspaper would get you just about everything you want.' He watched her worried face. 'What slot did you want to go for?'

'I thought regional news. At least to start with. *Look North*, perhaps.' She looked at him and the strength of her hope made her blush.

Godfrey pushed a wedge of fried bread around his plate, mopping up the juicy remains. 'Actually, I happen to have met the producer. I could have a word with him.' Suddenly he smiled, the genuine pleasure of being able to help her written clear in the lines of his face. 'Yeah, I think I could work something out for you. How about aiming for this lunchtime's programme?'

'Isn't that a bit optimistic?'

'Probably not if I make a call right now, and you're up for it. If we could get you on the lunch report, you'd probably go out again this evening as well. Catch a wider audience.'

Sadie wasn't used to sitting in her kitchen with a man who was not only helpful and sane but kind too. She wasn't used to being helped. She had been the helper for so long, she had got out of the habit of relying on anyone else. She put her hand out and touched his arm. 'Do you want toast? I've got some desperately sweet marmalade Dad used to lay on with a shovel.'

Whilst she cut more bread, Godfrey enquired as to whether she'd thought about talking with Jenny's friend Crystal again.

Sadie laid down her knife. 'I don't want to run the risk of upsetting her. I think she's got a lot to cope with at home, besides the shock of Jenny's murder. If there was something I was dying to ask her, something I thought could really move me forward in finding out what happened, I could see the point. But just having another chat . . . ' She slid bread under the grill.

'She's the only line you've got to grab onto at present,' Godfrey observed.

'Yes,' Sadie said slowly. 'You're right.'

*   *   *

Sue Sallis swung her car neatly into a slender parking space in the staff car park. It was her pride and joy, a six-year-old MGF in pristine condition purchased with careful savings and a little help from her bank. She patted its gleaming racing-green flank as she walked away. On the other public side of the park, a floridly good-looking man was heaving himself from a large sleek Mercedes. She recognized him immediately, although she had never before spoken to him in person. He paused momentarily, glancing towards the door of the station, a flicker of hesitation on his face. Sue walked forward.

'Mr Hoxton,' she greeted him courteously. 'Can I help you? I'm DC Sallis.'

He smiled at her, a man who made no secret of his admiration of a pretty woman. 'You're on Swift's team, are you?'

'Yes.'

He moved a step closer. 'Listen, this is rather embarrassing, but I think maybe you're just the one to help me. I came in last night and had a chat with one of your sergeants. Craggy chap, grey hair. Pretty grey all round, in fact.'

'Sergeant Fowler,' she suggested.

'That's the one. I'm afraid I was a bit the worse for wear. A couple of whiskies too many. I probably said a few things I shouldn't.' He gave her a plaintive and conspiratorial grin. 'Anyway, I needed to go to the boys' room and whilst I was there I think I must have taken off my signet ring and left it on the basin. I certainly can't seem to put my hand on it this morning.'

'Oh dear. Would you like me to have a look? Are you talking about the staff cloakroom outside the incident room?'

'That's the one. It has my initials on — JSH.'

Sue strode away, noting Hoxton's obvious relief at not having to enter the station. 'The boys' room,' she murmured to herself, smiling as she opened the cloakroom door and checked the absence of any boys before investigating further. The chunky ring lay on the first sink, closest to the door. Sue picked it up and went through to the reception. After a brief chat with the duty sergeant, she went back to the car park, handed Hoxton the ring, and asked him to sign the receipt book from the duty desk.

Having voiced elaborate thanks, Hoxton roared away leaving a faint trail of blue smoke to evaporate over the car park.

Sue, her curiosity burning brightly, went swiftly through to the incident room in search of Geoff. But he was already out and about, no doubt fruitlessly searching for any dog-leash-related clues which might lead to information on Ned Bracewell's possible abductor. Sue had to wait until the team meeting briefing, half an hour later before she saw him. And then she had to decide what to do about the fact that Geoff seemed to have left no record of his late-night conversation with Jeremy Hoxton. As far as her other colleagues were concerned, no such meeting had ever taken place.

It was 3.40 in the afternoon. The morning clouds had almost cleared and a frail lemon sun dodged its way through them. Sadie waited outside Middlewood School, standing back against a cluster of trees bounding the playing fields and keeping a close watch on the trickle of pupils who had begun to emerge from the rear doors of the basement of the main building.

The interview for *Look North* earlier on had left her both excited and drained. At last there was a sense of being proactive in fighting her dead father's corner. Sadly, whilst he was alive she had felt constantly on the defensive, feeling able to do little more than parry the blows being hurled at him. The BBC reporter had instantly sensed her anger and her courage. The resulting film footage had revealed a woman with a powerful conviction of wrong having been done and a lionlike determination to fight for truth and justice. Watching the image of herself on the monitor Sadie had found any self-doubts evaporating, leaving the path forward clear and inviting.

The trickle of pupils was growing into a steady flow. Her gaze flew back and forth over the girl pupils, searching for the small, lost-looking Crystal through the sea of blue-skirted, white-shirted girls, many of them already on the way to being young women. The flow became a flood, but Sadie still felt able to gain a quick glance at all the individual figures and faces. In time the flow began to dry up. It was coming up to 3.50 and there was only the occasional straggler leaving the building. The time moved on to four o'clock. Sadie moved forward and approached two gangly boys leaving together, one offering the other a cigarette from a crumpled packet.

'Excuse me,' she said, noting the sudden disappearance of the cigarettes into nearby pockets. 'Is this the only exit from the school? I'm supposed to be meeting someone and I don't know the school very well. Is there somewhere else where they could be waiting?'

The boys stared at her for a moment or two. 'Nah,' one of them said. 'This is the only place we're allowed to leave from.'

'The sixth form have a separate block,' the other boy said helpfully, probably hopeful of getting rid of her as soon as possible.

'Right, thanks.' She watched them amble away, pondering her next move. Walking back into the main road she tried to orient herself in relation to the church where Jenny's memorial service had been held and from where she had taken her walk with Crystal to the Coach and Horses.

She went back to her Land Rover and eased it into the school-leaving traffic. After a couple of wrong turns and some doubling back on herself she found the church and parked on a quiet side road nearby. Retracing the route she and Crystal had taken, she eventually arrived at the pub. A quick glance inside revealed two small groups of customers, none of them younger than forty. Chiding herself for not getting the details of Crystal's home address, Sadie crossed the road and wandered along, looking idly in the shops. At the minimarket she stopped, suddenly overwhelmed with grief, wretchedness and fatigue. She went into the shop in search of the sweet display and a chocolate bar to provide a sugar-kick of vitality.

And Crystal was there just in front of her, gazing at the lines of Bounty bars and Kit-Kats. 'Hi, there,' Sadie said.

The girl looked up, her pinched features anxious and hunted.

'It's OK,' Sadie said, smiling, summoning up from God-knows-where the energy she needed to make this encounter productive. 'I'm not stalking you.'

Crystal's eyes widened and flared. She

looked around her as though seeking some escape route.

Sadie selected a milk chocolate Aero and a Crunchie bar. 'Am I allowed to buy you something?' she asked.

'Yeah, OK.' Crystal picked two packets from the display and handed them to Sadie. 'My gran always used to tell me never to accept sweets from strangers,' she remarked, her face blank of either humour or irony.

'Quite right too,' Sadie agreed. 'My gran said the same. Shall we go and have a coffee at the Coach and Horses?'

Crystal wavered, suspicion and longing slogging it out in her haunted eyes. 'OK, then.'

Sadie thought she embodied the emptiness and despair of young people you saw sleeping in doorways. Those with no home, no families to love and quarrel with. No parents steady enough for them to kick against. She rested her arm briefly round the girl's shoulders as they left the mini-market. The bones of her shoulders were like a bunch of twigs.

In the warmth of the pub, with a foaming coffee on the table beside her and the promise of the fruit machine twinkling nearby, Crystal's edginess began to soften.

'How was school today?' Sadie asked, aiming to keep things neutral to start with.

'All right.' Crystal picked at the long strands hanging from the sleeve of her grey cardigan. Her shirt was speckled down the front with reddish brown marks. Her miniscule grey skirt rode over her stick-like thighs, which were encased in thick black tights.

'Do you have a choice of uniform at Middlewood?' Sadie asked, recalling the sea of royal blue she had seen on the girls leaving the school.

'What?' Crystal frowned and jerked her head. 'I don't go to Middlewood.'

'I thought you went to Jenny's school,' Sadie said, puzzled, and getting the feeling she'd made some sort of gaff.

'Nah! I go to The Dales school. It's a sink. There are inspectors crawling all over it, trying to kick it into shape. Some hope!' She gave a grim smile, as though she took a perverse pride in her school's inadequacies.

'Sorry. I thought you and Jenny went to school together.'

'Huh. Middlewood's far too posh for my family. Jen and I met at the fair last year and got to be mates straight away.' She eyed Sadie with thoughtful calculation. 'Have you got some change for the fruitie? Share the winnings?'

Sadie trickled coins into the girl's bird-like

hand. After the second try, a small shower of coins clattered into the tray.

'You bring me luck,' Crystal said, stacking the coins into little piles. 'Why have you come again? Did you want to know more about Jenny?' Her mood was lighter now, chummy and maybe potentially confiding.

'Yes.' Sadie wrestled with the choice she had been trying to make all day, a decision now being urgent. Taking the bull by the horns, she told Crystal the truth. About the police's suspicions regarding Jenny's murderer. About her need to prove her father's innocence. She did it gently and slowly, explaining as fully as she could without becoming tedious, or causing Crystal alarm.

Crystal listened, wide-eyed and entranced as though she were a child being told a fairy story. When Sadie eventually brought her exposition to a close, the girl dipped her head, letting out a sad sigh.

'The thing is, Crystal,' Sadie went on, 'I need all the help I can get. Any tiny bit of information that will give me something to work on.'

Crystal put her hands between her thighs, clenching the fingers with fierce determination. 'Yes,' she whispered.

'Is there anything you can tell me about Jenny, anything at all that might help me?'

'Like what?'

'I don't really know,' Sadie said. 'I'm not very good at this, am I?'

Crystal shrugged.

I should have planned all this out, Sadie thought, feeling a sudden panicky helplessness as she wondered how on earth she should go about prising information from this edgy, deprived girl. 'Did Jenny have a boyfriend?' she asked lamely, ashamed of her lack of creativeness.

Crystal picked up a coin from the piles on the table, turning it around in her fingers. 'There was someone she liked.' She looked up, gazing into some far distance. 'But I don't think he fancied her.'

'Do you know his name?'

Crystal fiddled with her cardigan sleeve and chewed on her lip. 'He goes to her school,' she said defensively.

'Have you met him?' Sadie asked gently.

Crystal shook her head. Her face had become a carving of tragedy. She dipped her head, seeming to withdraw it into her fragile shoulders. Sadie steeled herself to probe further. And failed.

'I'm really sorry about your dad,' Crystal burst out. Tears glistened in her eyes, and she gave a moist sobbing sniff. She jumped up in agitation. 'I'll just get a tissue.'

Sadie watched her make for the ladies cloakroom, a sad, lost little figure.

'Hell,' she murmured to herself, feeling as though she had been taunting an abandoned puppy.

Five minutes later she was prompted to murmur something rather stronger when it became clear that Crystal was not going to return for another dose of the medicine.

She went to the bar and slotted Crystal's winnings into the charity box for heart disease research. So much for my sleuthing skills, she thought grimly, gathering up her bag and walking out into the darkening February afternoon.

15

The next morning Constable Sue Sallis allowed Geoff Fowler a few minutes to settle at his desk before she went to tackle him.

'Hello there, love,' he said in a patronizing middle-aged male way that gave an instant boost to her courage.

'Can I have a word, Geoff?'

'Help yourself.' He gestured to the chair Hoxton had sat in two nights before.

Sue schooled herself to watch Geoff Fowler's face unflinchingly as she recounted her meeting with Hoxton the previous day. But the sergeant's impassive expression told her very little.

'Yeah, he came in. He'd had one too many and he wanted a shoulder to cry on,' Fowler said bluntly. 'Poor devil.'

Sue went on watching him. She wanted to ask to see his report. She wanted to ask if there actually *was* a report. But he was a senior officer. She was aware of her natural respect for rank and age and experience fighting it out with her natural directness and courage. And not doing very well.

'Hoxton mentioned to me that he'd said

things he shouldn't,' Sue ventured. The words were reasonable enough, and Fowler seemed unperturbed. Even so, she felt as though she had been highly provocative. 'I was curious.'

'Just the ramblings of a sad drunk,' Fowler said pleasantly. 'I'll put the report up on the screen for you, love.'

Sue stared at the bland sterile phrases and could think of nothing to say.

Swift's voice cut into her thoughts, calling out her name as he came towards the desk. The text shivered and then vanished as Fowler hit the close file button and the screen saver took over.

Sue's nerves gave a twitch. She looked up at Swift with a sense of having been caught out in some sordid conspiracy. But the chief inspector just smiled. 'Could we have a word in my office?' he asked her courteously.

He began to explain to her that the investigations the two of them had been pursuing regarding Jenny Hoxton's death would most likely be suspended. That Superintendent Lister was now confident to use the DNA evidence from Ned Bracewell to go public in identifying him as the killer.

Sue stared at him in dismay, some deep instinct telling her that this case did not hinge on poor dead Ned Bracewell and that to pin the crime on him and give up searching would be a terrible miscarriage of justice.

'What were you talking about with Sergeant Fowler?' Swift asked quietly, giving her nerves a further reason to twitch.

She put her hands on her knees, drew in a breath and then let it out.

'Come on, Sue. Loyalty to colleagues sometimes has to be balanced with the pursuit of truth.'

She lifted her head. 'I know that, sir. And I was going to speak to you. It's just finding the right way . . . ' In this atmosphere of calm truthfulness, her reservations fell away. She began to tell him of her encounter with Hoxton and what she had seen and learned. She had an excellent memory, both visual and auditory. The account was as clear and detailed as a video recording.

Swift nodded gravely as she came to the finish. She assured him that her account was fully written up and available for him to see.

'Conclusions? Theories? Future action?' he queried.

'Not fully developed yet, sir.'

'Then go and do it,' he instructed with a smile of dismissal.

★ ★ ★

236

Sitting at his desk some fifteen minutes later, having tersely summoned Geoff Fowler, Swift steeled himself for what was coming next.

Keeping his voice steady and his words rational he demanded of the sergeant why there had been no record made of the interview with Jeremy Hoxton the evening before.

Fowler was sullen now, stubborn in defence of his decisions and actions. 'He was drunk and mawkish. He just wanted to offload. And that's on record on the computer,' he finished with grim defiance. 'Sir.'

'You're saying an unrequested interview with the father of a murdered girl doesn't merit detailed reporting,' Swift rapped out. 'That it's not something to be shared instantly with the whole team? That it's not *important*.'

Fowler ran through the possibilities of disciplinary procedures Swift could proceed with. Not even the lefty milksop chief inspector could afford to turn a blind eye to this one. Agitation and consternation stabbed at him. Guilt too, for a job fudged.

'You should have taken Hoxton into one of the interview rooms and recorded the interview in accordance with our laid down procedures,' Swift said in dangerously soft tones.

Fowler saw that his senior officer's face was tight with a rage he had never displayed before. He saw that there was only one alternative available to him. 'I did tape the interview, sir. On my own recorder.'

Swift's eyes bored into him, but he said nothing. Fowler had the feeling the chief inspector couldn't trust himself. He took the tape from his jacket and laid it on Swift's desk. 'It's ready to go,' he said, activating the play button.

Swift listened to the tape with an attention which made Fowler's innards squirm. At the end he clicked the stop button and stared hard into the sergeant's face. 'We need to go and talk to the Hoxtons,' he said. 'Maybe you would like to go with me, Geoff. Or perhaps I should ask Constable Sallis?'

Fowler had never heard Swift use sarcasm. His legs felt liquid and quivery as he stood up. 'I'll go and see if Sue's free, sir.'

★　★　★

Watching the sergeant leave the room, Swift found that his heart was pounding so hard he had to press his hands against the edge of the desk to steady himself. He waited until his breathing quieted, slowly regaining control of himself, aware that the prospect of the forthcoming interview was gradually directing his mind away from his rage against Fowler.

Sue Sallis finished listening to the tape as Swift drove to the Hoxtons' house. 'Well?'

'This is potential gold dust,' she said slowly. 'It gives each one of them a motive.'

He nodded. 'But we're going to be lucky to find any of them in to enlighten us. Jeremy Hoxton should be at work. And Antonia at school.'

'And Mrs Hoxton will be playing golf or chairing a committee,' Sue speculated. 'Sorry, that is shameful stereotyping.'

'Probably true.'

In the event, it was Antonia who opened the door, barefoot and wearing cream satin pyjamas. 'Oh!' she said, looking none too pleased. She glanced up at Swift. 'Do you want to come in?' she asked in a way that silently queried whether this was really necessary.

She led the way into the drawing room, curled herself on one of the sofas and gestured the two officers to sit on the other. The central heating was luxuriously warm and Sue Sallis slipped her arms from her long navy wool coat.

'Are your parents at home?' Swift asked.

'No.' Antonia stared into his face, showing no signs of enlightening him as to where they were.

Swift let that pass. With some interviewees he would have used the tactic of letting a silence develop and waiting for what emerged when the void became too much to bear. He guessed that Antonia might well have the stamina to try to stare him out. He decided to plunge straight in.

'Jenny was your half-sister, is that right?' he asked.

Antonia stiffened, suddenly alert. 'That's always been a matter of debate.' Her eyes held his, hard and provocative.

Swift spread his hand, inviting elaboration.

'It's a family issue,' Antonia said, suddenly prim and buttoned up. 'Private.'

'This is a murder investigation,' Swift came back at her.

'I thought it was all wrapped up. You've got the killer, haven't you? The old farmer?' She wound a strand of golden hair around her finger. At the previous interview Swift had seen the hair twisting as an act of assurance, an indication of pride in the assets nature had bestowed on this fine-looking girl. This morning he had a sense there was a trace of agitation in the gesture.

'The investigation is not yet completely

'wrapped up',' he told her evenly, thinking that Lister would be roaring like an enraged lion if he could hear him now. 'We have reliable information that Jenny and you were not full sisters. So would you confirm that, please?'

Antonia put on an expression which suggested that she would be a truly formidable woman once she turned thirty. But she was not yet strong enough to resist Swift's quiet authority. 'My parents have always told me that Jenny was the result of an affair my father had with a much younger girl. My parents are against abortion and they felt the right and proper thing to do was to adopt the child as their own.'

Sue Sallis leaned forward. 'How old were you, Antonia, when they told you this?'

'I'm not sure. Quite young. Maybe four or five. It wasn't one of those TV soap revelations when you get to know during a family row when you're pretty well grown up. I've always known.' The answer rolled out as smoothly as an unfurling bolt of silk.

'Did they tell you about Jenny's background?' Swift asked.

'No. But I found out.'

'How did you do that?' Sue's voice was inviting and sympathetic.

'I worked on our cleaning lady. She's the sort of person who knows everything about everyone. She's got ears as big and flappy as an elephant's and she's been with our family since before I was born.' She gave a little smile — maybe to indicate satisfaction at her own wit and eloquence.

Swift and Sue Sallis resisted sharing a glance.

'There must have been times when you resented Jenny. Simply for being here in the family,' Swift suggested.

Antonia hesitated, as though considering the perils of answering the question. But only for a moment. 'Yes. You're right. In fact, I had begun to dislike her quite a lot. She was a total misfit here. She wasn't particularly intelligent, she was lazy, she was graceless and altogether devoid of cool.' She ran her fingers through her hair, lifting it and letting it fall again to lie around her shoulders in an arrangement of casual perfection. 'I'm sorry if I sound like a heartless, evil bitch. But that's the truth.'

Sue Sallis took in a breath. 'You told us you were with your friend Pippa in the days when Jenny was missing,' she said softly.

Antonia's eyes swivelled to the constable. 'Yes.' There was defensiveness now in her voice.

'Would Pippa and her parents vouch for you?'

'Yes!'

'On the afternoon Jenny was murdered? Between three and six?'

There was a protracted silence. A ripple of electric sensation ran around the room and its inhabitants.

Antonia murmured something, but her voice was so low neither Swift nor Sue Sallis could hear her.

'Antonia?' Sue prompted.

'No.'

'No, they can't vouch for you?' Sue prompted.

Antonia nodded.

'So who can?' Swift asked.

Antonia's throat moved as she swallowed. 'My boyfriend, the man I was with. I was with him all through lunchtime and the afternoon.' Her tongue moved over her lips. 'Oh, God! You've got to keep this to yourselves. He's married.'

Swift made a slight movement of his hand, indicating to Sue that they should keep quiet.

'You can have his name and his mobile number,' Antonia rushed on with panic-stricken eagerness, for the first time showing an emotion which was refreshingly human and understandable. 'But please, please don't let his wife know. Or my parents.'

'We'll be as discreet as we can,' Swift assured her.

The girl uncurled herself from the sofa and moved to a desk in the corner of the room where she scribbled on a pad. 'Here,' she said in a husky whisper, passing Swift the paper with a shaking hand.

He glanced at the writing on the sheet and then pocketed it. 'Did Jenny ever borrow your mobile?' he asked.

She stared at him, surprised and affronted. 'No! It's mine. Private.'

'Maybe she might have used it on the odd occasion without your knowledge?' Swift suggested.

'Well, yes, I suppose that's possible.' She looked at him suspiciously.

'Do you check through the accounts?' he asked.

'Well, yes. The account is in my mother's name but she gives the bills to me.'

'And you look through them?'

'Er, I just look at the total figure. My grandmother pays the account.'

Swift heard Sue Sallis blow out a tiny breath. 'Would you get me the recent accounts?' He gave Antonia one of his level looks and she sprang up, crossing back to the desk and pulling out one of the drawers. She wrenched out a plump A4 envelope and handed it to him.

He handed it back. 'I want you to have a look through the outgoing calls registered and see if there are any numbers listed that you don't recognize.'

'Oh! Right.'

'Take your time,' he invited her calmly.

There was a pause as Antonia rifled through the sheets. 'Yes! Here's one I don't know. And here it is again. Hell!' she exclaimed. She thrust the paper into his hand, indicating the number. He glanced down at the information and then passed the sheet to Sue Sallis, who noted down relevant details.

'And you're sure you don't know this number?' Swift prompted softly.

'Absolutely not.' Her face showed a mingle of bewilderment and indignation. Her dead sister's presumption to use her property clearly rankled, even now.

'It probably has nothing to do with Jenny,' Swift told her. 'Mobile phones have a tendency to be 'borrowed', or stolen, of course, however careful the owner.'

Antonia's face closed up. 'Is that all?' she said shakily.

He rose. 'I think so. Can you tell me where I might find your mother?' he asked.

She pressed her fingers against her forehead. 'Oh, Jesus! You're not going to tell her about . . . '

'To help us with our investigations,' Swift said coldly, correcting her self-absorbed anxieties. 'To help us further our knowledge of the circumstances of Jenny's death.'

'Yes, yes, I see,' she mumbled. 'She's at the church. Some family friends are getting married tomorrow and she's doing the flowers.'

At the door, Swift turned to confront the white-faced girl. 'Shouldn't you be at school, Antonia?'

'We've got a half day off for a staff meeting.' Her self-possession was already filtering back.

Swift nodded. 'Fair enough.' As he and Sue Sallis walked towards the car he began punching the number Antonia had given him into his mobile, keen to eliminate the calculating and cold-hearted Miss Hoxton from the list of suspects as soon as possible. His questioning was brief and to the point. 'Seems OK,' he told Sue as he clicked off the connection.

'She's got a secure alibi?'

'It'll do for now,' he said, his face grim as he slotted his key into the ignition. 'Get onto Geoff, will you, and ask him to check out that number from Antonia's phone bill.'

Sue nodded. 'Sure.' She glanced across at him.

'It'll probably be something and nothing. But I just can't believe a fifteen-year-old kid wouldn't have at least one friend in the world. Maybe a cosy bolthole to run to when the emotional temperature at home dropped below zero.'

★ ★ ★

Some hours earlier, in the later part of the night when dreams are deep and the dawn still seems an eternity away, Sadie had woken sweating and terrified. The darkness pressed in on her — she feared that when she opened her eyes she would discover that her sight had vanished, that she had been struck blind. Her throat dried, sweat rolled from her, drenching her hairline and trickling in sticky rivulets between her breasts. The pounding of her heart was so wild and uncontrolled she felt it would split open and burst into fragments. Her breaths were tiny stabs of pain.

Her eyes still tight shut, she groped in the blackness and found the lamp switch. Golden light flared behind her locked eyelids. She sat bolt upright, shivers of dread rippling over her skin.

Beside her, Godfrey stirred and then heaved himself up. He pulled her against him. 'Hey, calm down. It's OK. It's all OK.'

'No,' she muttered. 'No!'

'Deep breaths,' he declared. 'Right from the stomach. Come on . . . '

When she was quiet he went down to the kitchen and made tea. He brought up two mugs and handed her one. 'You know what, Sadie,' he said, 'I'm worried about you. You've been having a seriously bad time.'

She nodded. 'You could say that.'

'I know a panic attack when I see one.'

'You've probably acted dozens of them,' she said with a wry smile.

He ignored the brave attempt at humour. 'And I know it's none of my business, but maybe it's not a good idea to be doing this one-woman act trying to clear your dad's name when you're still in shock and mourning for him. You were shattered after the TV interview and going to talk to Crystal again. You need to cool things a bit. Take care of yourself for a change.'

She stared into her tea. 'Supposing, just supposing, Dad did it,' she said in a low, flat voice. 'Killed little Jenny.'

He took a moment to react, then stared at

her in astonishment. 'Well, go on, don't stop there.'

She frowned into her tea. 'There's a story to tell — from way back. When I was a kid my parents always impressed it on me and my brother that we weren't to have anything to do with our neighbour, Bernard Gough. He was a dairy farmer and his fields bordered on our fields on the north and east sides. There'd been a long-running feud between Dad and Bernard because of some boundary dispute in one of the northern fields. They hated each other's guts. Then one day things blew up because Gough shot one of Dad's dogs which had got in with his cows. He claimed it had upset one of the calving heifers, which Dad said was absolute rubbish. Dad was in such a mood. For days we hardly dared speak to him. And then Bernard Gough was found dead — drowned in the cattle trough. The word went around that he'd had too many pints at the pub and had fallen in on the way home.' She stopped, trying to get on a grip on those days from the past. 'I remember thinking the story made perfect sense, and that Bernard Gough probably deserved to be dead — he was my dad's enemy. A few days later the police came to the house. They took Dad to the police station. Mum was in a real state. The atmosphere in the house was awful.

I knew something bad was going on, but I didn't know what it was. Dad was away for a couple of days. When he came home he simply carried on as though nothing had happened.'

'Did he ever tell you why the police had taken him away?'

'He never said a thing. But I got a load of teasing at school. One or two of the kids had obviously picked something up from their parents. They made up a song about Bernard. 'Poor old Bernard Gough, Got well pissed and fell in the trough. Did he fall or was he pushed?' You know the sort of thing.'

'I can hear it all now,' Godfrey commented. 'And what did you make of the message they were trying to get across?' he asked with tender concern.

'I never believed it for one moment. I had that sure childish belief in the goodness of my parents. I rewarded the teasers' efforts with some pretty hard thumps. I was a big girl and they were weedy boys. They soon backed off.'

'And now?' he prompted softly.

'It's like there's a worm of doubt has begun to eat away at me, making me wonder if all my protests about Dad's innocence have been some kind of defence against asking myself whether it's possible that what the police think is true. I've tried to push it away, but let's face it, if the police heard what I've just told you now, they'd be jumping for joy, thinking their case was rock solid. Their prime suspect not only had his DNA all over the dead girl's clothes, he had a possible violent history, had maybe literally got away with murder. And then if I were to tell them he'd had blood-covered gravel in his pocket when he came back from the quarry that day. And a strand of the girl's hair, like some kind of grim trophy . . . '

A violent tremor shook her body from head to toe. Godfrey held her against him, stroking the back of her neck. 'Sadie, you need to give yourself a break. You've got to stop running so hard.'

She shook her head. 'No! I've got to go on. For his sake. Deep, deep down I can't believe Dad killed that poor girl.'

'Fine. But you're in no fit state to play Sherlock Holmes.'

She sighed. 'I can't argue with that. I don't seem to be in a fit state to do very much at all at the moment.'

'This Chief Inspector Swift guy,' Godfrey said. 'From what you've told me he's not convinced that your dad's their man.'

That's right. So?'

'I think you should go and talk to him.'

'I have done.'

'I mean talk to him about what you've found out.'

'Which is just about nothing,' she said, disgusted at what she saw as her wretched failure.

'That's not true. You've found the only person who's admitted to being a fully paid-up pal of Jenny's. Someone who thought Jenny had her eye on a possible boyfriend. Someone who might just hold some keys to what happened.'

'Mmm, but it's a long shot, isn't it? And if the chief inspector follows up what I tell him, poor Crystal won't be too happy. Her family hate the police.' She closed her eyes and rubbed her hand over her forehead. 'I'd just be stirring up more trouble for her.'

Godfrey knew when to back off. 'Fair enough. So why don't you just chill out for a while? No need to rush into anything right this minute.'

★ ★ ★

Having dented the smooth arrogance of ice maiden Antonia, Swift and Susan Sallis were now standing in the chill of a Victorian town church, facing up to Anita Hoxton and attempting to find a chink in her impeccable defences. Immaculate in grey trousers and a

252

cream cowl-neck sweater, surrounded by buckets of longiflorum lilies and willow branches, she listened politely to their probings and answered in clean, considered phrases.

'It's true that Jenny was adopted,' she told them. 'But I don't think that has any bearing on the current tragedy. And if my husband gave such an impression when he came into the station last night, then I'm afraid that was more a result of drunken ruminations than anything of substance.'

'Your daughter indicated that Jenny was a misfit in the family, an outsider,' Sue Sallis pointed out, struck afresh at this mother's coolly detached attitude to her dead daughter.

'That too is true,' Anita responded. 'Sadly.'

'You must sometimes have felt resentment for her,' Sue continued, feeling like a swimmer struggling against an opposing current.

'Many times, I'm sorry to say. She was a fretful baby, a dissatisfied child, and a sullen, unforthcoming teenager.' She pulled a lily from the bucket and considered its folded petals with a faint frown.

'Did it ever trouble you that she might not have been your husband's child?' Swift asked.

'No.' The answer was offered with perfect calm.

'You never thought of requesting DNA testing to find out?' Sue suggested.

Anita Hoxton let out a sigh of exasperation. 'What purpose would that have served? Jeremy and I agreed to take on the child of the young girl he had been . . . involved with. We made a commitment to Jenny, to give her a home and to care for her and protect her. The issue of paternity was immaterial as far as I was concerned.'

Swift watched her with hawk-like concentration. It was a matter of honour, he thought, half admiring this gracious but affectionless woman who could well have belonged to some lost world of courtly chivalry. 'And did you care for her?' he asked quietly.

'I take it you're asking if I loved her.' Anita Hoxton gave further consideration to the furled bud of the lily in her hand. 'That's a hard question. I'm not a loving, warm, demonstrative kind of person, as I'm sure you've gathered. However, I did care for Jenny in the sense of trying to guide her into adulthood with an appreciation of the responsibility we all have to our fellow beings. And I tried to gently encourage the development of the higher human qualities: honesty, moral courage, service to those less fortunate than ourselves. Qualities that bring self-fulfilment.' She clipped the end of the lily's stem with shiny scissors then dropped it back in the bucket. 'But I have to say that I felt saddened at her lack of response, her aimlessness and her predisposition to drift.'

Swift and Sallis considered their next line of approach. Unspoken maxims hung in the air between them. Thoughts of bad blood and how it will out. Thoughts of sows' ears and silk purses. Thoughts of how daughters grew up to be like their mothers.

'I'm presuming,' said Anita, 'that you are here asking these questions because you are considering the possibility that Jeremy or myself — or both — were involved in Jenny's killing.' She froze them both with the steadiness of her gaze. 'Because if that is not the case, then you have no business to be here, questioning me in this way.'

'No, indeed,' Swift agreed. 'You're quite right, Mrs Hoxton. Can you provide an alibi for the time Jenny was killed?'

Anita gave him a long, steady look, the look of a head-teacher disappointed in the performance of a previously well-regarded student. 'On the day Jenny was killed, Jeremy and I lunched with friends at a small hotel on the shore of Lake Windermere. We didn't leave until around four o'clock. Jeremy was over the limit for driving so we took a walk beside the lake. We arrived back at our hotel in Bowness around 6.30. I think the staff at both hotels would be able to provide you with satisfactory corroboration.'

Swift nodded. 'Thank you, Mrs Hoxton,' he said gravely.

Anita took up another lily and clipped its stem. 'Good day, Inspector,' she said, inclining her head. 'Constable.'

Dismissed, Swift and Sallis walked in silence down the knave to the west door.

Outside, Sue gave vent to her feelings. 'When I have kids, I'm going to be really hands-on. I'm going to be there for them, caring and keeping them safe and loving them to bits.'

Swift smiled. 'They probably won't thank you for it.'

In the car Swift checked the messages on his mobile phone. There was quite a harvest. A man had arrived at the station with information on Ned Bracewell's abductor. The mother of Imogen Barclay had called to ask to speak to Swift urgently. And Geoff Fowler thought that he might have come up with something interesting from the mystery number on Antonia's mobile account.

Even Lister would have to concede that all of these needed to be followed up. He set the phone to replay and handed it to Sue Sallis.

Things are moving, he thought, firing the engine. At long last.

16

The man waiting at the station to talk to Swift was sitting in the reception area, his calm, resigned manner reminiscent of an injured patient waiting to see a doctor in the accident and emergency department of a hospital.

His name was Arnold Lightowler. He was a retired post-office worker who lived locally and he believed that his son, Lewis, was the abductor of Ned Bracewell.

Swift guessed his age at around sixty-five and had the strong impression that this was a man of strong moral integrity who was finding himself under considerable strain as he embarked on his grim story.

'He's my only child,' Arnold said sadly. 'He never had an easy time. My wife became ill with breast cancer shortly after he was born and she died a year later so I brought Lewis up on my own. My mother was good with him and helped, but she died eight years ago when the boy was only fourteen. He'd always been a bit odd, even as a little boy, standoffish and not very sociable, but when I look back I think it was when he lost his gran that Lewis's problems really began to show. He became very withdrawn and depressed. There were difficulties at school. And then he got involved with psychiatrists and counsellors and social workers.' Here he stopped, blowing out a long breath as though he had been running. 'Autistic spectrum disorder, they called it. I've never really known what that meant. It's just a label, isn't it? Like 'fragile' on the wrapping of a parcel. You don't know what's in there, but you know to be gentle with it.' He looked at Swift with bleak appeal.

After that Swift had to gently coax out the rest of the story. It came in halting phrases interjected with heavy sighs and the occasional sign of being in danger of petering out completely. It was a story whose bare bones Swift had become familiar with during his police career. Lewis had been in and out of psychiatric care, sometimes voluntarily, sometimes under the requirements of the Mental Health regulations.

'The really tragic thing is, he does so well when he's in care,' Lightowler said. 'And of course when he's 'stable', as they call it, they find him a flat or a hostel. And then gradually he goes downhill, and the whole cycle starts again. You see, I don't think he takes his drugs regularly when he's on his own, not even with his care-worker visiting regularly.'

Swift sensed that this story could well go on for a very long time. It was not unusual for the relatives of disturbed young people to convince themselves their offspring was the perpetrator of a high-profile crime. Not unusual for them to long to tell their sad story to a sympathetic listener. As gently as he could, he tried to direct Arnold Lightowler to the essential points pertaining to Ned Bracewell's abduction. 'Mr Lightowler, have you any evidence that your son was involved with Ned Bracewell in the past week?'

Lightowler dug in his pocket and brought out a dog leash. As far as Swift could tell it looked identical to the one which had been used to tether Ned Bracewell.

'It was seeing the news last night that made me think,' Lightowler explained. 'You see, some time ago I helped Lewis get a dog from one of the animal rescue centres. It was a nice dog, a collie-labrador cross. Lewis was as pleased as a box of monkeys with it. He took the coins he'd saved in jam jars to the pet shop and bought it some smart matching collars and leads and rubber bones and suchlike.' His voice died away and he shook his head in sorrowful memory. 'But the dog never took to him. I think it sensed that he was different, odd. It kept running away and coming back to me.' He looked across to

259

Swift. 'It arrived on my doorstep a couple of days ago, early that morning the old man was found.'

'Ah.' Swift nodded. 'And where is Lewis now?'

'At his bedsit. I've been to see him a couple of times. He seemed quite calm, but he wouldn't tell me nothing about what he'd been doing. Just said he'd been away and living rough for a bit.'

'Does Lewis have a history of going off on his own?'

'Oh, aye. He once went missing for two weeks. He can be quite self-sufficient when he puts his mind to it.'

'Where does he go?'

'Up on the moors usually. There are one or two abandoned shepherds' crofts up there where he can shelter. He seems to like to get away into the hills from time to time. Just be alone.'

'And how long was he away for this last time?'

'Eight days.'

'You didn't think to alert Social Services or us?'

Lightowler shifted in his chair, unease puckering his features. 'Oh, I did a lot of thinking. But he's been doing really well recently. He's been in the bedsit for five months, and there've been hardly any problems. I didn't want to cause trouble for him,' he finished simply.

Fair enough, Swift thought.

He leaned forward and spoke more slowly. 'And you didn't connect Lewis's disappearance with that of Ned Bracewell? It was in all the newspapers and the TV. In connection with a murder?'

A nerve buzzed in Arnold Lightowler's cheek. 'No,' he answered with firm simplicity. 'No, I didn't.'

'Does Lewis have a history of violence?' Swift asked evenly.

Lightowler's body now jerked in shock. Ashen-faced, he looked at Swift, his eyes wide and staring in horror. 'No, no. He's a gentle boy. He can get frustrated and he's got a temper on him . . . ' He stopped, his mouth working for a moment but producing no sound.

'Tying an old man to a lamppost with a dog lead could be described as violent,' Swift pointed out. 'Also hanging an accusing label around his neck. You did know about that, didn't you, Mr Lightowler?'

Lightowler flinched and nodded. 'But that wasn't real violence, not like thumping and kicking. Or knifing.'

Swift sat back. 'No.'

Lightowler crumpled. 'You're not thinking he could have killed that little lass up at the quarry? Oh no, not Lewis. No.' Distress had shaken him to the roots, like an old tree pierced with lightning.

'Lewis was obviously aware of the murder case, otherwise he wouldn't have written the label?' Swift suggested with soft challenge.

'Oh, aye. He likes to read the papers. Reads some articles over and over again. But that doesn't mean . . . '

Swift took up the calendar on his desk and pointed to the date on which Jenny Hoxton had died. 'Where was Lewis on that day?'

Lightowler shook his head in despair. 'I don't know,' he whispered. 'I truly don't know. That was the day he went missing.' He stared at Swift with pleading eyes. 'What are you going to do?'

'I shall need to talk to Lewis. Just talk to him to see if he can help us with our enquiries.'

'Oh dear. He soon gets upset. Frightened.' The pleading was still there. *Do you really have to do this?* his eyes were begging.

'I'll bear that in mind,' Swift said reassuringly.

'When will you be going?'

'Now.' Swift rose to his feet and reached for his keys.

★ ★ ★

Mrs Barclay was waiting at the door as Sue Sallis brought her car to a halt at the gate. 'Are you by yourself?' she asked, looking behind Sue as though a whole battalion might be arriving.

Sue's confirming nod brought a sigh of relief from the overwrought mother. 'Oh, thank goodness. It's always easier to talk to a woman. Well, that's my view.' She led the way into the sitting room. 'Do sit down,' she invited, her manners not forgotten even at this time of intense maternal stress. 'Can I get you some tea? Coffee?'

Sue shook her head. 'Mrs Barclay, what is it you wanted to tell us?'

'We've had such a time. Imogen cut her wrists last night,' Mrs Barclay said baldly. 'I still can't believe it. What an ordeal.'

'How is she?'

'She's shaken and shocked, but she's going to be all right. And I thank God for that.' Tears sprang up in Mrs Barclay's eyes. 'They told me at the hospital that there was never any real danger, but I still say it's a mercy I caught things in time. I've been telling my husband for days now that I was worried something was going to happen, but he said just to let things settle down, that she'd come round back to her normal self.' She perched on the edge of a chair and began to twist her fingers together in the compulsive way Sue had seen at the previous interview.

'Is Imogen here?' Sue asked gently, wanting to clarify this important issue at the outset, mindful that Mrs Barclay seemed pent up with a good deal of information. 'Here at home?'

Mrs Barclay blinked. 'Oh yes, they let me bring her home from the hospital at lunchtime.'

'Could you tell me what happened?'

'Well, I was getting really worried yesterday. She still wasn't eating, and she'd been crying. Not sad sort of crying, more . . . frustrated, if you know what I mean. I kept asking her if there was something I could help with, if she'd only talk to me, because that's what mothers are for. But I couldn't get a thing out of her, she just turned her face away. Anyway, when I took her up a mug of cocoa at bedtime I got the feeling she'd changed her mind and wanted to tell me something. I tried to get her to open up. But the more I asked, the more she went into herself. They're like that, aren't they, at this age? So secretive. Although I never was myself. I used to tell my mum everything.' She bit down on her lip.

'And then?' Sue prompted.

'I went downstairs and talked to my husband, but he said not to worry. Let her have a good night's sleep. Well, I can tell you, *I* didn't have a wink myself. It was about 5.30 when I heard her going along to the bathroom. I thought it was a bit strange, because she's got an en-suite of her own and she normally uses that. Anyway, I lay there listening for the sound of the loo, or water running. But it was just so quiet. Dead quiet. After a bit I just couldn't stand it any more. She'd locked the door, so I had to kick it in. And she was sitting there on the bath side, holding up her hands and staring at her wrists. She'd cut herself with one of my husband's old razor blades. There was so much blood — I just went to jelly.' Her face crumpled and she dabbed at her eyes and nose. 'And then my husband came in and he rang for the ambulance. And I sat there next to Imo with my fingers pressed over the bleeding to try and stop it.'

'I'm so sorry,' Sue said.

'Nothing this bad has ever happened to me,' Mrs Barclay said. 'I never realized before how lucky I'd been never to have had a real tragedy.'

'So,' Sue said after a respectful pause, 'you

still have no idea what has been troubling Imogen?'

'Not really. Although I think it could have something to do with her boyfriend, Nick. She's been refusing to take his calls. He's phoned twice on the landline and he told me that he's left messages on her mobile. But she absolutely refuses to speak to him. They must have had some kind of a fall-out. It's very odd, though — he seemed so sweet and concerned when he came round a few days ago. And on the phone as well.' Her fingers twined together in ever-growing agitation. 'I think she might talk to you, though.' She gazed in appeal at Sue. 'She told me there was something she needed to talk about, but she couldn't tell anyone but the police.'

Sue felt a fizzing buzz of speculation. 'I see. Do you think I could speak to her now?'

Mrs Barclay frowned, her instinct to protect her child making her anxious about any new stress in the offing. 'Well, I suppose just a few minutes won't do any harm. I told her someone was coming to see her, and she seemed relieved. In fact, she's very much calmer altogether than she has been for days. I did wonder if they'd given her some kind of tranquilizer at the hospital, but do you know,' she went on with frowning consideration, 'I've begun to think that cutting herself has somehow brought things to a head, like lancing an abscess.'

Sue found Imogen propped up in bed on a mountain of frilled pillows, her face ghostly pale, her bandaged arms stretched out in front of her. She smiled hesitantly as Sue walked into the room, and then, without warning, began to cry. 'Oh!' she exclaimed after the first rush of tears subsided. 'I feel such a fool. And now I'm bawling like a little kid.'

Sue sat beside the bed and pulled a bunch of tissues from the box thoughtfully placed on the white embroidered counterpane. 'Here,' she said. 'I'm not surprised you're bawling. You must be in shock, and a lot of pain.'

'Yeah, and all of my own doing,' Imogen commented bitterly. 'I just can't believe how stupid I've been.'

Looking into the girl's face, even though it was tight with strain, Sue felt that she was seeing a different girl altogether from the withdrawn, hunted creature she and Swift had interviewed only two days before. She was not sure about Mrs Barclay's lancing the boil theory, but it certainly seemed that in some way Imogen's clumsy, abortive attempts at harming herself — and then being rescued — had precipitated some watershed of decision-making. 'Your mother said there was something you wanted to speak about,' she prompted with gentle invitation.

Imogen closed her eyes and sighed. 'Yes. Oh God! I don't know if I can do it.' She winced as she raised her arm in order to run trembling fingers over her brows.

Sue waited. The tension in the air was heavy. 'Is this a problem about betraying someone's trust?' she asked, hoping that vague phrase might cover a number of possibilities, one of which would be appropriate to encourage Imogen to proceed further.

'Yes. That's just it. Exactly. Betrayal.'

'Imogen,' Sue prompted, 'is this connected with Jenny Hoxton's murder?'

'Yes.'

'Then it's serious. And we need to know.'

A beating pause. 'I think I know who killed her. And why.' She dipped her head, avoiding Sue's gaze. There was a long, long silence.

'Would it help to write it down?' Sue asked. Glancing at Imogen's bandaged hands, she instantly cursed herself for such a stupid suggestion.

'Not really. The person I'm talking about is my boyfriend, Nick. Nick Ashton,' Imogen said in a rush. She glanced up at Sue with darkened eyes, as though expecting the constable to register surprise and shock.

Sue nodded calmly, although her pulse had

quickened. 'You think Nick killed Jenny?'

'Yes. She knew something about him. Something really awful.' Imogen's voice had fallen to a whisper.

'Take your time,' Sue reassured her.

'It's something no one knows,' Imogen said. 'Just me. And Nick, of course.' She paused. 'And Jenny.'

'I want you to tell me,' Sue said, her voice low and urgent.

'It happened a few months ago. The day before bonfire night,' Imogen said. 'It was dropping dark and there was already the smell of smoke in the air.' She looked down at her bandaged wrists and hands, tentatively trailing the fingertips of one hand over the dressing covering the other palm. 'I was walking home from school with Nick. It had started to rain so we decided to take a short cut across the bridge that crosses the main Bradford road. The cars go really fast there.' Again she paused. 'Oh, God, this is so hard.'

Sue frowned, her memory instantly throwing up a recent horrific road accident in that area. Superintendent Lister had unofficially code-named the incident Mischief Night. In his day, apparently, the doing of mischievous deeds on the evening before Guy Fawkes night had been something of a ritual. 'Are you talking about the place where a young driver was killed?' she demanded. 'A heavy object was thrown down from the bridge. There was a pile-up?'

Imogen swallowed and croaked out a faint, 'Yes.'

Connections began fitting into place in Sue's mind. She recalled that no witnesses had come forward to describe the shadowy figures on the bridge, one of whom must have tossed down the brick that shattered a windscreen and brought about traffic mayhem. Nor had there been any useful forensic evidence. 'Imogen, are you saying that Nick threw that object?'

'I think so,' she confirmed, adding hurriedly, 'but he didn't really mean to. He was just fooling around. And then suddenly there was the crack of glass shattering. The cars all started braking, skidding and hitting one another. The noise was terrible.' Her voice dwindled away. 'It was horrible. Grotesque. I've been thinking about it ever since it happened. I couldn't get it out of my head.' She pressed two fingers against her closed eye sockets.

'What sort of object was it? That Nick dropped?'

'It was a brick. Just an ordinary red building brick. There's a new estate going up

270

just near the bridge. There's loads of building stuff around.'

Sue was scribbling furiously on her pad, aiming to record every detail. She looked up, coming eye to eye with her informant. 'So you're saying that Nick Ashton was the person behind that major accident?' She looked hard at the stricken girl. 'Imogen, did you see Nick Ashton throw a brick down onto the dual carriageway?'

'I didn't actually see him throw it. I think he . . . kind of let go by mistake. It was all a ghastly accident.'

'Indeed it was,' Sue said grimly, recalling the event in ever greater detail as time passed. Her body was flooding with adrenalin now, fuelled with the prospect of nailing the callous perpetrator of that terrible accident and its subsequent personal tragedy — whether intentional or not. But it looked as though there was going to be more — the uncovering of the truth behind Jenny Hoxton's murder, the identifying of the real killer. Killing two birds with one stone didn't go anywhere near describing the coup that might be made.

Sue phrased her words carefully. 'You told me that you thought Jenny also knew about the cause of the accident?'

'Yes,' said Imogen, her voice just a breath.

'I'd like you to explain that. In your own words.'

'Jenny was there. On the bridge.'

Sue's heart bucked as she scribbled the words down. This was pure gold. She couldn't wait to tell Swift. 'Was Jenny walking along with you and Nick?'

Imogen let out a little snort of disbelief. 'No way. We thought we were alone. We didn't realize she was there until I dashed away from Nick to the other side of the bridge to see what was happening there. She was pressed back against the wall. I could tell she was scared, trying to make herself invisible.' Her handsome features were twisted with dislike and fury. 'I told you before,' she protested to Sue, 'she had a habit of tagging along.'

'Was she in love with Nick?' Sue asked quietly.

'She fancied him something rotten,' Imogen said. 'Like just about every girl who laid eyes on him.'

Sue's sympathy for the self-centred, self-harmed girl was steadily dwindling. 'So Nick decided not to tell anyone about his part in an accident which took the life of a young woman? And you decided to collude with him?'

'We didn't just decide, just like that. We

272

talked about it,' Imogen said desperately. 'You know . . . '

'The pros and cons,' suggested Sue. The moral rights and wrongs, she thought grimly, hastily checking herself from saying it out loud and ruining her rapport with this vital witness.

'Nick's going to study law; he's got a wonderful career ahead of him,' Imogen protested. 'If he'd gone to the police he could have been done for manslaughter, or maybe . . . worse. We looked up lots of law stuff on the internet. Nick could have gone to prison, for a long time.'

A shorter time if he'd pleaded guilty than he's likely to get now, Sue thought. And that's just taking into account the girl in the traffic accident.

She leaned forward and touched Imogen's upper arm very gently. 'It must have been very hard for you to tell me all this,' she said. 'But it was the right thing to do. Believe me.'

Imogen did not look convinced.

'How did Nick react when he realized Jenny was on the bridge when the accident happened?' Sue asked.

'He went to talk to her. He said it was a terrible thing that had happened.'

Just like that! Sue thought. Surely no one implicated in such a serious accident could have been so cool and self-possessed. But, then, maybe Imogen was simply being truthful to what she remembered, however damning her account sounded. Maybe she was still in love with Nick Ashton. 'And then what?'

'Jenny said, yes, it was terrible. She said she wondered how it could have happened, as though she'd seen nothing.'

'Did you believe her?'

'We weren't sure. I thought she might be frightened to say what she'd really seen.'

'Did Nick threaten her in any way?'

'No. He was very gentle, very charming. He hardly ever loses his cool.'

'What happened after that?'

'Jenny kept repeating she hadn't seen anything. And then she went home. Well — none of us wanted to hang around.' She bowed her head. 'God, if only that awful day had never happened.' She eyed Sue speculatively. 'Will I get put on a charge for what I did?'

'Possibly,' Sue said carefully.

'I don't care,' said Imogen with sudden defiance. 'I'll pay. I'll pay for being a spineless coward. I'll pay whatever it costs, even going to prison. Anything's better than keeping it all inside, bottled up. Feeling terrible.'

'Did Jenny make contact with either you or

Nick after the crash?' asked Sue, wanting to move on.

'She kept away from us at first. For weeks. Nick began to think he was in the clear. She had a crush on him, you see. A really big thumping crush. She'd have done anything for him, we both knew that. And then, out of the blue, she wrote Nick a letter. Asking if he'd let her have some money.'

Sue came on full alert. 'How much?'

'Ten pounds. She said her parents had stopped her pocket money. But it was obvious it was some kind of blackmail. Nick couldn't believe it at first. He tried to persuade himself she was just a needy, cranky kind of girl. Which she was.'

'He gave her the money?'

'Yes. She asked him to put it in her sports bag in the cloak-room. Inside her running shoes. Ugh.'

'Wouldn't it have been odd for him to be seen in the girls' cloakroom?'

'Yes. Except he always went there late on in the afternoon when everyone had gone and the cleaners had finished. And head boys can get away with taking quite a lot of licence,' she pointed out.

'Mmm.' Sue raced to complete her scribblings, her brain now fizzing with conjectures, striving to make the connections which would fit all the pieces of information into a complete picture. 'You said 'always'. How many times were these 'deliveries' made?'

'It started off with the occasional one-off request. But by the time . . . well, later on it was every week.'

'And the amounts?'

'They went up slightly. But she didn't go mad; she was clever, I suppose. She used to leave little notes for him in her shoes, saying, 'Thank you.' I began to think she was seriously scary,' Imogen remarked reflectively.

'Was Nick worried?'

'I'll say. He was getting really rattled. He wondered what she was going to do next. She'd been such a little nonentity. She'd had no clout, no friends, no cool. And now suddenly she had the head boy of the school, the idol of all the most groovy girls, dancing like a puppet when she pulled the strings.'

'Did Nick ever mention the idea of killing Jenny?'

She winced. 'No! He's very together, very reasonable. But someone like Jenny could really get under your skin.'

Sue made a swift mental review of the previous interview with Imogen. 'You told us last time that Jenny wasn't down for the Dales trip, that she wasn't there. But her body was found only a few miles away. She must have been there.'

The girl's lips moved. A faint confirming sound emerged.

'She gatecrashed the trip, didn't she?'

'Yes — she just wouldn't leave him alone. It was horrible. He was getting really uptight.'

'And what about you, how did you feel?'

'I just knew . . . something awful was going to happen.'

Suddenly her body sagged as though she were exhausted. She threw herself back on her pillows. 'Oh God! I've branded him a murderer.' She closed her eyes, blotting the world out.

'Listen, Imogen. You've been battling with a massive conflict,' Sue told her. 'And now you've chosen the only path.' Her easy ability to moralize surprised her.

Imogen let out a protracted and extravagant sigh. 'Yeah. So at least when this is all over I'll be able to get on with my life.' She sank back against the pillows and closed her eyes.

Sue left Imogen to contemplate her future and went down the stairs, resisting the urge to run, to get to the privacy of her car as fast as she could and make contact with Swift. Mrs Barclay, predictably, was waiting for her.

How to deal with this as quickly and kindly

as possible, Sue thought, eyeing the mother's ravaged face.

'I heard,' Mrs Barclay said. 'I was listening in. I'm sorry.' She was holding herself very still, struggling to deal with all the implications of her new knowledge. 'What's going to happen now?' She stared at Sue with a mingle of fear and hope.

'We shall need to take a full statement from Imogen.' She was about to add 'as soon as she's well enough' and then thought better of it. It would be bad for the furthering of the investigation if Mrs Barclay were to seek medical support to suggest the girl was too traumatized to make any formal declarations. 'It will go in her favour that she has voluntarily admitted to her part in the cover-up of the circumstances of the road crash.'

'And that she's been able to name Jenny's murderer?' Mrs Barclay added, her eyes shining with horror and a gleam of anticipation.

'That is just supposition, Mrs Barclay. As yet.' Sue put on a reassuring smile. 'I think you just need to concentrate on helping Imogen to return to full strength.'

'Yes, yes, of course.' Mrs Barclay obviously wanted to ask much much more, but mercifully Imogen called down to her and

Sue was able to make her exit with gravely smiling dignity.

Sue drove her car around the corner into the next road then re-parked and punched out Swift's number on her mobile.

Her pulses pounded; ambition and fantasy took wing. She knew the procedure of arrest and she was word perfect on the recital of the caution. And suddenly she wanted it really badly — the bringing to book of the killer of the flawed and despised Jenny Hoxton.

★   ★   ★

On meeting Lewis Lightowler, Swift was immediately impressed by the young man's ready understanding of his questions and his solemn determination to answer them with as much detail as he could. Lewis had the darting brittle glances typical of those who are emotionally disturbed and not fully connected with reality, but his recall of events and his ability to recount them appeared flawless.

Swift arrived to find Lewis drinking coffee and devouring doughnuts in the bedsit that was his home. He sat himself down opposite the thin and bony young man, filing the details of his appearance into his detective's memory. The face was drawn and skull-like, the remnants of boyish good looks now rapidly fading, but the dark eyes were alive and shrewd, their whites clear and shiny.

Lewis did not appear in any way troubled by Swift's arrival and his questions. He was neither friendly nor defensive. He showed no emotion as Swift proceeded through his list of questions. He listened carefully to each question and then, if he was able, supplied a clipped and succinct answer. If he did not have the information, he simply said, 'I don't know.'

Swift was inclined to believe that he was answering with impeccable honesty.

'So, Lewis,' he concluded, when the bare bones of the questioning were completed, 'you're saying that you left your flat on February 13th with the intention of walking up to the shepherd's croft towards the top of Black Moor? Two days later an old man turned up at the croft in the evening — '

'It was the old farmer, Mr Ned Bracewell,' Lewis interrupted. 'He arrived at ten minutes past nine.'

'But you didn't know he was Mr Bracewell until later, when you saw his picture in the newspapers?'

'No. That's correct.'

'Mr Bracewell came into the croft. He was hungry and so you gave him food?'

Lewis listened, his attention intense, as though constantly waiting for Swift to make an error.

'Yes. I think he liked me.'

'After two days you ran out of food. Ned Bracewell had some cash and he gave it to you to go down into town and get supplies. When you came back you found him wandering about on the moor near to the croft. You took him back inside.'

'He was lost,' Lewis explained. 'He was very cold and he was crying. I put more wood on the fire to get him warm again.'

'Right. And when you left on subsequent occasions you locked the door on the outside?' Swift stopped and levelled a glance at the raptly attentive young man who nodded his head vigorously, urging Swift to continue.

'You say that Mr Bracewell slept a lot of the time and spoke very little, apart from asking for food and to know where his mother was and when she was coming to fetch him.' He looked up again. There were more active nods. 'You say that at no time did you use violence on Mr Bracewell.'

'I never hurt him,' Lewis confirmed in his flat mechanical voice. 'He was an old, old man.'

'You and Mr Bracewell were in the croft

together for six days — '

'Five days, five hours and twenty-seven minutes,' Lewis corrected him.

'Ah, yes.' Swift flipped over the sheets of his notepad, making a rapid review. Every new item of detail Lewis offered checked out with his previous account.

Lewis jerked his head up and down impatiently. 'Go on.'

'On the fourth day you went down into the town for more food. You saw newspapers with Mr Bracewell's face on them and a story about a girl who had been murdered.'

'Murder is an evil act,' Lewis stated. 'The papers said the old man had killed a girl at the Arkwright quarry. Killing is wicked and evil. There is nothing more sinful than killing.'

Swift found this mechanical recital strangely chilling. He returned to his notes. 'You stayed in the town, buying food and thinking what you must do. Then you went back to the croft. You stayed there with Mr Bracewell until the food ran out again. On the morning of February 21st you left the croft whilst it was still dark, taking Mr Bracewell with you.'

'He didn't want to go,' Lewis interjected. 'It was dark. He wanted to stay asleep. But I knew what I had to do. I pulled him to his feet and I put the dog lead on him so that he would walk with me. I tugged at it to make him come along.'

'You walked back into the town and you tied Mr Bracewell to a lamppost.'

'Yes. I knew the police would find him. They look for people who stay out on the streets.'

Swift did not argue with that. 'You hung a notice around his neck.'

'Yes. I wanted the police to know that he had done wrong.'

Swift gave an inaudible sigh. 'On the day you set off to the croft, you didn't leave your flat — '

'Bedsit,' Lewis corrected him.

'You didn't leave your bedsit until 2.30 in the afternoon — is that correct?'

'Yes. That is correct.'

'Lewis, didn't it worry you that it might soon be getting dark and that you had a long way to walk up the moor to get to the croft?'

'No. I don't mind the dark. I've got a torch. My dad bought it for me. He said it's the best torch you can buy.'

Swift had already mentally tracked the young man's likely route from the town centre to the base of the moor and upwards to its higher reaches. The whole journey would take around three hours walking at a steady pace. And halfway along the route he would most likely have passed the entrance to the Arkwright quarry. Perhaps at around 4 to 4.30 in the afternoon.

Lewis Lightowler had, on his own free admission, every opportunity to meet and murder Jenny Hoxton. He was an emotionally disturbed young man with a disordered personality. There could be an argument made for his having attacked, possibly abducted, and killed the girl on a whim. Alternatively it could be argued that some stress or trauma he had suffered in the past had been triggered by meeting Jenny. It was even possible that she had behaved towards him in a way he had found upsetting or threatening.

Swift's instinct was that Lightowler had played no part in Jenny's murder. But the evidence he had provided was highly significant and could not be ignored. Further investigations would be required: forensic testing and psychiatric assessments. All of which would take time. Time during which Lister would have no option but to keep the Hoxton investigation open and to concede that the case against the dead Ned Bracewell was by no means open and shut.

17

Excitement shone out of Sue Sallis's face as she watched Swift read through the neatly word-processed account of her interview with Imogen Barclay.

'This is good work,' he said quietly, laying the sheets on his desk, his face grave and thoughtful.

Sue's elation suffered a small puncture. 'Should we go and see Ashton right away, sir?' she asked, careful to tone down the eagerness she still felt.

'Let's think this one through,' he said, refusing to be hurried. 'Imogen's information and her implied allegations are of great interest. But so far, that is all they are. As yet we have no corroborative evidence.'

'But that's what we would be going to get, sir. When we see Ashton.'

'If I were to play devil's advocate,' Swift told her, 'I could argue that Imogen Barclay's outpourings reflect the turmoil of a girl under great stress, a girl in shock having committed an act of serious self-harm — which could have had fatal consequences.'

Sue's face fell.

'Or maybe,' he continued, 'Imogen's insinuations are the result of some kind of conflict between her and Nick Ashton. We don't know anything about the relationship between Imogen and Nick, do we? Suppose they've had a recent bust-up — a row about something quite unconnected with Jenny Hoxton. Or suppose Nick's recently dumped Imogen for someone else. How do we know her allegations aren't motivated by some kind of revenge for hurt he's caused her?'

'OK,' Sue said, 'I accept those are possibilities. But we've already established Ashton had the opportunity to kill Jenny. He admitted that himself. Now we have a likely motive. *And* why would Imogen make up a story about the Mischief Night incident? It was so convincing. I really believed her.'

Swift smiled. 'I think I would probably have believed her too. But we have no hard evidence as yet. And Nick Ashton is a highly intelligent young man. This forthcoming interview is going to be crucial. We shall need our full armoury about us, which includes being aware of all the chinks.'

★   ★   ★

Lister listened to what Swift had to tell him of the day's interviews, his face registering a

286

weary resignation at the chief inspector's stoic determination to remove Bracewell from the frame in the Hoxton case. But at the point where the account brought in Nick Ashton, linking him in as possible suspect to the discovery of the perpetrator of the Mischief Night crash in addition to the Hoxton girl's murder, his demeanour underwent a transformation. He snapped upright in his chair, his eyes burning with anticipation. 'You're a cool one, Ed, making me listen to all that preamble before getting to the point. If we can open up this can of worms . . . ' His hands swiped at the air in a gesture of triumph, words failing him. 'I take it you'll be wanting to interview Ashton right away?' Without waiting for an answer, he got to his feet. 'And I think I'm going to go along with you. After all those press conferences and PR paraphernalia, some hands-on policing will do me a power of good. Not that I'm going to trample on your toes, Ed. You're the SIO in this case. I'll just be back stop.'

'I need to include Sue Sallis as well,' Swift pointed out, knowing that Lister was going to be in on this possible coup, whether he, Swift, liked it or not. 'She's done a lot of the spade work. And she's dead keen.'

'Sharp lass, that,' Lister agreed. 'A touch of the terrier about her. We'll make a good threesome. Tell you what, get her to put her uniform on. There's always something intimidating about a good-looker in full regalia. And we'll go in one of the blue-light wagons.'

While Sue, bemused but ready to go along with whatever was required, was changing into uniform, and Lister was skimming through interview transcripts, Swift telephoned Naomi.

'You're onto something, aren't you?' she commented, instantly picking up on the tense anticipation in his voice.

'It's looking hopeful.'

'Is it a male or a female you're after?' she asked.

'Why do you ask that?'

'Oh, I don't know. A girl gets killed, an old man gets abducted and dies. His daughter goes on TV protesting his innocence. It's like a restoration melodrama.'

'So what have you to offer on the likely sex of the villain?'

'My money's on the girls. Women can be devils when they're roused. Leave the blokes standing.'

'I'll remember those wise words,' he said, smiling.

'On the other hand,' she offered, 'where girls are concerned, maybe one should 'cherchez le garçon'.'

'Indeed,' he agreed drily. 'Are you all right?' he asked, worried as usual and trying to conceal it. 'I'm going to be late.'

'Dad! It's Friday night. I have a date. With a young guy you seem to approve of.'

'OK. Fine.' He smiled to himself. 'Don't be late.'

★　★　★

The Ashtons' house was similar in period and style to that of the Hoxtons. Small orange lamps gleamed at the edges of the long gravel drive and as the car approached the house a trio of security lights snapped on. Looking up after he had pressed the bell, Swift saw that there was a video camera pointing directly at him.

'Can't fault them on security,' Lister commented.

The door opened to reveal Nick Ashton, framed against the golden light in the hallway. He was wearing jeans and a red and white striped rugby shirt. His thick, dark hair gleamed and the angle of the light showed up the sculpted carving of his facial bones. His eyes swept over the small waiting group. 'Hello. How can I help?'

Swift took a step forward and showed his warrant card. 'I'm Detective Chief Inspector

Swift and this is Detective Superintendent Lister. I think you already know Constable Sallis.'

If Ashton was worried by the arrival of three police officers, he gave no sign of it. He nodded to the two men and bestowed a smile of sweet charm on Sue. 'Hello, again. Won't you come in?'

Passing the entrance to an impressive drawing room, he took them through into a smaller room at the back of the house — a snug den lined in light oak panelling and lit by softly dimmed spotlights glowing from the ceiling. A large TV was showing a period film.

'*Richard III*, Olivier's version,' Ashton explained, poising the remote at the screen and zapping the picture. The action took no more than two to three seconds, but allowed Swift to notice that the young man's hand was not quite steady.

'Please, sit down,' he invited them.

'Are you planning a career in acting?' Swift asked conversationally.

'Film direction is my dream,' Ashton said. 'But I'll probably end up going into the family firm. My father's an estate agent,' he reminded them.

'Yes.' Swift paused. 'Are you alone in the house, Mr Ashton?'

'Er . . . I'm baby-sitting.' He smiled. 'My

parents are at the opera in Leeds with my sister. The baby's hers. I volunteered to keep guard.' His eyes swivelled between the three visitors. 'Is this about Jenny?' he asked. He glanced across at Sue. 'I spoke to Constable Sallis a few days ago.'

'Yes, you were very helpful,' Swift said. 'And now we'd like to talk to you about another incident.'

'We'd like to know, Mr Ashton,' Lister put in, 'what you were doing on the afternoon of November 4th last year.'

It was a timely intervention and Nick Ashton was taken offguard. His features tightened as though pulled by wires. He took a breath and then rallied. 'Well, it's hard to say, exactly. Was it a weekday?' he wondered, in polite tones.

'Yes,' Swift said quietly.

'I'd be at school, maybe until around four or maybe later. Then I'd walk home. Probably do some reading or browse the net until supper.'

'What route do you take when you walk home?' Swift asked.

'I go down the main road to the big roundabout. Then past All Saints church and through the park. That brings me to the end of our road here. On the south side.'

'And how long does it take you?'

'Around twenty minutes.'

'Do you always use that route?' Swift asked.

There was a slight hesitation. 'Yes.'

Swift unfolded a street map of the area. 'You could knock around five minutes off the journey by walking through the new Jubilee Road estate and across the footbridge over the Bradford road.'

Ashton looked down at his feet. 'I suppose I could.' His unease was unmistakable now.

'We have reason to believe you did take the route over the footbridge on that afternoon,' Swift said with deadly calm. 'That you dropped a brick down onto the motorway.'

Ashton stared at him for a moment, frozen. 'No. Of course I didn't!'

'We have a witness,' Swift said.

The room went very quiet as though the world had stopped for a moment.

Ashton erupted from his chair, his cool completely deserting him. 'Oh God! NO. No, you've got it all wrong.'

'Listen, son,' Lister said with full menace. 'We've got forensics on this. All we need is take a sample from you . . . '

'No!' Ashton shouted. 'It was raining. You couldn't have got anything . . . ' He stopped, horrified at his blunder.

Lister fixed him with a long stare before

bowing his head and making a show of recording every word in his notebook.

'We also have reason to believe that Jenny Hoxton was on the bridge that afternoon,' Swift said. 'And that she witnessed what happened.'

Seconds passed. Ashton stumbled to his chair and sat down again, his face rigid with shock and anxiety.

'She was blackmailing you, wasn't she, Nick?' Sue Sallis said. 'Making you pay for her silence?'

'No. Oh God!' His voice caught in his throat, throwing him into a fit of choking coughs. He jumped up. 'Got to get water,' he wheezed, making for the door.

Lister put out an arm to stop him. 'You stay right there, son. I'll get the water.'

Ashton stood, dazed, as though stunned with a blow.

'She'd got a real stranglehold on you, hadn't she?' Sue persisted. 'There was no escape, no way out? Except killing her.'

The horror in Ashton's eyes diminished him to the state of a terrified child. His hand clutched at his throat. He couldn't or wouldn't speak.

Lister returned with water in a white mug. 'Here. Take a few slow sips.'

Ashton drank. His eyes darted over the

walls then flew up to the ceiling, filled with fear and misgiving. 'I think I need to call my dad's solicitor,' he said. 'I don't think I should answer any more questions.' He looked around at the three officers, his mouth working silently. The misery on his face suggested that he considered this last move yet another blunder.

'Then call your solicitor,' Swift said steadily. 'We'll meet up with him, or her, at the station.'

He let out a low cry. 'I can't leave the baby,' he said desperately.

'We'll call a WPC to come and mind the baby,' Lister said. 'Constable Sallis will stay until she comes.'

'Are you going to arrest me?' he whispered.

'No,' Lister said reassuringly. He left a cruel pause. 'I think we'll let the constable do that. She's done all the spade work on this one. We'll go for suspicion of causing a fatal accident, failure to report an accident, perversion of the course of justice. And first degree murder.' He turned to Sue. 'Constable?'

Sue stepped forward.

Ashton backed away and held up his hands in surrender. 'All right, all right,' he moaned. 'I *was* there on the road bridge. I *did* drop a brick onto the motorway. It was an accident. I was fooling around. I was a damn fool. But I didn't kill Jenny. I swear to you, by everything I can think of that's sacred, I did not kill her.' Panic flared from his eyes. 'I'm not a bad person. Truly, I'm not.'

* ★ ★

At the station Fowler stayed on late, wondering what his colleagues were up to visiting Nick Ashton. The duty sergeant had nothing to say except that the three officers had left looking as though they had the bit between their teeth. All of which had left Fowler feeling excluded, redundant and sour. It rankled that Swift had not considered the message he had left on his mobile of sufficient interest to follow up. Which, of course, would probably turn out to be the case — given Fowler's rotten luck.

He recalled the thrill of excitement he had experienced a few hours before on discovering that the telephone number he had been given to follow up had corresponded with that of a young villain well known to the drug team. Rocky West was nineteen years old. He lived — on and off — with his mother and sister at a local address in the unsmartest part of town. Master Rocky (what sort of name was that, for goodness' sake) had apparently been a very slippery boy and was an even craftier young man. He'd been caught twice in possession of cannabis but never with the harder stuff, and they'd never been able to nail him for supplying. When things got tough he moved on and melted into the ether for a while. But he'd always kept in touch with his mam.

Fowler had read the lad's file with mounting excitement. What if Jenny had fallen into the hands of Mr Rocky? Got mixed up with druggies? He had felt himself seized with determination to squeeze this particular orange until the pips popped out. He had a sense that the case against Ned Bracewell was a dead duck, like the man himself. But now there was a juicy new suspect, he was damn well going to be in at the kill.

He'd gone out, all guns blazing, taking with him the burly jobbing PC who'd accompanied him to the Bracewells' place that morning he'd helped himself to the hairs on Bracewell's brush. They'd battered on the door to the Wests' run-down flat, but there'd been no reply. The neighbours said they hadn't seen Rocky for a week or so now. The sister was sometimes around but they couldn't say when she'd be back and the mother wasn't one to spend a lot of time in the place. Liked to be out enjoying herself.

There was nothing for it but to leave the PC on watch and return to the station. Seated again at his desk, aching for action and glory, he had no option but to embark on the routine background checkouts of Rocky West's family (which Swift would expect to have to hand) and wait . . .

★　★　★

Swift arranged for Nick Ashton to be put in interview room one under the supervision of a duty constable until the solicitor arrived. Sue Sallis was on her way back to the station, having been relieved of her child-minding duties. Lister, having disseminated the information of Ashton's arrest throughout the staff, was in his office, ostensibly tidying up the forest of paperwork on his desk. His self-satisfaction at having acted as the vital catalyst in getting Ashton to confess to the Mischief Night incident was frank and undisguised. 'Best night's work I've done in years,' he'd commented as he and Swift drove away from the Ashtons' house. 'Who'd have thought the lad would just open up easy as that, gushing like a full-on tap?'

Privately Swift was worried that the confession had come out too fast, too easily.

Ashton had not been under caution, not in strict interviewing conditions. No tape or video recording. With the support of a good solicitor Ashton could well retract his admissions about the road incident. And whilst it had been a shrewd move of Lister's to drop in the mention of 'forensics', they would be in bother if they had to rely on DNA evidence to link Ashton with the brick which had been found on the road at the place of the pile-up. Ashton had been quite right, it had been raining on the night of the crash and the forensic team had found no usable human traces which could be used as evidence to build a case.

Moreover, the denial about Jenny Hoxton's murder seemed to have a cast-iron quality about it.

Pretty well exhausted with the day's events, and a lack of food, he went into the incident room with the intention of going through into the corridor to coax something hot out of the coffee machine. Geoff Fowler was sitting behind his desk, frowning at the computer screen. On hearing footsteps he looked up. 'Sir!' he called out, attracting Swift's attention.

'You're working late, Geoff,' Swift commented, interested to note that the sergeant's face registered something akin to animation.

'I think I might be on to something, sir. Relating to the phone number you asked me to follow up.'

'Ah.' Swift chided himself for forgetting to follow up Fowler's earlier call. 'And?'

Fowler gave him a swift run-down on Rocky West and the subsequent abortive home visit.

'Is there any evidence he was involved with Jenny Hoxton?' Swift asked.

'Not directly. But he's got a sister called Crystal who's around the same age as Jenny. This little lass isn't down on the Middlewood registers, so I tried the head at The Dales school, telephoned him at home. He gave me chapter and verse about her. She's been in quite a bit of trouble recently. Bunking off, setting fire to paper towels in the girls' cloak-rooms, some petty thieving. Typical deprived profile. Can't stand authority figures.'

Through his weariness, Swift felt a prick of curiosity. 'And Jenny phoned this girl's number from her sister Antonia's phone just days before she died. Twice, in fact.'

'Aye.' Fowler's characteristically dour face was now lit with energy. 'And according to our lad who's been watching out at the flat, she came back home around half an hour ago.'

'Right.' Swift frowned in thought.

'Shall I take along a WPC and hear what

she has to say?' Fowler asked. 'She might be able to fill in some background. It could help you with the Ashton questioning.'

Swift glanced at his watch. It was past eleven. Getting late. But he had an instinct not to delay until morning. 'Do that, Geoff. For starters it would be interesting to know if Crystal was the friend Jenny stayed with in the days before she died. And if Jenny had voiced any thoughts of 'unofficially' joining the school trip and hanging around with Ashton. Take it from there.'

'Right.' Fowler's eyes gleamed. 'And while I'm at it,' he said, his irony for once untinged with bitterness, 'I'll remember that she hates authority. Try not to make her detest us even more.'

★ ★ ★

In the interview room Swift and Sue Sallis sat opposite Nick Ashton and Clive Watson, the family solicitor. Watson was in his fifties, lined and cadaverous, with a face like a poker. Nick's skin looked white and pasty under the harsh overhead lighting. His face was raw with fear and alarm, as though the seriousness of what was happening to him was gradually eating away at his habitual self-confidence and the life-long belief that he was one of the world's lucky winners.

'Mr Ashton, earlier on you gave us some information regarding a serious road accident on the evening of November 4th last year. Is that right?'

Nick swallowed, his Adam's apple moving up and down as though he was trying to swallow a lump of rock-hard toffee. He glanced at the solicitor, who gave a minute nod.

'Yes.'

'Would you repeat that for us now? What you told us?'

The solicitor leaned towards the young suspect and whispered in his ear, a cautionary expression on his face.

Ashton shook his head vigorously. 'It's pointless to make no comment,' he burst out. 'They've got it all down on paper — what I said.'

Sue Sallis laid the point of her pen on her pad and began to read in a low, steady voice. 'The suspect said: 'I *was* there on the road bridge. I *did* drop a brick onto the motorway. It was an accident. I was fooling around. I was a damn fool.''

'Yes,' Ashton muttered, causing his solicitor to close his eyes briefly. 'Yes, that's what I said. And that's the truth.'

Watson drew in a breath. Swift guessed

that he was beginning to regret giving up his Friday night.

'Look,' Ashton exclaimed, defiant anger showing in his face, 'I'm not going to mess anyone about. I was the person who caused that crash. I didn't do it on purpose, it was a dreadful, shocking mistake. I was a stupid, careless idiot — and I'm prepared to confess that to a jury if necessary. And I'll take the consequences. But I did not kill Jenny Hoxton.' His voice rose to a yelp of panic as he spoke the last sentence.

Is this some kind of trade-off? Swift wondered. Did Ashton think that by being cooperative and confessing to one crime he would be more likely to get away with the other? Was he calculating that a prison sentence for causing the road crash was going to be less than for first degree murder? Swift felt the tension tightening his spine and made himself relax.

'It is true that Jenny Hoxton saw you and Imogen Barclay on the footbridge over the dual carriageway on the evening of November 4th?'

'Yes.'

'And afterwards you spoke to Jenny about what she had seen?'

Ashton's pupils dilated. Swift guessed that it had only recently dawned on him that

Imogen Barclay had not only betrayed his secret, but had furnished a good deal of detail. 'Yes. I think anyone in my position would have done the same.'

'In your position?' Swift asked.

'Well, feeling totally sick about what had happened.'

'But you didn't know at that time that a twenty-two-year-old mother had been killed,' Swift commented. 'Did you?'

'I knew there was one god-awful mess going on down in that road,' Ashton protested. He threw himself back in his chair, raking his fingers through his mane.

'Jenny started asking you for money — is that right?'

'Yes.'

'You decided to give it to her. Why was that?'

The solicitor issued a low warning.

'Let me handle this,' Ashton growled like a cornered dog. He faced Swift. 'I thought she might tell someone what she had seen on the bridge. I thought she might spice it up a bit, make things look really bad for me.'

'Why would she do that?'

'She was that sort of girl. Mean and devious. A born manipulator.'

'Did she have something against you personally?' Sue Sallis asked.

'Not that I know of.'

'Maybe she'd made overtures to you and you'd rejected her,' Sue persisted.

Ashton shook his head, his eyes dull now and weary. 'No. She never came on to me. Not in a girly way.'

'But after what she'd seen, then all of a sudden she had a lever on you?' Sue suggested.

'Yes.'

'You, the head boy. The one all the girls fancy.'

He said nothing.

'She was wanting to scare you,' Sue said. 'Or maybe she was simply wanting you to notice her?'

'She was on a power trip,' Ashton said. 'I don't think she was bothered about the money. She never asked for any really scary amounts.'

'But blackmailers escalate, don't they?'

He shrugged.

'And was she scaring you?' Swift asked.

He took a long time to answer. 'Yes.'

'I'd say you were in a terrifying position,' Swift said. 'She could have ruined your chances for Oxford. Put you in prison for a long time. Wrecked your hopes for a decent career.'

'That's all going to happen now anyway,' Ashton pointed out in a flat voice. 'But I didn't kill her.'

'I would think you sometimes wished she were dead,' Sue offered.

Ashton dropped his head on to his hand.

'On no account dignify that with a response,' the solicitor hissed. 'I think Mr Ashton needs a break,' he told the officers. 'Maybe you could provide us with a hot drink.'

Ashton's head jerked up. 'You won't find any evidence,' he burst out. 'DNA or fingerprints or whatever.'

'Why is that?' Swift asked, wondering if the despairing young man was going to invoke the intercession of the rain once again.

'Because I never touched her. Not once. Not on the day she was killed, not before. Not ever. If you want to know the truth, she made my skin crawl.'

★   ★   ★

Fowler saw the hand of poverty and neglect all over the flat in which the girl Crystal lived with her mother and her brother. Although lived with seemed not quite the appropriate term.

Not only were neither the mother nor Rocky present at the flat but Crystal claimed not to know where they were or when they were coming back.

The place smelled of old cigarette smoke and partly washed clothes that had never quite dried. The carpet was tacky with unwiped spills and as Fowler sat on the fraying settee he felt a mysterious dampness creeping along his thighs.

Crystal was sitting on the floor watching a gangster film on TV. A plate of half-eaten supper was in front of her: cream crackers and an open carton of cheap margarine smeared with jam and unidentifiable black specks.

The girl seemed indifferent to the arrival of Fowler and the WPC. She'd shrugged her shoulders as he asked if they could come in. And now she was acting as though they were not there. Fowler's questions, posed with commendable restraint, were mainly ignored as she stared fixedly at the figures who ebbed and flowed across the screen.

'How old are you, Crystal?' he asked.

Crystal turned slowly to face him. 'A lady never tells her age,' she told him. 'That's what me mam always says.'

'Fourteen? Fifteen?' Fowler persisted. It was pretty hard to tell. Could be thirteen going on twenty.

'Aye, one of those,' Crystal said, slanting him a glance of pure insolence. 'What's it to you, anyway? I've told you, our Rocky's not here. You're just wasting your time.'

'We were really wanting to see you, love,' Fowler said.

The girl's face hardened, defensive and sullen. 'I ain't done nothing.'

'No, we know that. We just wondered if you could help us. It's about Jenny Hoxton.'

The girl's shoulders stiffened. 'What about her?'

'Was she a pal of Rocky's?'

The girl swivelled her head, aggrieved astonishment twisting her features. 'No way!'

'Was she a pal of yours, Crystal?'

There was a silence. 'Mebbe,' the girl muttered.

'Did you know Jenny Hoxton, love?' Fowler prompted, his voice soft as a summer breeze.

'Yeah.'

'And you and Jenny Hoxton were pals?'

'Yeah. I already said so. Don't you listen when someone's talking to you?'

Fowler pulled in a breath and held it. He mustn't mess this up. And he was on well trodden ground here, pitching his wits against the underclasses. 'Where did you meet Jenny?' He aimed for a conversational tone.

'At the fair. She loved the fair. That's where her real mum used to work.'

'Did you ever go and stay with Jenny? At her house?'

Crystal shook her head in sorrowful disdain. 'No way. Her parents are dead posh — and rich too. And her sister's a right cow. Jenny couldn't stick her.'

'Did Jenny come to stay here, then?'

There was a flicker in her eyes, a spark that instantly died. 'What do you think? It's an effing dump.'

'Jenny was missing for a few days before she was murdered,' Fowler reflected in neutral tones. 'No one knew where she was. Not even her sister and her mother. But *you* knew where she was, didn't you, Crystal? You were her best mate, and you knew everything about her.'

Crystal was suspicious, but unable to resist the seductive flattery of the notion of an exclusive friendship. 'No. I never knew all about her,' she said, in a manner suggesting exactly the opposite.

'She was staying here with you, wasn't she?'

'Give over!'

'Her parents were away. She could do what she liked. And I'll bet your mam and brother were out of the way too. What did you do together, Crystal? Have a bit of fun? Invite a few lads round, eh?'

'Don't be daft. I'd never invite *anyone* here. I'd be ashamed.'

'So maybe you met your boyfriends out somewhere?'

'I haven't got a boyfriend. I hate boys. Great stupid lumps.'

'But I'll guess Jenny had a boyfriend?' Fowler suggested with silky cunning.

Crystal's eyes hardened. 'You're not getting me to tell any tales on Jenny. It's wrong to speak of the dead. Didn't you know that?'

'So she did have a boyfriend — or someone she liked?'

'No.'

'Oh yes, she did, Crystal, and we know his name.'

Crystal's head snapped up. 'It was that Sadie told you, wasn't it? She said she was Jenny's cousin or summat. And then she said she was the daughter of that old man who everyone thinks did it. Bitch! I thought she were me friend. She's one of your lot, isn't she?'

Fowler spread his hands. 'Nothing to do with us.'

'Huh! Tell me another one!' Crystal's pupils swivelled from side to side. She was rattled now. 'So what if Jenny had someone she liked? That's no big deal.'

'Lads and lasses get keen on each other. They fall out. And sometimes . . . things turn nasty,' Fowler commented with slow speculation. 'Come on, Crystal, if you know something about this bloke, you've got to say. It's only fair to Jenny. You know that, don't you?'

Crystal's mouth opened slightly and there was fear in her eyes. 'I thought the old man must have done it,' she muttered.

'We're not sure yet. We need to be sure, Crystal. To find out who really killed her. And put him inside for a long time.'

She stared at him, transfixed, her lips pressed tightly together

'We're talking about a young man called Nick,' Fowler told her in a low, intense voice. 'Nick Ashton. He's the lad Jenny fancied. Isn't that right?'

Crystal flinched and hunched up her shoulders as though in self-protection. 'Don't know.'

'Yes, you do, love. You just don't want to say, do you? You don't like us police lot and you think it's safest to keep your mouth shut. Well, that's fine, but you see we already know things about Jenny and Nick. We know that Jenny saw something that could get Nick into big trouble if she ever told on him.' He leaned forward. 'And then Jenny gets found dead, only a few miles away from where her school mates were on a trip. And one of those mates was Nick Ashton . . . '

Crystal gazed at him in horror. 'You mean you think *Nick* killed her?'

'We're just asking questions, Crystal. Trying to get at what really happened.'

'Oh, no, not Nick,' she murmured, her eyes wide and staring. 'Listen, I'll tell you,' she said desperately. 'I'll tell you what happened that weekend. Jenny came here instead of going to those other friends. It were Sat'dy evening and we went out and got cider and crisps. Quite a lot of cider 'cos I got the jackpot on the fruitie.'

'Where was that?'

'At the pub just down the road. The Coach and Horses.'

'I thought pubs didn't serve underage drinkers,' Fowler said with a conspiratorial grin.

'They don't. But I said it was for me mam. The girl on the bar just laughed. We played the fruitie for a bit and then we came home and drank the cider and watched TV.' She looked wistful. 'It was nice.'

'And then?'

'We went to bed and I didn't wake up until gone ten. Me head was thumping.'

'And what about Jenny?'

Crystal's face blanked over. 'She'd gone. Taken all her stuff and gone.'

'Where to?'

'I don't know,' Crystal said. 'That was it. She didn't leave no note, no nothing.'

Fowler felt like someone on the point of reeling in a fish and suddenly seeing it flashing away through the water. 'She hadn't mentioned where she was going?'

'No. She was like that sometimes, Jenny. Just did her own thing.'

Fowler let his eyes rest on the girl's pathetic weasel face. She's just getting fanciful now, he thought, wondering if the whole of her account had been nothing but a pack of lies. Disappointment settled like lead in his stomach.

As he was considering a possible new line of attack, a woman with a cascade of 1980s swept-back curls lurched into the room. 'What's going on?' she barked at Crystal, before turning on Fowler. 'And what do *you* think you're bloody doing in my flat?'

'Just having a talk with your daughter, Mrs West.'

'God! You're never away from my door, you lot. First you're after my lad and now it's her. What's she been up to?'

'Nothing that I know of. We came to talk about her friend Jenny Hoxton.'

'That poor little kid,' Mrs West said, throwing herself onto the opposite side of the couch to Fowler and kicking off her stiletto-heeled shoes. 'Jesus, there are some filthy perverted bastards around these days. Nobody's safe. Crystal has been that upset. She's cried buckets for poor little Jenny.'

'Did you know Jenny at all, Mrs West?' Fowler asked.

'No. Only what Crystal told me. Kids don't like hanging around at home any more, do they? They like to be out and about. Well, don't we all?' She gave the sergeant a drunken, saucy smile.

Fowler gave an internal sigh of disgust. There seemed little point going any further whilst the room was filling with the alcohol fumes of Mrs West's exhalations. He got up. 'I think that'll be all for now,' he said, nodding at the WPC.

Crystal was once again absorbed in the TV. She poised the remote and turned up the sound full blast. Mrs West shouted at her to turn it down.

'Good night,' Fowler said into the crossfire.

★　★　★

Nick Ashton held to his story. Through two further sessions of questioning, he refused to say any more about his relationship with Jenny Hoxton than he had already revealed. There was nothing more to say, he insisted.

His solicitor made a pointed exit at 2 a.m., having explained to Nick's bewildered and angry parents — who had come post-haste from the opera to issue a number of demands — that the police were entitled to detain their son for forty-eight hours, after which he must be charged or released. Sue Sallis and Lister returned to their homes. Swift stayed on and talked with Geoff Fowler about his interview with Crystal.

'She knows more than she's saying,' Fowler told him, his face dragged down with the frustration of not being able to offer the DCI something more significant.

'We'll go and see her again in the morning,' Swift said. Exhaustion was swirling through him like a crushing wave, impossible to resist. He left the building and fired the engine of his car, then pulled out into the deserted road and forced his eyelids to stay open. The earlier elation of the day had worn itself out. He had felt they were on the brink of cracking this case. And, indeed, it was possible that all the pieces were already there, but sometimes pieces could take a long time to fit together.

18

The telephone woke Geoff Fowler at 7.30 the next morning. He had to drag himself up into consciousness, having dozed only fitfully until around six, and then fallen into a deep, calm sleep.

'You're wanted, Geoff, lad,' the morning duty sergeant told him.

'Uh! What?'

'A young lady to see you.'

'Get on with it,' Fowler growled, not in the mood for jests and teasing.

'A Miss Crystal West. Asking just for you!'

Fowler shot upright. 'I'll be right there! Don't let her out of your sight. And make sure there's a child protection officer on tap — the kid's maybe no more than thirteen.'

His hands shook with anticipation as he showered, shaved and dressed. Anticipation was fizzing in the marrow of his bones. He told himself to calm down. What was the point of getting keyed up like a kid on Christmas Eve? Expectation invariably ended in disappointment. This Crystal kid was lonely, deprived and bored. She'd probably turned up for nothing more than a bit of attention, a chance to play a walk-on part in the Hoxton drama and shine a little.

At the station, Lorna Price, the child protection officer assigned to assist with any child witnesses in a case, was waiting for him. She was a calm, motherly woman who had proved herself highly successful in persuading terrified young children to talk about their horrific experiences. She had been following the Hoxton case and there was no need for a lengthy briefing.

'Oh, by the way,' Price told Fowler, 'she's fourteen.'

'You did well to worm that out of her. She was very cagey with me.'

'Woman to woman stuff,' Price said, smiling.

'Aye, well. She's no more than a kid, is she?'

Crystal had been invited to make herself at home in Price's pleasant interview room, and given tea and ginger biscuits. She looked up as Fowler and Price entered.

'Are they on?' she asked, pointing to the video cameras in the corners of the room.

'Yes,' Price said. 'Is that a problem for you, Crystal?'

'No. And the sound — is that on too?'

'Yes.'

'It's just like they do on the TV, then?'

'I suppose so.' Price smiled and swivelled a glance at Fowler.

'Right.' The girl seemed satisfied with the information. She sat very still, her hands on her knees, her body rocking very slightly from the base of her spine.

Fowler noticed that she had washed her hair. It hung in long strands around her neck and cheeks, gauche but glossy. Both her well-worn jeans and her grey sweatshirt looked freshly laundered. Her face and hands were scrubbed clean. She had made a big effort.

'How did you get here, love?' Fowler asked her with genuine curiosity. It was a desperately cold morning. Winter had kicked in once again and the sleet had been blowing in horizontal sheets as he had driven in. Yet Crystal showed no signs of having battled with the elements. It would have taken her around forty minutes to walk from Eden Terrace, there was no direct bus route and he doubted that Mrs West would run a car, even less drive it to a police station.

'In a taxi,' Crystal said.

'Oh, my!' said Price, smiling.

'Lucky for some,' Fowler chuckled, aiming for chumminess.

'I can afford it.' She sounded affronted. 'I had another win on the fruitie this week.'

'Fine. Congratulations.' He made his face grave and thoughtful. 'So, what is it you wanted to tell me?'

The girl put her head down and rubbed her knees harder. The rocking became more pronounced. 'It was me,' she said. 'I killed Jenny.'

On a reflex, both police officers straightened their spines.

It flashed through Fowler's mind that detective work was a bit like playing the fruit machines: you put your money in, and more often than not, you lost. But just at this moment he felt as though he'd got three plums. Nevertheless, he was an experienced officer and he knew better than to take confessors at face value. Especially needy, nervy adolescent girls.

'How did you kill her?' Price asked very gently.

A silence. Price and Fowler held themselves rigid. 'With a sandwich wrapper,' she whispered.

'What sort of wrapper?' Fowler was aware of literally holding his breath. He made himself breathe normally.

'One of those clingfilm ones.'

'Why did you kill her, Crystal?' Price asked, her voice caressingly soft.

The rocking continued. The girl shook her head.

'We talked about Jenny and you having a good time together at half term,' Fowler said. 'You'd had some ciders and watched a video. It was good, and you were mates?'

A nod.

'Then next day, Jenny went off. You didn't know where she'd gone. You felt bad about that, didn't you, love?'

She shook her head. 'No,' she breathed.

'You didn't feel bad?' he followed up.

'She didn't go and leave me. We went together.'

'And where were you going?' Fowler made his voice as hushed and soft as a cat's paw.

'To see Nick. To find him.'

'On the school trip?'

'Mmm. Jenny knew where they were going. She knew everything about Nick.

'She used to follow him about. You know, stalking. She got really excited about joining up with the trip and seeing him. She could talk about nothing else when she was staying at the flat wi' me. How we'd go and find him at that place where the Brontë sisters lived.'

'So, when did you set off?' Fowler asked, striving to get a mental picture of the outline of the action.

'Umm, on the Monday about eleven. Me mam was away with her boyfriend in Manchester until Wednesday morning. Me

319

brother was supposed to be minding me, but he'd pushed off to Bradford on the Sunday night for a couple of days. So we knew we could go where we liked without anybody missing us. We decided to go to Haworth and find Nick. And then we'd come back on the Tuesday afternoon.'

'What were you going to do when you found Nick?' Fowler asked with genuine curiosity.

'Oh, you know. Just hang about. Gawp at him. Jenny was going to give him a letter she'd written.'

'What sort of letter?'

'Just a letter. She was always writing him letters.'

'Did you see the letter, Crystal? Did Jenny show it to you?'

'No. She said it was secret.'

'Even from you, her best mate.'

'I weren't her best mate,' Crystal said slowly.

'So who was?'

'No one. She didn't really want a best mate. She was the sort who can do things on her own.'

'So you set off on Monday morning,' Fowler continued. 'How did you travel?'

'By bus. It took four buses to get there. Jenny had a map. She'd got it all worked out.

She's quite clever really.' Crystal stopped, and there was a flutter under the skin of her cheek. 'She always said she was a dimbo, but she wasn't.'

'When did you arrive in Haworth?'

'It was late. Well dark.'

'Did you take food with you?' Price asked.

'Oh, aye. Chocolate bars and crisps and cider. Loads of stuff.'

'Did you call in anywhere for a snack?'

'No. I told you, we had plenty. But we did kip down in the ladies toilets at a pub just outside the village. They never noticed us going in. And we got out through the window in the morning.'

Fowler suddenly recalled that there was a song or a play called *Lock Up Your Daughters*. Wise words, indeed. 'That was on the Wednesday morning?' he asked.

'Yeah. Jenny said the trip had stayed the night somewhere further up the Dales. So we hung around waiting until the coach came.'

'Into Haworth?'

She nodded. She was rocking hard now, as though to keep the momentum of her tale going. 'They all got off. We kept watching for Nick; we could hardly wait. He was last to come off. He was with that lass Imogen.'

'Nick's girlfriend?' Price prompted.

'Mmm. Jenny said she was a stuck-up evil bitch.'

'What time was this?' Fowler asked.

'It were dinner time. They'd all got sandwiches and drinks with them. Some of them stood around the coach eating their dinner.'

'And what about Nick?'

'Him and Imogen went off down the road, back the way we'd come. Jenny thought they might be going to the pub we'd crashed out in.'

Fowler leaned forward. 'You followed them?'

'Mmm.'

'Didn't they notice you?'

'It were a twisty road, so we stayed just behind the corners, so they didn't see us. Anyway, they were all over each other, snogging and stuff. They got to the pub and went in. Jenny said, 'Come on, we'll go and see what they're up to.' But I didn't want to. I felt — Well, sort of scared.'

'Was Jenny scared?' Price asked.

'No way. She was having a great time. She marched in and went to the bar and got some sandwiches to take out.'

'Did you go in?'

'No, I scooted off into the car park and kept well out of the way. It seemed like ages, and then she came out with the sandwiches. She was looking around for me. She was grinning all over her face. And then Nick came after her. He had the letter she'd given him in his hand. He started shouting at her. He was really mad.'

'What did he say, Crystal?' Fowler's nerves were taut.

She closed her eyes, the rocking now soft and thoughtful. 'He told her to eff off.' Her face was twisted with feeling, her mouth moving, but no sound emerging.

'What else?' Price murmured.

'He said, 'Bloody leave me alone. I'm sick to death of you.'' Her body was rigid now, and the words were bellowed out, conveying deep, raw anger. 'That was it, really. It went on for a bit, same sort of stuff, telling her to get lost.'

'And what did Jenny say?'

'She laughed at him. She said she was going to stick to him like glue. She wasn't afraid or nothing. He went back inside, and Jenny waved for me to come over. She was as pleased as anything because she'd got loads of cider besides the sandwiches. We walked along the road and ate one lot of sandwiches. We drank some cider and got giggly, and she said why didn't we walk up to the top of the big moor we could see in the distance, right to the top. And I said yes, because I'd never walked up a moor. So we set off, but it took ages and the top of the moor still seemed miles away. We saw this turning to a quarry and we thought we'd go there and sit down for a bit and finish the sandwiches and have another drink, and I was hoping Jenny'd forget about going up to the top, 'cos I was knackered.' She was suddenly very still. 'That's when I did it.'

Neither officer spoke for a time.

'What did you do, Crystal?' Fowler said, speaking as though walking on eggs.

'I wrapped the clingfilm from the sandwiches round her head, right tight. There were loads of it.'

'Didn't she struggle?'

'No, she'd gone dozy with the cider and then she'd laid back and banged her head on a stone. She was all muzzy and giggly, waggling her legs in the air and talking on and on about Nick and saying how he was never going to be rid of her. She said she could make him do what she liked. And how . . . she was going to . . . you know . . . ' Colour rolled into her face.

'You mean, have sex with him?' Price said gently.

'Yeah.'

'And what happened after that?'

'She went all quiet, dropped off to sleep. I'd finished me sandwich and I was going to squash the wrapper into a ball. And then I smoothed it out. And then I spread it over her face, as smooth as smooth.'

Fowler and Price looked at each other, beginning at last to understand the pathetic wilful circumstances of a killing.

'What made you want to wrap the clingfilm round her face?' Price asked.

Crystal stared at her. 'She was getting right on my nerves.'

Price sat forward. 'Was it because of Nick?'

Crystal's features gave a twitch. 'Nick was nice. He used to help me with my reading when I was at primary.'

Fowler was baffled. 'How come?'

'Some of his year group were doing community projects and stuff. He used to come to my school to listen to me practising my reading. He was lovely and kind.'

'You loved him?' Price spoke softly.

The girl frowned, considering. 'Sort of. I never saw him again after the project finished.'

'Until Jenny Hoxton got involved with him?'

'Yeah.' She gazed at the two officers in tragic appeal, a small lonely being impoverished in body and spirit.

'What did you do with the sandwich wrapper?' Fowler wondered. 'And the cider cans?'

The girl's eyes flickered. 'Put them in the bin when I went to the bus station.'

Fowler wondered if she realized that was one of the best ways to get rid of small items of evidence. He was impressed with the girl's account. It had a clear ring of authenticity, as did the girl's emotional state given the nature of the crime. But as yet there was no hard evidence to point to Crystal as the killer; perhaps never would be.

He'd talk it over with Swift. The thought of presenting Swift with this confession awakened a sense of inner bliss he had not felt for years. Not just three plums, the whole bloody jackpot.

He turned back to the pathetic, tragic girl, with the intention of asking if she'd go with him and a woman officer to show them the exact place where Jenny had died. That would surely clinch the matter. But Crystal was fast asleep, her head thrown back against the chair, her mouth slightly open, moving with soft breaths.

19

Swift looked through the one-way mirror. Beyond, in the juvenile interview suite, the girl was still sleeping. Lorna Price sat nearby. An hour had gone by since the startling confession had been completed.

Swift had watched the tape. Speculations had been humming and he was keen to set up a party to walk along the route Crystal claimed to have taken with Jenny at the earliest opportunity. 'Send a car for the mother, will you, Geoff,' Swift told the anxiously waiting sergeant. 'She'll need to give permission for the walk to take place. And probably to come along.'

Chance'd be a fine thing, Fowler thought to himself, unable to imagine Mrs West tottering to the nearest pub, let alone up the side of a moor. 'Right.' He gave a jerk to his tie. 'I'll get that sorted out pronto.'

Left to himself, Swift checked the map of the local area, then telephoned Sue Sallis to put her in the picture, leaving a message on her voicemail when there was no answer. He rather hoped she'd pick it up too late to do anything about it. It was Sunday, a time for at least some of the team to have a break.

Lister, in the office bright and early to have another go at Nick Ashton, was mildly supportive of the venture, clearly hopeful of a result which would show the girl to be an attention-seeking time-waster. Having come to grief with one prime suspect, Lister had his sights very firmly on Ashton for promotion to the hot seat.

Glancing again through the one-way mirror, Swift saw that the girl had woken. Lorna Price was gently escorting her to a door which led through to a small cloakroom. When they returned the girl sat down again, leaning forwards and dropping her hands between her knees. Swift made his way to the main door of the suite. As Lorna Price stood aside to admit him, the girl raised her head, her eyes darting over him. Her cheeks were pink and damp, her eyes heavy with sleep.

Swift drew up a chair and sat beside her. 'My name's Ed Swift,' he told her. 'I'm one of the detectives who work here.'

She stared at him, her eyes taking in each detail of his face. His hair, eyes, nose, mouth, ears.

'Oh, aye.' She was suspicious, on the defensive.

'I'd like to talk to you about Jenny,' he told her. 'I've seen the tape, Crystal. And I've listened very carefully to all you said.'

'Will they lock me up?' she asked, her face intense. 'Will I have to go to court?'

'We need you to help us some more before we know what's going to happen,' he said.

'Are the cells cold?' she asked. 'Do they stink?'

'They're not the most pleasant of places. Are you worried about that, Crystal?'

'No. I'm tough, me. I don't look it, but I am.'

'Right. That's good, because I'm going to ask you to do something that'll need you to be both tough and brave.'

'What's that?'

'Show us exactly where you and Jenny went that day she was killed. We want you to go with us in a car to the place where you set off. And then we want you to take us on exactly the same walk you and she went on and show us where you ended up.'

'Up to the quarry?'

'If that's the place you ended up, yes.'

'It's a long way,' she said.

'We don't mind,' he said, 'Your mum can come along as well. You needn't feel as though you're all on your own with us police people.'

'Me mam!' Crystal frowned and then her face took on a look of devilment. 'Walking on the moors! She ain't got any shoes with less than four-inch heels.'

★ ★ ★

Mrs West, none too pleased at being roused from her Sunday lie-in, and suffering from a stonking hangover, veered between bewildered confusion and outbursts of rage against the police. They were bullies, they were cunning devils, they incorporated all that was evil in mankind for intimidating her daughter and getting her to confess to murder. And at the same time they were gullible idiots for believing a word the girl said. The kid had always been one for romancing, living in a dream-world. She couldn't tell real life from the rubbish they put on TV any more than she could tell her arse from her elbow. Moreover, she wasn't going to let her daughter out of her sight for one minute now them police bastards had her down for a capital offence. She was going to stick with her through thick and thin. She wanted a lawyer for her Crystal. The best. And now.

'Mrs West,' Swift explained patiently, 'we simply want Crystal to show us what she remembers about the day Jenny died. Where they went, what they did.'

'No way did our Crystal do away with

anyone,' Mrs West insisted. 'It's bloody outrageous all this dragging her off to some godforsaken moor.' She glanced down at her own short skirt and her stiletto heels. 'It's snowing, for goodness' sake! I wouldn't send a dog out in this.'

'We're not accusing Crystal of anything,' Swift reminded her, as he had done several times before.

'Not much you're not,' the disgruntled mother muttered, lighting up a cigarette and retiring behind a cloud of smoke.

★   ★   ★

The wind was bitter, tearing in from the north and lashing the grains of sleet straight into the faces of those brave enough to leave the warm comfort of the car and set out on foot.

Mrs West had cried off at the last minute, despite Swift's offer of a thick fleece-lined raincoat he had found in the lost property store, together with a pair of commendably stylish Hunter wellingtons. 'To tell the truth I'm not feeling too bright,' she said, glancing out of the window and grimacing. 'I get bronchitis in this kind of weather if I'm not careful.' She gave a smoker's graveyard cough and banged on her breastbone. 'You'll be all right, love,' she told Crystal. 'The lady officer'll take care of you. And don't you let any of 'em make you say anything you don't want to.'

Crystal, now kitted out in a borrowed windproof anorak with a huge furry hood, climbed out of the car, registering undisguised relief that her parent was not going to join the party of walkers.

Swift had decided they should start out from the pub car park where Crystal claimed to have waited whilst Jenny went inside to get food and drink and attempted to inflict some further damage on Nick Ashton's peace of mind. She stood on the tarmac, looking around at the looming moors and trying to orient herself, her face tense with concentration, her thin frame hunched against the wind.

Swift walked back to the waiting police car and asked the driver to wait until the pub opened and then order rounds of sandwiches for everyone and be ready to bring them along to the walking party when he got Swift's request call.

'We went down that way,' Crystal told him as he returned to stand beside her. She gestured towards the road that led eventually to the village of Haworth. As she moved forward the small party of police followed on:

Swift, Fowler, Lorna Price and a uniformed female constable.

'You said Jenny had a map,' Swift observed.

'Aye, but she didn't use it when we were walking up to the moor.' She stopped and gestured to the skyline ahead. 'We just fixed our sights on that big black moor and . . . sort of went that way.'

Swift's glance followed her pointing finger. He looked around. 'They all look like big black moors to me.'

'I know. But I'm sure it were that one. It's the biggest, and the nearest. It's got to be that one.'

They reached a crossroads. Crystal swivelled and hummed to herself, chewing on her lip. 'We went down that way,' she decided eventually. 'I remember that tree stump in the hedge. It looks like an old man with a hunchback.'

Swift gave an internal sigh. Inside his wool coat his body felt numb and miserable with cold: the weather in the north was truly terrible, not at all suited to uncharted ramblings. He reminded himself that on the day of the murder the two girls had been drinking cider, and that Crystal's memory of the route they took could be hazy. He trudged on.

An hour and a half later, having dived

down several unpromising-looking side roads on the instructions of their young guide, the party were now on the flanks of the moor she had had in her sights. For a time they scrambled over rough moorland grass and shallow pools of water packed with grains of ice and sleet. Then they were back on trodden paths.

Fowler came up beside Swift, who was banging his gloved hands together, trying to coax some life back into his frozen fingers. 'She's on the right track, sir,' he murmured softly, so the girl couldn't hear. 'If she cuts up the hill on the unmade road next on the left, it's only another forty minutes or so to the quarry.'

Swift's mental map of the terrain was nowhere near as knowledgeable as that of Fowler. He had been beginning to lose hope and the sergeant's words sent a new surge of anticipation through him. He flipped open his mobile and asked the PC driver at the pub car park to make his way up to the quarry and wait for further instructions. He detected a note of relief in the young constable's voice as he chimed a hearty, 'Will do, sir.' In the background Mrs West's voice droned on in full complaining mode.

Half an hour later Crystal faltered and then stopped, shoulders slumped, head hanging.

Lorna Price stepped forward. The girl turned her face up, miserable with cold and exhaustion. 'I'm not sure this is the right way,' she said.

'Do you recognize anything here?' Price encouraged. 'Look around, you might remember something . . .'

The girl shook her head. 'I'm whacked,' she said.

Price glanced across to Fowler. 'Minutes away,' he mouthed.

'Do you want to have a rest?' Price asked the girl.

'No, I'll go on a bit.' Crystal turned and looked back the way they had come, hesitating, wondering. Each member of the team held their breath. Swivelling back, she continued her tramp. Then suddenly her pace quickened. The road met a narrow curving limestone track. At the divide there was a rough-hewn sign pointing the way: 'ARK-WRIGHT QUARRY', it said, in clumsily styled capitals. In an instant the mouth of the quarry was revealed. 'This is it! This is the place!' she called out in triumph. Price was about to give a gentle prompt about the precise location of Jenny's final moments, but Crystal was already running forward, making her way around the shallow curve of the quarry to the place where its edge was most cliff-like. 'Here,' she said. 'This is where we sat. I know because of those trees behind us. Look, there are three stood together, and then a space and then two more.'

Swift looked and saw that the front line of trees did indeed make a formation some observers would remember if that kind of thing interested them. Moreover it struck him that, rather than being a 'romancer' as Mrs West had put it, Crystal seemed to be something of a careful observer. 'Well done,' he told her.

'Can we go back now?' Crystal asked, suddenly hunted and anxious. 'Where's the car?'

'Just at the end of this road here.' He gestured to the wide frozen track which had been a sea of trodden mud on the day he and Fowler came to look at the body. 'I'll call the driver to come along. He's got sandwiches and drinks. I should think you're hungry, mm?' She shook her head and walked towards the line of trees, leaning up against one of their trunks.

The car arrived. The constable got out and placed the sandwiches and drinks on the bonnet of the car. The team moved forward. Mrs West opened the car door and stuck her head out. On finding her beautifully styled waves sucked at by a greedy biting wind, she promptly withdrew.

Swift chose two packets of sandwiches and walked across to the shivering Crystal. 'Which would you like? There's cheese and pickle or bacon and egg.'

'I'll have the bacon.' She reached out a thin, cold paw.

'What did you and Jenny have?' Swift asked in conversational tones.

'She had tuna mayonnaise and I had egg and cress.' She began to unwrap the sandwiches. Swift noted that the amount of clingfilm wrapping was extremely generous, quite enough for the purposes of a would-be murderer. Crystal crumpled the film into a tidy ball and put it in her pocket.

Swift took a bite of his cheese and pickles. 'So you finished eating your sandwiches, and then you talked . . . '

She nodded. She seemed unable to speak, shrunk within herself and hiding away.

'And where were you then?'

She gestured to the spot where Jenny Hoxton's body had been found, but her eyes veered away from the site of the killing, as though she couldn't face up to the powerful memories it might awaken.

'Did you sit on the ground?' Swift asked.

Another nod. Her fingers picked at the

sandwiches, sending a shower of bread-crumbs on to the ground.

'Crystal,' he said with a degree of sternness, 'you brought us here because you wanted us to believe what you told us. What you recorded on to the tape. You have to help us understand exactly what happened. You have to talk to us.'

Her head seemed to hunch even further into her shoulders.

'Was it wet, sitting on the ground?'

She considered. 'It were dry that day, and not really cold.'

'And what happened then?'

'I've told you,' she exclaimed, edgy and defensive once more. 'She started going on and on, saying stuff and giggling . . . '

'And then?'

'I just . . . I just wanted her to shut up.' Her voice had faded to a whisper. She pressed her lips together. 'That's it,' she said with finality. 'That's all.' She sank down against the tree, clasping her hands around her knees and pulling her chin down against her chest. Swift was fairly sure they weren't going to get another word out of her until they took her away from the killing scene. He looked across to the waiting team who had been attending carefully to the brief interchange and shook his head to indicate they'd gone as far as they could. 'Let's get back,' he said, 'before we all perish from hypothermia.'

★   ★   ★

By the time they reached the station, warmth had begun to seep back into Swift's frozen limbs and a revised theory of the Hoxton killing was taking shape in his mind.

Leaving Mrs West to kick her heels in the reception area as she flatly refused to step any further into the bowels of a police station, Swift arranged for a uniformed female PC to take Crystal to one of the adult interview rooms and wait there with her. 'Give her a hot drink,' he told the officer. 'I doubt if she can stomach anything more substantial at the moment.'

Lorna Price raised her eyebrows. 'She's a juvenile, sir,' she reminded him.

'I think it would be in her long-term interests to have the chance to experience the reality of custody, and consider her position,' he said with a wry smile. 'We'll bring her back to the juvenile suite when she's up to further questioning.'

'So, what are your thoughts so far, sir?' Fowler asked as they made their way to Swift's office and got their hands around steaming mugs of coffee. 'She's obviously well versed on the terrain and the method of killing.'

'Indeed she is,' he agreed. 'And in addition her knowledge of where and how Jenny was killed indicates that she was present at the killing scene. But that doesn't automatically mean she was the killer.'

As they paused in thought, Lister came in, his face creased with tiredness and irritation. 'I hope you lot are making some progress,' he protested, 'because I'm wasting my breath trying to get Ashton to cough. That damn solicitor chimes in at every verse end, telling the lad to keep his mouth well and truly zipped.' He sat down heavily on a vacant chair. 'I'm beginning to feel about as lively and useful as a tanker grounded in mud.' He paused to allow his subordinates to digest this distressing information. 'So then, Ed, what have you got on our young lady confessor?'

Slowly, patiently, Swift began to fill in the details.

*   *   *

By the time Swift and Lorna Price considered Crystal ready to be on the receiving end of further questions, Sue Sallis had turned up at the station, eager not to miss any of the action which she suspected was hotting up nicely. She, Lister and Fowler sat in the viewing room whilst Swift and Price talked with Crystal in the reassuring ambience of the juvenile suite.

Crystal sat facing Swift, with Lorna Price sitting beside her. On the table between them was a container filled with coloured felt-tip pens, some pads of paper and a selection of soft drinks with plastic cups lined up beside them.

Swift leaned forward, folding his arms on the table. 'We're very grateful that you came here to talk to us this morning,' he told the wary-looking girl. 'Because our job in the police is to discover the truth when a crime has been committed, and to make sure the criminal is brought to justice. And you've been helping us to do that.'

The girl's eyes rounded and then contracted. 'Yes.' She took a pen from the holder and began to stab tentatively at a pad of paper.

He left a long pause. 'Now. You told us you were responsible for the death of Jenny Hoxton. You didn't say it was an accident. You told us that you wrapped her face and her head in plastic until she could no longer breathe. Until she was dead. You murdered her.' His gaze levelled with hers and her eyes slid away from him.

'Murder is the most serious and wicked of

all crimes. The worst thing one person can do to another. Do you agree with that?' he asked.

She nodded, her face bleak and desperate. She drew a circle on the paper, digging in deep, going over and over the outline.

'Murder is an act of terrible wickedness and injustice,' he went on in a reflective tone. 'Think of it — to deprive a person of their life, to cut them off from the living world. And in Jenny's case to deprive them of becoming an adult and being able to make choices about what to do with their life.'

The pen slid from Crystal's fingers. She put the tip of her thumb in her mouth and bit down hard.

'Murder is a cruel and heartless act,' Swift continued, soft and relentless. 'I don't know if you are a cruel and heartless person, Crystal. I don't know you well enough. But you told us earlier on today that you had done this cruel and heartless thing. You didn't tell us it was an act of self-defence. You didn't say that Jenny had been threatening you in such a way that you had to retaliate. In fact you told us that she was drowsy, half asleep. She was defenceless and you took advantage of her. You committed a crime of cold-blooded killing, with no thought of the years of life you were taking away from Jenny, just for the sake of a few moments of irritation with her behaviour.'

In the viewing room Fowler shifted in his seat and Sue Sallis leaned forward in rapt attention.

'He deserves an Oscar for this performance,' Lister muttered. 'I just hope it's leading somewhere useful.'

'Do you know what they do with the bodies of people who are found murdered?' Swift asked the dumbstruck girl, gazing steadily at her so she cringed away. 'They put them on a table with a cold steel top and they cut them open. From here,' he said, putting his fingers against his throat, 'down to here.' Another graphic gesture. 'They take out their heart and their liver and their kidneys and all their important organs in order to weigh them and examine them. They cut open their stomachs. They can even find out what the person had for their last meal. With Jenny, it was tuna sandwiches. Just as you told us, Crystal.'

'*Bloody hell!*' Lister hissed.

Crystal folded her arms on the table and lowered her head on to them, soundless and still.

'I don't think you murdered Jenny,' Swift said evenly. 'I believe that you were there when she was killed. And I believe that just before she died there were moments when you felt angry with her. But you were not the person who murdered her.'

The girl was as still and silent as a corpse.

'I'll tell you what I think,' Swift said, his voice soft and comforting. 'I think that when you got upset with Jenny, you jumped up and ran behind those trees where we stood this morning. I think you were cross and sad and upset and you wanted somewhere quiet to think. And while you were wondering what to do next, someone else came along to the quarry. Someone who felt very angry indeed with Jenny. Someone who found Jenny lying on the ground giggly and sleepy. Someone who very much wanted to shut her up — for good. Someone who smoothed a sandwich wrapper around her face and held it there until she was dead.'

He stopped and waited. The atmosphere fizzed with tension.

'Am I right, Crystal?' he whispered.

The girl's head moved. A low muffled 'Yes' slid through her lips.

20

'So, what now?' Lister demanded of Swift an hour later. 'Our confessor has retracted, by implication anyway. But it doesn't look as though she's going to speak another word for a very long time.'

'She's lived through a traumatic couple of weeks since Jenny died,' Swift pointed out. 'And for the past eighteen hours or so she must have been at emotional breaking point.'

'She just needs time, eh? Is that what you're trying to tell me? Or maybe she's never going to spill the beans. Especially if it was Ashton she saw and she's got a thing about him.' He let out a mammoth sigh. 'If she'd just identify him as the killer, we'd be home and dry. She could give a bona-fide witness account; she was clearly there at the scene. And she's certainly one who notices things, as you pointed out earlier.'

Swift nodded. 'I'd like to talk to Imogen Barclay again, sir,' he announced quietly.

Lister's head jerked as though wrenched by a wire. 'What? When was she in the frame?'

'All along.'

Lister raised his eyes to the ceiling. 'Oh,

why not? The more the merrier. We could soon have a football team of prime suspects!'

★   ★   ★

Swift set up a brief planning meeting with Sue Sallis, Fowler and Lorna Price. He had decided that Sue was to accompany him to talk to Imogen, Fowler was to visit as many of the pupils who went on the Dales trip as he could manage in the next couple of hours, with two specific questions, and Lorna Price was to continue working with Crystal, aiming to tease out more details of what the girl had seen and heard during Jenny's last few living moments.

★   ★   ★

Imogen took a long time to answer the door. As she opened it her face registered surprise and discomfiture to see the two officers on the doorstep. She explained that her mother had gone to visit an aunt in a nearby nursing home and her father was playing in the finals of a snooker tournament at a nearby sports club. She did it in such a way as to suggest that perhaps they would be better to come back when one or both parents were present.

'We just want to come in for a quick word,'

Sue Sallis said reassuringly, moving smoothly forwards.

'Oh, well. All right.' Imogen led the way into the front room, switching on the lights and perching stiffly on the nearest chair. Her long dark hair gleamed where the beam fell on it.

'Are you feeling better?' Sue asked. 'Since I last saw you?'

'Yes. I'm OK, thank you.' In fact she looked fragile and on edge. Her wrists were still bandaged and she tugged at the sleeve of her sweater in an effort to cover them up.

Swift and Sue watched her with sympathetic faces, quietly determined to place the ball in Imogen's court and see where she lobbed it.

'Er, I heard that you got Nick in for questioning,' she said at last.

'Yes, that's right,' Swift confirmed.

'Oh . . . Is it . . . Is it going well?' she asked.

'We can't make any comment at this stage,' Swift told her with a regretful smile.

'Imogen,' Sue Sallis said, 'we'd be glad if you could confirm for us that you were at the Brontë museum on the afternoon Jenny died.'

A muscle twitched in Imogen's cheek.

'We're asking everyone on the trip the same question,' Sue hastened to reassure her.

'Oh, I see. Yes, I was. I told you that before.'

'What time did the visit start?' Swift wondered.

'At two o'clock. There was an introductory talk and then we could wander about as we liked. We went back to the coach about 4.15.'

'That's very precise,' Sue commented. 'Excellent.'

There was a thoughtful silence. 'Haworth's a bleak place, isn't it?' Sue said conversationally. 'It's always cold and windy there. Even in summer.'

Imogen frowned. 'Actually it was quite warm that day. There were a few days like that in the middle of February, weren't there? Some people were saying it's global warming.'

'It makes it difficult to know what to wear,' Sue said. 'Do you remember what you were wearing on the day of the Haworth visit, Imogen?'

She thought for a while. 'No.'

'It would quite help us — with our questioning,' Swift said meaningfully, 'to know what various people were wearing.' The implication that the questioning referred to Nick Ashton was patently clear.

Imogen dipped her head in thought. 'I think I was wearing grey tracksuit bottoms, and a grey sweatshirt. And trainers.'

Swift's mobile chirruped in his pocket. He took it out, glanced at the display, and slipped quietly from the room.

Imogen sat in silence. Sue could sense her deep unease. Her eyes would occasionally dart across to the constable's and then slide away. 'Do you think Nick did it?' she asked suddenly. 'Killed Jenny, I mean. I can't stop thinking about it.'

'We need to find out much more before we can say anything for definite,' Sue told her. 'It's pretty bad for everyone concerned, isn't it — waiting to know?'

'You can say that again,' Imogen agreed, glancing up at the doorway as Swift re-entered the room.

There was a moment of stillness. 'Imogen Barclay,' Swift said in formal tones, 'I am arresting you on suspicion of the murder of Jennifer Hoxton — '

Imogen sprang up as he continued his recital. 'No! You can't do this. It wasn't me. It was him. I didn't do it!' She let out a long chilling scream and twisted away as Sue stepped up close to restrain her.

'We shall continue our questioning at the police station,' Swift told her. 'You will be entitled to the services of a lawyer if you wish. And to contact your parents to let them know where you are.'

Imogen's eyes blazed with fury. 'I don't want to go with you!' She squared up to him.

'Why should I go? You can't force me.'

'We can, in fact, do just that if you refuse,' Swift told her. 'There's a squad car on the way.'

She drew herself up, powered by outrage and terror. 'Then let them do their fucking job,' she shouted, folding her arms. 'Because no way am I going like a lamb to the slaughter.'

★   ★   ★

Before starting the interrogation with Imogen, Swift slipped into the juvenile suite. Crystal and Lorna Price were working together on a crossword puzzle from a bumper book of 'Speedies'. Beside the book was the drawing which Swift had been advised about in his telephone message earlier. Whilst crude and cartoon-like, it conveyed a strong and primitive power. Against a roughly sketched grey background, a kneeling scarlet-clad figure with long dark hair bent over a smaller figure lying prone on the ground. Neither of the faces were detailed, but for Swift, who was familiar with both Jenny Hoxton and Imogen Barclay, there was no doubt whom the artist had had in mind.

'Can you tell me something about this picture, Crystal?' he asked.

She looked up. Her earlier infantile defensiveness had left her. She looked calm and tired and sad. She drew the paper towards her. 'It's not very good,' she said. 'That's Jenny there on the ground. And that's . . . the girl who put the stuff over her face.'

'You saw her do it?'

She nodded. 'I wanted to tell her to stop. Make her stop. But I couldn't. I was frightened. For me own self, you see. I was a coward.' She examined her hands, picking at a patch of red ink on her fingers. 'She's a big strong lass, that Imogen. She was spitting mad, shouting and yelling.'

'You're not being a coward now,' he told her.

'It's all on the tape,' she said sadly. 'I told Mrs Price everything. No lies this time, it's the truth.'

Lorna Price gave a confirming nod. She handed him the transcript from the tape.

★   ★   ★

Imogen sat in the interview room, her face rigid with horror at the situation in which she found herself. A grim, harshly lit mini-jail, reeking of old cigarettes, fear and despair.

Swift and Sue Sallis sat opposite her. She had opted not to have a lawyer and to speak for herself. Swift switched on the audio tape and fed in preliminary remarks.

He handed Imogen a typed list. 'These are the names of some of the pupils who were at the Brontë museum at the time Jenny died. Two of them confirm that they spoke to you towards the close of the visit around four o'clock.'

Imogen narrowed her eyes suspiciously. 'What a surprise! So why have you dragged me here to be questioned?'

'They said that you were wearing red tracksuit bottoms piped with white and a sweatshirt to match,' Sue commented.

'Human memory is not one hundred per cent reliable,' Imogen said, her face touched with arrogance. 'Far from it. I've read a lot on psychology.'

'Red piped with white is rather distinctive, wouldn't you say?' Sue asked. 'You don't see much running gear in those colours, do you?'

'Tracksuit bottoms are hardly running gear,' Imogen pointed out. 'They're for jogging, or just simply casual wear.'

'You're a runner, aren't you, Imogen?' Swift commented. 'On our first visit to see you, your mother mentioned that you came second in the Yorkshire Junior Ladies' Marathon last summer.'

'Yes.' For a moment she was wavering. 'So?'

'It takes around two hours to walk from the pub, ten minutes away from the Haworth parsonage, to the Arkwright quarry where Jenny was killed,' Swift told her. 'I know that first hand. I did that walk with my team this morning. We were walking at a fairly relaxed pace. The distance we covered was around four miles.' He looked hard at the internally squirming girl.

'I've no idea what all this is about,' she said.

'Anyone setting out from the pub and walking up to the quarry would take around two hours. It would take them perhaps ten minutes at the most to kill Jenny. And then two hours to walk back.'

Imogen sat stony-faced. 'Which puts me out of the picture.'

'But marathon runners can do as much as thirteen miles in an hour,' he pointed out. 'And fell runners going downhill can clock up even faster times.'

Imogen tugged irritably at her sleeves. 'That's beside the point when I haven't even the faintest idea where this quarry you're talking about is.'

'No, I suspect you didn't. Which is why you would have needed to follow Jenny to get there,' Swift agreed.

A tiny pause. 'I was at the Brontë museum. People saw me there. You just said so.'

'We have information,' he continued, 'that Jenny and a companion set out from the pub near the Haworth village a few minutes before one. That means they would have reached the quarry around three.'

'But how could I have followed them when I was at the Brontë museum?' she cut in, her voice beginning to rise in pitch.

'I'll deal with that in a moment,' Swift told her curtly. 'Assuming that a person with running skills such as yours had followed Jenny, then they would have had time to kill Jenny and get back to the Brontë museum perhaps as early as quarter to four.'

'But I didn't go to the quarry. I was at the museum, people saw me . . . ' She faltered and stopped.

'Not until four o'clock,' Sue reminded her.

'I spent a lot of time wandering about on my own,' Imogen protested. 'I was worried about Nick. I wasn't in the mood for chatting. Just because no one actually says they saw me at the start of the visit doesn't mean I wasn't there!'

Sue glanced at her notes. 'The two witnesses who saw you later on — wearing your red track suit — said you looked 'agitated' and 'out of sorts', and that you didn't want to talk to them.'

Imogen blinked. 'But surely that proves what I just said.'

'Possibly,' Swift agreed. 'Or perhaps some other matter was causing you agitation.'

She flashed him a cold pitying look. 'No.'

'Let's go back to the lunchtime of that day,' he continued. 'I'm going to paint a scenario. You and Nick were at a pub near Haworth. Jenny turned up. She gave Nick a letter suggesting she could get him to do anything she liked in order for her to stay quiet about the incident at the road bridge. Including have sex with him. Nick was angry. So angry he stormed off to walk on the moors, leaving you to go to the museum. But you were pretty angry too. And sickened, and jealous. You followed Jenny and the person with her. You hadn't any particular plan in mind, just an overwhelming urge to have things out with Jenny once and for all.'

Imogen listened, her face a mask of arrogant scorn.

'You kept well behind the two walkers. When you reached the Arkwright quarry you saw Jenny and the other person having a row. The person with Jenny was crying and shouting at her to shut up. You saw the companion run off behind a clump of trees and down one of the several foot tracks which lead out of the quarry. You, quite naturally, assumed they were going back down the moor. You waited a little. Jenny was alone now. She was lying on the ground kicking her legs in the air and giggling. And then she went quiet and dozed off to sleep. You walked up to her. This girl who had been making your and Nick's life a misery for months. Because she was blackmailing you too, wasn't she Imogen? Little threats and hints that were steadily escalating. Neither you nor Nick were ever going to be quite sure of your security for the rest of your lives. You were seized with an overwhelming wish to silence her for ever. You saw the sandwich wrappers lying on the ground. You placed them over Jenny's face and held on tight until she stopped breathing. And then you unwound the clingfilm and put it in your pocket. By the time you reached the Brontë museum around four o'clock you had disposed of the wrappers in a public bin.'

'Not true,' said Imogen in a flat, bored voice. 'Any of it.'

He placed a copy of Crystal's drawing in front of her. Her features froze.

'There was a witness to Jenny's death. This is their representation of what they saw. They captured you on paper. And they've named you.'

Imogen interlaced her hands in front of her, squeezing the fingers with vicious power as her brain hummed. 'This means nothing. That girl just wants to put the blame on me for what happened to Jenny. She could have done it herself.'

'That girl,' Sue echoed reflectively. 'I was under the impression you thought Nick had killed Jenny.'

'And you've told us you didn't follow Jenny and her companion,' Swift followed up. 'That you were never at the quarry . . . ' He stopped to allow the implications of her mistake sink in.

Got her! Sue Sallis thought.

Imogen, deadly white and clearly shaken, had nevertheless pulled back her shoulders and assumed a demeanour of contemptuous arrogance. 'I want to see my parents,' she said. 'And I'm not going to say anything else.' She let her steely glance move from Sue Sallis to Swift. 'That's something even you can't force me to do.'

★ ★ ★

Sue caught up with Geoff Fowler as he attempted to bully and coax something hot and wet from the drinks machine. 'Hey, how did you get that information from two witnesses with such lightning speed?'

Fowler grinned. 'Pretty good eh? And it's all kosher, love. Sometimes even a miserable beggar like me gets lucky. First house I went to was filled with young 'uns having a bit of a knees-up. Parents away, the mice will play, you know. Quite a few of them had been to the Brontë place on the day in question. They were all a bit tiddly and over-excited, falling over themselves to be helpful. I wouldn't be surprised if we don't get some more useful stuff once they've had time to sober up. So how have you and the boss been getting on with Miss Barclay? Have we got the right one this time?'

'Oh, yes,' Sue said slowly. 'Yes, yes, yes.'

'Will she crack?'

'I doubt it. Since she pulled herself together after the cut wrists incident, she seems to have gained a mantle of queenliness and a will of iron.'

'Oh aye,' Fowler said. 'That's hardly the kind of attitude to appeal to juries, is it now?'

★   ★   ★

Imogen took in deep breaths, forcing herself to focus as her athletics coach had taught her. Her parents would save her; they would get her the best defence lawyer money could buy.

She would walk away from this. There was no real evidence. She'd bagged up the red track-suit and the trainers caked with limey mud; they'd gone with the rest of the household rubbish into the churning jaws of the refuse lorry. She smiled at the memory. But then what if police searched her house? They'd know what she had done. It would come out in court. Her heart began to beat with wayward force. Rational thought and terrified confusion jostled with each other so that her head felt as though it were filled with screaming voices. Negative thoughts crowded into her mind like wayward children.

She tried again to focus, picturing herself walking out of court. Walking free. But a cruel inner voice was speaking now, low and insistent. 'Guilty, guilty, guilty.'

★ ★ ★

'Have we enough to charge her, Ed?' Lister demanded, thumping the transcripts of the two vital tapes sitting on his desk and fixing Swift with a raptor-like gaze.

'We've got motive in spades. She's already tripped herself up during questioning. We've got Crystal West's eye-witness description of the killing, a very detailed account. But no forensics — well, not as yet.'

'That'll do.'

'I agree. But will it convince the CPS?'

'A lot depends on the witness account. Will this little lass have the bottle to work with us? And then stand up in court and face a fancy defence barrister? Tell it as it was?'

'Yes,' Swift decided slowly, 'I think she will. Six, seven months on, she'll have had time to reflect in the cold light of day. She lost a friend, she saw twisted anger and evil up close. She will want justice to be done. Yes, she'll tell it as it was.'

21

Swift booked two weeks of leave for the end of July. Imogen Barclay's trial was scheduled for September and he felt the need for a break from police work before that. He had thoughts of getting a late package deal for Italy or Spain. Naomi said she would go with him.

'There's no obligation,' he said. 'You might have something more exciting to do.'

'I'll be able to do that as well.' She eyed him beadily. 'It'd be nice for us to go off together, father and child. Sweet! You know thirty years ago men used to take a bit of totty to Rome or Valencia and people would think, how touching, a father and his daughter. And now dads and daughters go off together and everyone thinks, What does that lovely girl see in *him*?'

'I hope you don't treat Marcus with such scorn!'

'With him, I'm pure Cruella DeVil. It's the only way.'

Thoughts of a break prompted him to look back over the past few months. On balance he felt the move to Yorkshire had worked well, both on a personal and professional level. Naomi seemed happier, making progress in her fight to come to terms with the absence of Kate, forging a new life for herself. And he too felt a slow change within himself, a move away from the despair and desolation of those early months after Kate's death.

He had recently completed a batch of staff appraisals and both Fowler and Sallis had come out well in terms of progress made. Sue, of course, was on her way up, studying hard for sergeant exams and interviews. Geoff, inevitably at his age, was winding down. But Swift sensed he had a new enthusiasm in the work. The Hoxton case and the part he had played in the final unravelling had given him a significant boost. They were a good team.

Reminders of the Hoxton case had stayed with him, a sadness lingering. Young deaths were always especially troubling, a point Sadie Bracewell had made when he talked with her after the charge against Imogen had finally been brought.

Later he had looked through the file once again when the date of the trial came through. His glance had lingered on the photographs of the dead girl. He was reminded that at first the case had seemed to be a tragedy resulting from the vagaries of senility. But in the end it had turned out to hinge around the whims and wilfulness of youth.

Jenny Hoxton, Crystal West, Nick Ashton, Imogen Barclay. His Naomi and her Marcus. A diverse group, yet each one a prisoner of their youth and its many desires.

Other titles published by
The House of Ulverscroft:

A KIND OF JUSTICE

Angela Dracup

Josie Parker is found drowned in the bath on her wedding night. The circumstances indicate murder and DCI Ed Swift is forced to regard the distraught bridegroom, Jamie, as chief suspect. But Jamie claims to have lost all recall of the time leading up to his bride's death. When Swift investigates the family dynamics of the newlyweds he uncovers a shocking trail of deceit and treachery. Then Swift takes Jamie back to the scene of the crime and the young widower recaptures his buried memories. Swift must reveal the truth behind Josie's killing if justice is, finally, to be done.

THE ULTIMATE GIFT

Angela Dracup

Following a heart transplant, Kay becomes disturbed by a menacing and recurring dream. Convinced that her new heart is carrying messages from its previous owner, she determines to discover the truth about his death. When she finally meets the donor's family, Kay is horrified to find herself triggering off further heartbreak in their lives. However, the charismatic family head, Majid, agrees to help her unearth the dark secret that marked the end of his cousin's life. But as she discovers the shocking truth, Kay finds herself in terrifying danger. Will the donor's killer seek to put a final end to the heart that survived?

THE SURROGATE THIEF

Archer Mayor

Brattleboro is the epitome of scenic Vermont. And yet there is darkness here, too. Veteran cop Joe Gunther has battled drug pushers and foiled gangs . . . but hasn't always won. Thirty years earlier shop owner Klaus Oberfeldt was robbed and beaten senseless. When Klaus died six months later, the case became murder. The guilty man appeared to be a well-known crook who had since vanished. Gunther, distracted by his wife's losing struggle with cancer, let the case go cold. Now reopened, the Oberfeldt investigation forces Gunther to open old wounds. For on the idyllic Brattleboro streets stalks a murderer who has good reason to kill again . . .

OXFORD LETTERS

Veronica Stallwood

When Kate Ivory hears that her mother, Roz, is unwell, she finds it hard to believe; her mother doesn't 'do' ill. But when Kate sees Roz it's obvious that something is wrong, and not just with her health. A married couple, the Freemans, have moved into her house to 'look after her' and Kate suspects they are more concerned with her mother's wealth than her well-being ... Increasingly disturbed, Kate decides to look into the Freemans' background and uncover the truth — and soon realises that her mother may not be the only one in danger.